A Little Piece of Paradise

T. A. Williams lives in Devon with his Italian wife. He was born in England of a Scottish mother and Welsh father. After a degree in modern languages at Nottingham University, he lived and worked in Switzerland, France and Italy, before returning to run one of the best-known language schools in the UK. He's taught Arab princes, Brazilian beauty queens and Italian billionaires. He speaks a number of languages and has travelled extensively. He has eaten snake, still-alive fish, and alligator. A Spanish dog, a Russian bug and a Korean parasite have done their best to eat him in return. His hobby is long-distance cycling, but his passion is writing.

Also by T. A. Williams

Chasing Shadows
Dreaming of Venice
Dreaming of Florence
Dreaming of St-Tropez
Dreaming of Christmas
Dreaming of Tuscany
Dreaming of Rome
Dreaming of Verona
Dreaming of Italy

Escape to Tuscany

Under a Siena Sun
Second Chances in Chianti
Secrets on the Italian Island

T. A. WILLIAMS

A Little Piece of Paradise

CANELO
US

San Diego, California

 Canelo US

An imprint of Printers Row Publishing Group
9717 Pacific Heights Blvd, San Diego, CA 92121
www.canelobooksus.com

Printers Row Publishing Group is a division of Readerlink Distribution Services, LLC. Canelo US is a registered trademark of Readerlink Distribution Services, LLC.

First published in the United Kingdom in 2021 by Canelo. This edition originally published in the United Kingdom in 2022 by Canelo.

Published in partnership with Canelo.

Correspondence regarding the content of this book should be sent to Canelo US, Editorial Department, at the above address. Author inquiries should be sent to Canelo, Unit 9, 5th Floor, Cargo Works, 1–2 Hatfields, London SE1 9PG, United Kingdom, www.canelo.co.

Publisher: Peter Norton • Associate Publisher: Ana Parker
Art Director: Charles McStravick
Senior Developmental Editor: April Graham
Production Team: Beno Chan, Julie Greene

Design: Brianna Lewis

Library of Congress Control Number: 2022946081

ISBN: 978-1-6672-0466-6

Printed in India

27 26 25 24 23   1 2 3 4 5

To Mariangela and Christina with love as always

Chapter 1

'Stop that, Jeeves!'

Jeeves looked up with a guilty expression on his face, but he didn't stop what he was doing.

'Are you listening? I said, stop it, Jeeves! I'm trying to pack and I need that box.'

'Leave him alone, Sophie. He's enjoying himself.' Chris was grinning.

The big black dog returned to the systematic destruction of a cardboard box. Fortunately, unlike most of the other boxes piled around the room, this one was still empty.

'Well, he's the only one round here who's enjoying himself.' Sophie straightened up, ran her hands through her hair and stretched. 'I hadn't realised I had so much stuff.'

'Well, it's almost all packed now. Sit down and have a rest. I'll go and put the kettle on.'

The young Labrador, seeing that his mistress was now down at his level, abandoned the tattered remains of the box and wandered over to the sofa. Keen to capitalise on the opportunity that now presented itself, he decided it would be a very good idea to climb onto her lap.

I

'Jeeves, you great lump, get off. You weigh a ton.' Sophie's words would have carried more clout if she hadn't been giggling at his antics.

Sophie's protests attracted Chris's attention and his head appeared around the door. 'Glad to see the dog training classes are paying off. Jeeves, I've found a packet of biscuits. Interested?'

Jeeves looked up. Somewhere in his food-obsessed Labrador head, the word 'biscuits' registered and he relinquished the sofa and padded off towards the kitchen. Relieved, Sophie fanned herself as she reflected yet again on the magnitude of the step she was about to take. Not only was she moving out of this little flat here in south London, but she was moving back to Italy, only a year after she had come running back to England with her tail between her legs. But even this paled in comparison to the prospect of being reunited with Rachel. Ever since the shock letter from Uncle George's solicitors three months ago, she had been able to think of little else.

'Your tea – I made it strong.' Chris pushed a steaming mug of tea into her hands and took a seat beside her, reaching across to clink his mug against hers. 'Here's to your Uncle George. I wish I had an uncle who felt like leaving me a whopping great castle.'

Sophie nodded and managed to produce a smile. 'You're forgetting all the strings attached.'

Chris blew on his tea to cool it down. 'How could I? It does sound a bit Machiavellian, I must admit.'

News of her much-loved uncle's death had come as a real blow to Sophie. They hadn't spoken much for a year or so and the arrival of a letter from his lawyers informing her of his death and of his decision to have a simple, fast cremation rather than inconvenience his friends and family had come as a bolt from the blue. The letter had also given details of his will but when she had read the conditions of the bequest, she had been rendered almost speechless. Uncle George had hatched a cunning plan to bring her and her sister back together again after so long apart.

Six years ago, when Rachel had stunned everybody by dropping out of university and disappearing, Sophie had been worried sick. She had called, emailed and texted her over and over again for days, but with no response. She had even started to believe that something awful might have happened and was on the point of contacting the police when, finally, she had received a two-line message from Rachel. All it said was that she was alive and well and in Puerto Rico. No address and nothing else. Since then, Sophie had heard nothing more from her and had eventually given up trying.

Uncle George wanted to change that – from beyond the grave. His cunning plan involved his Italian holiday home. He had been an extremely wealthy man and, apart from his amazing apartment overlooking New York's Central Park and his vast waterside property in the Hamptons, he had also bought himself an old Italian castle on a hilltop overlooking the Mediterranean. His American properties and business interests had gone to other beneficiaries over there, but the Italian castle was to be for the sisters. It was apparently worth a lot of money and according to the terms of his will, it would become the property of Sophie and Rachel to do with as they wished but – and this was a big *but* – only after they had both lived there under the same roof continuously for three full months starting this summer. If either of them refused or gave up partway through, all bets would be off and it would revert to his American heirs.

'A *bit* Machiavellian?' Sophie shot a glance across at Chris and shook her head ruefully. 'It's diabolical.'

'Don't say that, Soph. I'm sure he felt he was doing it for the right reasons. Obviously he was hoping you and Rachel won't be able to live together for a long period of time without patching things up between you.'

'I hope you're right, but I'm not holding my breath. Rachel turned her back on mum and me six years ago and then cut off all contact. She couldn't even be bothered to come to mum's funeral, and as far as I'm concerned, that was the last straw.'

'But you got on well with her before?'

'Yes, of course, she is my sister after all. We sometimes quarrelled, but that's normal for siblings, isn't it? The thing is, though, we're very different people. She's always been far more interested in having a good time. She's prettier than me and the boys all loved her – they probably still do.'

'I've met Rachel and she's definitely a pretty girl, but you're gorgeous and you should remember that.'

Sophie looked up at him gratefully. 'I don't know what I'd do without you to boost my confidence.'

'Well, it's true. I think you're every bit as attractive as your sister.'

Chris had always been so very encouraging and she knew she owed him a lot. They had known each other since the first year of university when he had started going out with her flatmate, Claire. In fact, if Claire hadn't already nabbed him, Sophie might well have done, and she had remained very close friends with both of them, even after he and Claire split up. Having him as a shoulder to cry on over the past year had been invaluable. She reached over and gave his hand a squeeze.

'Thanks, Chris. For everything.'

'Any time, Sophie, you know that.' He caught hold of her fingers and squeezed them in return before releasing them. 'Anyway, physical appearance aside, the thing is you've always been the brainy one. Maybe she resented that.'

'I'm no brainier than her; I just work harder. Boring as it sounds, that's the way I'm made.'

'And that's why she went off? To have a good time?'

'I expect so, but I honestly don't know. At one point it wouldn't have surprised me to find out she'd been abducted by aliens.'

'So you aren't looking forward to seeing her again?'

Sophie considered the question. 'Half of me is. Like I say, she's my sister and apart from anything else I'd love to know why she just upped and left. But the other half of me still can't forget or forgive the hurt she caused – to me and to mum.' She took a sip of hot tea and adopted a more positive tone. 'Anyway, hopefully the castle's so big we'll be able to cohabit without seeing too much of each other if she hasn't changed for the better. I imagine I'll be okay.'

'Just you wait and see. I reckon you'll work things out, but if you don't, remember all you've got to do is stick it out until the end of September and then you can sell the place and, suddenly, you'll be a millionaire.'

'The end of September can't come soon enough, that's all I can say.'

Sophie must have sounded a bit despondent as the next thing she knew, sixty pounds of bone and muscle had started to climb onto her lap in a show of canine solidarity.

In so doing, Jeeves managed to make her spill the last of her tea in her lap and she squealed.

'Oh, God, Jeeves, did you have to?'

Unperturbed, the big dog did his best to put his paws on her shoulders and lick her face before she chased him off.

'Well, you know you'll have at least one friendly face over there with you.' Chris was laughing at the dog's antics.

'Yes, causing havoc as usual.' Still, she reached down affectionately and gently stroked Jeeves's ears. 'I'm glad I've got you, Jeeves. Somehow I've got a feeling I'm going to need all the support I can get over the next three months.'

'I'm sure it'll be all right, Soph, but let's face it, if you've got to be miserable, spending the summer in a historic castle on the Riviera coast's about as good as it gets.' Chris was still doing his best to cheer her up. 'And anyway, you love Italy, don't you? How many years did you live there?'

'Four, almost five. I went over there almost straight after finishing university, and you're right, I do love the country.' While still a very young journalist, she had been given a dream job as Southern European correspondent for an online news channel and this had meant being based in Rome. It hadn't paid very much but it had been exciting and a lot of fun. 'It's just that I've only ever lived in Rome, and Uncle George's place is way up in the north, almost in France.'

'But with a name like Paradise it can't be all bad. What more could you ask for?'

'True. Paradiso is quite a name. Let's hope the place lives up to it – but, like I say, I'm not holding my breath.

Paradiso looks good on Google Earth with the sea nearby, but it's the whole Rachel thing that's freaking me out.'

'It'll be fine. And you know that if you ever need anything, even if it's just somebody to shout at, you can always count on me.'

She smiled back at him. Chris really was a good friend. He had been immensely supportive after her three-year relationship with her Roman boyfriend had come to a very sudden end the previous year, followed just weeks later by the loss of her dream job when her employer had gone bust. After that, she had returned to London where she had been eking out a precarious living as a freelancer, searching fruitlessly for a new job and licking her emotional wounds. When Chris had heard she was moving back to Italy, he had immediately offered to come and help her with the packing, volunteering to store her unwanted stuff in his attic until she needed it again.

She reached over and caught hold of his arm, giving it another little squeeze. 'Thanks for everything, Chris. You're a star.' For a moment it looked as though he even blushed a little and she felt a real surge of affection for him. 'Thanks for being there for me.'

'There's nothing so attractive to a man as a maiden in distress – especially if they happen to be living in a castle.' He winked at her. 'I bet you'll be fighting the Italian men off within days of your arrival.'

Sophie screwed up her nose. 'No more Italian men for me – in fact, no more men of any nationality. I'm quite happy with Jeeves. As long as I feed him and take him for walks, I can rely on him to love me.' She sighed. 'Unlike Claudio. Until last summer, I really thought he was the man of my dreams, but I was wrong.'

'Maybe you should have given him dog food and taken him for walks. Besides, the guy was clearly an idiot to cheat on a lovely girl like you, Soph.'

'I know I'm far better off without him.' She did her best to sound resolute. 'He was a two-timing toad and I had to dump him. I had no choice.'

'And you really didn't suspect anything?'

She hesitated. She had spent almost a year now pondering this question time and time again. 'If I'm honest, I suppose I always had some suspicions. He was often away overnight or had late night business dinners. I was away quite a bit myself and caught up in my work, so it was easier just to believe what he told me. Looking back on it, I was probably a bit gullible, a bit too naïve, really. You know something? What I've been feeling isn't so much regret at losing him, but anger – anger at myself for being so stupid. I've always thought of myself as a grounded, pragmatic sort of person and the fact that I could be fooled so easily really grates.'

'Do you ever hear from him?'

'No. I've severed all links with him on social media and I delete all his emails as soon as they come in.'

'Did you say "all his emails"? Is he still sending them?' Chris was clearly surprised.

'Every now and then. Fewer and fewer as the months have gone by. Hopefully he'll give up soon.' Sophie was trying to sound positive but wasn't sure she was pulling it off.

'I never met him, but I remember Claire saying he was a good-looking guy.'

Sophie nodded ruefully. 'Didn't he know it! As did half the female population of Rome. No, I'm happy on my own, at least for now. The thing I miss most is Italy – you know, the lifestyle, the weather, the food… It'll be good to get back to that again – even with Rachel lurking in the background.'

'That's the spirit, Soph, and don't worry about Rachel. I'm sure you'll be able to get on together.'

'I seriously doubt that, after what she did…'

'A lot of time's passed, Soph. Maybe she's changed.'

'I'm prepared to bet good money – which I haven't got – that this particular leopard hasn't changed her spots one bit. She's always been selfish and always will be.'

'Well, you're seeing her next week, aren't you? You'll soon find out when you get to paradise.' He grinned at her. 'Paradiso – what a name! I bet the place turns out to be a little piece of paradise.'

Chapter 2

Paradiso

Sophie spotted the village of Paradiso ahead of her long before she reached the motorway turnoff. It was situated on top of an imposing promontory, perched high above the Mediterranean, and the handful of red roofs looked even smaller in reality than it had done on Google Earth. There couldn't have been more than a couple of dozen houses up there amid the trees, clustered around the solid bulk of the castle.

After wasting several minutes and annoying the driver of a motor home behind her as she struggled with the self-service pay toll, she finally emerged from the *autostrada* and arrived at a roundabout where she was relieved to spot a little sign to Paradiso. She was even more relieved to find that her car – which had been making ever more sinister noises for almost an hour now – had managed to get her here from London. Since losing her job, money was very tight and she had been dreading an expensive breakdown.

She turned left onto a narrow road that wound its way up the hillside in a series of sharp bends. The higher her car climbed, the worse the awful racket and spluttering became and she hoped it wouldn't let her down at the last minute. Looking back down over the rows of vines and olive groves, she couldn't miss the unsightly sprawl of urban development in the valley below. Thanks to Wikipedia she now knew that fifty years earlier there had been virtually nothing there. What was now the popular seaside town of Santa Rita had been little more than a hamlet, whose inhabitants had made a precarious living out of producing olive oil and wine, growing vegetables, and fishing for anchovies in the warm waters of Italy's Riviera coast.

Since then, Santa Rita had been adopted by families from the big northern Italian industrial cities like Turin and Milan for their second homes and had ballooned into a chaotic mix of modern villas, shops, restaurants and a multitude of apartment blocks that threatened to swamp the handful of remaining old houses. The good news was that it looked as though modern development had been restricted to down there in the valley. The higher Sophie climbed, the clearer it became that the developers had yet to reach up as far as Paradiso, unlike the mass of new houses all over the hills behind Nice and other parts of the Côte d'Azur she had seen on the way here.

Even the urban mess below couldn't spoil the sheer beauty of the deep green of the tree-clad hills and mountains behind the coast and the perfect azure blue of the sea stretching out in front of her. From up here Sophie could see the coast arching back the way she had come in the direction of the French border and Monte Carlo, with the Maritime Alps a distant smudge on the horizon. Just like Chris had said, as a place to be miserable, this took some beating. Her breath escaped in a frustrated sigh as she hoped yet again that things wouldn't be too awful once she was reunited with her little sister. Wonderful as it was to be left a valuable property, why, oh why, had Uncle George decided to add those pesky conditions?

The road levelled out as she reached the t
ridge and ran along between a high stone wall to
and olive trees on her left, through whose branches she
caught glimpses of Alassio and the curve of the coastline
stretching off to the east in the direction of Genoa. The
road grew ever narrower and a minute later made a sharp
turn to the right and abruptly ended and she found herself
in a small piazza, little bigger than a couple of tennis
courts, surrounded by ancient stone buildings. There was
what looked like a bar/restaurant in one corner, right
alongside a tiny old church. A stone horse trough full of
geraniums added a touch of colour to the scene.

Sophie drew up in front of a pair of ornate iron gates
set into the same high stone wall she had been following.
A discreet sign on one gatepost informed her – just in case
there could have been any doubt – that she had arrived at
the Castello, her Uncle George's holiday residence. The
wall and the gates were so high she could see no sign of the
castle itself, which remained discreetly hidden from view
beyond them. She turned off the engine and stretched.
As she did so, she heard movement from behind her and,
glancing in the mirror, saw Jeeves's head loom above the
rear seat. She swivelled round towards him.

'We're here, Jeeves. I bet you'll be glad to get out.'

In response the dog shook himself, wagged his tail
hopefully and gave his trademark half-whine-half-sigh,
one of his familiar ways of communicating with her.

Sophie glanced across the square to the handsome
clock set into the main façade of a fine old building
directly opposite the castle gates. It read half past twelve.
Her watch told her it was a quarter to four. She decided
to trust the more modern technology.

'Right, Jeeves, we've just got time to stretch our legs before four o'clock. Fancy a quick walk?'

The Labrador's tail started wagging more enthusiastically as he recognised the magic word, so she opened the door and climbed out. The heat hit her like a physical slap after the car's air con and she could feel the hot arid air dry her throat as she breathed in and coughed. There was a very definite smell of burning coming from her little car and her heart sank. Still, she reminded herself, at least it had got her here. She opened the tailgate and the dog leapt out eagerly, stopping to shake himself again before turning back towards her, front legs splayed, raring to go.

'Come on, let's go and take a quick peek at our new home before we have our little walk.' Over the past year since getting Jeeves as a puppy, she had got into the habit of talking to him quite a lot. What he lacked as a conversationalist, he made up for as a listener, and he definitely knew the meaning of the words *walk* and *food*. He also probably knew the words *stop it* and *get down*, but his memory for these regularly failed him.

She wandered across the square towards the castle and looked around but she couldn't see another living soul. This was no doubt partly because most sensible Italians were still resting after their lunch and partly because of the heat. She hadn't needed the regular updates on the radio in the car to tell her that July was kicking off with a heatwave all along the Riviera. She felt sure the temperature gauge was correct in indicating it was thirty-six degrees here in Paradiso today.

When they reached the gates of the castle, Jeeves stopped to pee on an ancient stone bollard and Sophie wished she had thought of stopping at the last service station on the motorway to do the same – with or without a bollard. It had been a long drive. In fact, it had been a hard couple of days, driving down from England via the Channel Tunnel, stopping only now and then for fuel, food and to give Jeeves a chance to stretch his legs.

They had spent last night in a cheap hotel in a *centre commercial* outside Vienne, to the south of Lyon, where Jeeves had pleasantly surprised her by behaving almost like a grown-up – apart from an unfortunate episode involving him trying to hump the poodle at the next table at dinner. Still, she couldn't complain, apart from the habit he had developed of erupting into paroxysms of barking every time they stopped at a motorway pay toll. Because she was driving a British-registered car, the steering wheel was now on the wrong side and she had to shuffle across to the empty passenger seat each time she came to a toll and this clearly bothered her dog. The series of pay stations around Nice had been particularly harrowing and his vocal accompaniment to her recent struggles with the self-service machine at the motorway exit here meant that her ears were still ringing now.

The castle gates were closed and locked but she managed to peek through the narrow gap between the gate and the gatepost and what she saw was mightily impressive. The castle was an imposing stone fortress, no doubt dating back many, many centuries, with crenellations on top and a huge arched doorway flanked by arrow slits at the front. It looked very old indeed and she hoped there would be internal sanitation and at least a few creature comforts. The idea of spending three months in medieval squalor did not appeal one bit – although she pinned her hopes on a wealthy man like Uncle George having made at least some modifications to render it habitable.

The castle was surrounded by a host of magnificent trees, chief among which was an absolutely enormous umbrella pine that was almost as high as the castle itself and cast welcome shade across the gravelled area directly below the main entrance. Just along from it was a huge fig tree, beneath whose broad leaves Sophie could see luscious figs just waiting to be picked and many more already littering the ground at its feet. There was no doubt about it: this was quite some place.

She turned away and accompanied Jeeves across the square to a pair of old horse troughs. The one filled with flowers looked delightful and the one alongside it was full of water, fed by a constant stream pouring out of a narrow metal pipe. The water was crystal clear so she let her dog have a good drink before heading over to a narrow track that led directly away from the castle in the direction of the sea. Within seconds, they were away from the houses and in the midst of a mixture of rough scrubby bushes and weather-beaten trees, their branches bent backwards by the prevailing wind over decades.

Today, however, there wasn't so much as a breath of wind and Sophie was glad to be in the shade cast by the foliage around her. It was very quiet up here and all she could hear was the distant clucking of hens and the cooing of a pair of amorous doves somewhere in the branches above them. There was a heady cocktail of scents in the air, among which she identified wild thyme and rosemary, and as the trees began to peter out and she could look out over the open hillside towards the sea, she had to admit it was quite some view. It came as no surprise to see that the local council had thoughtfully put a bench here, perfectly positioned to take advantage of the spectacular panorama.

She suddenly realised that she wasn't alone. There was a figure sitting there and the penny only dropped as the woman on the bench turned in her direction and rose to her feet.

'Hi, Soph. Long time no see.'

'Rachel!' Sophie couldn't get another word out.

She just stood there. Rachel was still unmistakably Rachel, although she looked, and of course was, six years older than the last time they had set eyes on each other. Her hair was still long, still that same lovely golden colour and still far glossier than Sophie's had ever been. She had shed what little puppy fat she had had and she looked good, in spite of the wary expression on her face. It took some time before Sophie managed to kick her brain into gear, genuinely torn between screaming at her sister and hugging her. In the end she did neither.

'Hello, Rachel. I was beginning to think I was never going to see you again.'

'And you probably didn't want to either, I bet.' By now Rachel was bending down, making a fuss of Jeeves, who looked delighted to meet a new friend.

'I...'

Sophie choked off the upsurge of emotion she could feel welling inside her and came close to going over and giving her sister that hug, but finally restrained herself. There would be time for reconciliation as and when they had had a chance to talk the whole thing through. So much had happened in both their lives over the intervening years, starting with their mother's illness and death. Instead, Sophie transferred her attention to the Labrador. He was a naturally friendly dog and normally a good judge of character so the fact that he was cosying up to Rachel was a promising sign. In fact he was getting very affectionate already and she stepped in to protect her sister's clothes.

'Jeeves, don't jump all over her. Come here.' She was pleased to see him turn and come trotting amiably back to her, tail wagging.

'Jeeves – cool name.'

Sophie didn't respond. She just glanced at her watch. 'It's almost four. We need to go and meet the lawyer.' She slipped easily back into her big sister role and Rachel just nodded and shouldered her heavy-looking backpack before they set off together back along the path.

When they reached the piazza, they saw a middle-aged man in a suit hugging what little shade was cast by a branch of the umbrella pine that extended out over the wall. He was wearing glasses, carrying a briefcase and he looked hot. They walked up to him and he gave them a little smile and shot a nervous glance at the Labrador.

'Good afternoon, ladies. Are you the sisters Elliot? My name is Massimo Verdi. Is this your dog? Is he friendly?' He was speaking comprehensible if heavily accented English. Sophie could probably have saved him a lot of trouble by telling him to switch to Italian which she now spoke fluently after her years in Rome but, although their maternal grandparents had been from Italy and the girls had grown up speaking to them in Italian, she wasn't sure how much her sister still remembered.

She adopted a reassuring tone and replied in English. 'He's very friendly, Signor Verdi, probably too friendly. I'm Sophie and this is Rachel.'

They shook hands, after which he removed a hefty bunch of keys from his briefcase and turned towards the gates. He inserted a long key into the lock and not without difficulty managed to make it turn with an ominous grating noise. He pushed, but nothing happened. He pushed harder, adding a hefty kick with his foot, and the gate finally swung open, producing an alarming screech of ancient hinges as it did so. Jeeves took two apprehensive steps backwards, pressing himself against Sophie's thigh. He had never been the bravest of dogs. She gave him a reassuring pat on the head, and she and Rachel followed Signor Verdi into the gravelled courtyard. An intoxicating scent of resin and roses filled the air. Here, in the shade of the big pine tree, it felt delightfully cool after the blistering heat of the piazza and she felt a smile forming on her lips.

Half a dozen stone steps led up to the imposing front door which was set back inside the arched entranceway. All the way along the front of the castle were shrubs and plants as varied as cactus, palms and a spectacular display of roses, most smothered in aromatic blooms. The flower-beds had been meticulously maintained and, although the main gates didn't appear to have been used for some time, it was clear that somebody had been coming to look after the plants. Presumably this meant there was another access to the property. Sophie was pleasantly surprised to find the garden so well cared for. She had never been interested in that sort of thing and didn't really want to have to start getting involved in it in a temperature of thirty plus degrees. Thinking back on it, gardening had been one of Rachel's interests as a girl – along with boys, of course.

'Ladies, if you would like to follow me...'

Sophie looked back to see that Signor Verdi had already managed to open the massive wooden front door a lot more easily than the gates, and that was a relief. She glanced across at Rachel and indicated to her to go ahead but, as it turned out, the first across the threshold after the lawyer was Jeeves, followed by the two sisters.

They found themselves in a large, dark hallway with huge flagstones covering the floor. A couple of full suits of armour against the walls added a rather intimidating feel to the place and Sophie and Rachel exchanged apprehensive glances. It was like stepping back into a bygone age and the initial impression was more daunting than welcoming.

'The living room's through here.'

Evidently Signor Verdi knew his way around the castle. Rachel shrugged off her hefty backpack and left it in the hall before they followed him through a pair of double doors into a large room with a high, vaulted ceiling. It was equally dark in there but as Sophie and Rachel stood apprehensively by the doorway, Signor Verdi went around opening windows and pushing the shutters outwards so that more and more light gradually filtered into the room through the narrow openings. As for the contents of the room, these were also rather disconcerting. The various pieces of furniture had been covered with white cotton dustsheets, creating strange amorphous shapes. It looked spooky in the half-light and Sophie made a resolution not to come in here at night – or at least not until the furniture had been uncovered. Hopefully the rest of the castle would be a bit less scary.

After opening the windows, the lawyer busied himself pulling the dustsheets to one side so as to reveal a set of comfortable-looking leather armchairs with an antique coffee table positioned in the midst of them. He laid the covers carefully onto the stone floor and indicated they should take a seat. Sophie and Rachel chose armchairs side-by-side facing him while Jeeves plonked himself happily on the pile of dustsheets, raising a little cloud of dust as he did so and sneezing as a result.

'Welcome to Paradiso castle.' The lawyer set his briefcase down on the table and his face adopted a formal expression. 'In accordance with the instructions left to me by your uncle, I now have to explain the exact conditions surrounding his bequest to you. Have you any initial questions or shall I proceed?'

Sophie glanced across at Rachel who gave a little shrug and a shake of the head.

'Please continue, Signor Verdi.'

He opened his briefcase and pulled out a thin file. 'First, merely as a formality, please could you both confirm your dates and places of birth?' They both did so and Sophie saw him do a bit of mental arithmetic. 'So, Sophie, you were twenty-nine in April and you, Rachel, are twenty-seven and you'll be twenty-eight on the first of October?' They both nodded and he reached for the file in front of him. From it, he extracted a single sheet of paper. 'This is a letter from your Uncle George to you both and I'm instructed to read it to you. I must assure myself that you understand the full implications and obligations outlined in it, and then give you each copies to be signed and returned to me for my files. You should be aware that you are about to enter into a serious legal undertaking. Is that clear?'

Sophie and Rachel's eyes met for a moment. Implications, obligations and legal undertakings sounded ominous, but neither of them commented. Taking this as consent, the lawyer reached for his reading glasses and read the letter out loud to them. It was dated February of that year and Uncle George had written it shortly after having been handed his terminal diagnosis. It wasn't long, but it contained three main criteria to be observed.

The first – which Sophie, and presumably Rachel, already knew – was potentially the trickiest. The two of them had to live together in the castle for three full months, until midnight on the thirtieth of September, the day before Rachel's birthday. Whether this date had deliberately been chosen by their uncle because it was directly prior to her birthday wasn't stipulated but Sophie wouldn't have been surprised. He had always remembered their birthdays and marked them with a card and a gift. By the sound of it, this year's gift was going to be way bigger than anything he had given them before. The onus was on both of them to observe this cohabitation stipulation rigorously. If either of them wavered – even missing one single day – both of them would lose any chance of ownership of the property. In order to guarantee they adhered to this, one of the boffins in one of Uncle George's highly successful companies had come up with an ingenious solution as the lawyer explained.

'In this digital age, your uncle has devised a way of ensuring you abide by his instructions. Upstairs on the first floor you'll find his study. In there is a computer with a touch screen, on which there is a special app. Every day you must both lay your hands on the screen at the same time to prove that you are indeed here and together. No exceptions will be permitted, for whatever reason. He was adamant about this. In a moment we can go upstairs and try it out, but first I need to know that this is quite clear.'

Once again the two sisters exchanged glances. Uncle George was taking no chances. They both nodded to the lawyer.

The second stipulation consisted of a list of works that needed to be carried out on the castle before the end of their stay, ranging from selecting and arranging installation of new kitchen units and appliances, to remedial work on the lead flashings around the chimneys, repairing crumbling stone arches, and a number of other tasks, including sifting through the bric-a-brac on the uppermost floor, disposing of anything unwanted and selling anything of value. Sophie nodded slowly. It was inevitable that an ancient place like this would have no shortage of repairs to be undertaken and junk accumulated over the centuries to be sorted. Presumably this was some sort of test of their initiative to see if they could be trusted to look after the property and, of course, a necessary preparation for the day when the castle could hopefully be put up for sale. She nodded to Signor Verdi.

'We have three full months to get the work done, so I don't see any great problems there.'

He nodded but added a word of caution. 'Good, but be aware that many businesses here in Italy close down for all or part of August, so do plan accordingly. Again, satisfactory completion of these tasks forms an integral part of the agreement.'

Finally, they had to oversee the harvesting of the grapes in the castle vineyard, the production of this year's wine, and the donation of fifty litres of last year's red to the local church. That, too, seemed fairly straightforward on the face of it – the letter said *oversee*, after all, not do all the work themselves. Both of them assured the lawyer they were happy to comply with the full complement of points their uncle had laid out.

The letter indicated that 'sufficient funds' had been deposited in a bank account, to which they would both be signatories, to pay for all the stipulated works and, most pleasing of all, he had also left enough cash to keep them 'in comfortable style' for the next three months. This was really good news. Sophie had been barely ticking over financially since returning from Rome and her savings had been dwindling fast, but three months rent-free and without household expenses would mean a considerable saving, even if this project went belly up and they didn't get the castle to sell after all. She signed the agreement willingly and saw her sister do the same.

After signing duplicate copies of the letter and returning the originals to the lawyer for safe keeping, they followed him up an imposing flight of stone stairs to Uncle George's study. Up here on the first floor the window openings were considerably wider and the rooms far lighter – and in consequence less intimidating – than downstairs. Here, for the first time since arriving in Paradiso, Sophie began to feel emotional. Their father had died when they were both very young and Uncle George, their mother's unmarried brother, had played a big part in their lives, despite having settled in America. Seeing his study with his chair and even a pair of reading glasses on top of a year-old copy of the *Wall Street Journal* suddenly brought home to Sophie that he, too, was dead, just like both her parents. There was an old photo on the desk of a smiling Uncle George with their mother and the two little girls on the beach at Perranporth where they had often holidayed together. Her eyes filled and she scrabbled in the pocket of her jeans for a tissue.

With the help of her faithful hound who started poking her with his cold wet nose, she gradually regained control. When she finally wiped her eyes and blew her nose she was touched and secretly pleased to see her sister had been similarly afflicted. She cleared her throat and they both went across to join the lawyer at the computer where he was tactfully averting his eyes from their grief.

'I'm sorry, Signor Verdi, but I was... we were very close to Uncle George, even if I hadn't heard from him for a while. He was a lovely man and we thought of him as a sort of replacement father after the death of our dad.'

The lawyer looked up again and nodded soberly. 'I knew him well and I had considerable respect for him. He was indeed a good man. Such a shame.' He checked that they were both sufficiently recovered to continue. 'Now, if you would like to stand side-by-side in front of the screen, I will explain.'

It was simple. First Sophie had to put her left hand on the screen, fingers splayed, and then Rachel had to place her right hand on top of Sophie's, similarly splayed, pressing down so that the ten digits were all touching the screen together. This was the first time Sophie had had any physical contact with her sister for six years and she felt the tears stinging in the corners of her eyes again. She wondered if Rachel was similarly affected but resisted the temptation to glance across to see. Apparently oblivious – or maybe just being diplomatic – Signor Verdi carried on with his instructions.

'The computer has now registered and recorded your handprints, so it's all set. When you see the thin red line around the fan shape of your fingers on the screen change from red to green, a message will appear.'

The screen flashed green and a note sounded on the computer. As it did so, a box appeared in the top corner:

Day 1 registration successful. 91 days remaining.

Signor Verdi nodded approvingly. 'So you can see that the time and date have been recorded. Today is Tuesday the first of July. It's imperative that you repeat this procedure every day up to and including the thirtieth of September. Including today, that adds up to a total of a ninety-two days. You can sign in at any time within each twenty-four-hour period, but it must be done. Like I told you before, I have strict instructions to inform you that missing even one day will invalidate your claim and the property will revert to other beneficiaries. If you run into any problems, you should contact me at once. Here's my card. You can always get hold of me on my mobile. Are we clear? Good.'

Back downstairs he passed on additional useful information before leaving. There was a man who did the garden on Thursdays and a lady who lived in the village who would come in most mornings to keep the place tidy and to look after the laundry. Once again, 'suitable remuneration' for both of them had already been arranged through the lawyer. The lady, Signora Morandi, would also be able to give the girls all sorts of practical information, from where to eat – Signor Verdi assured them the Vecchio Ristoro, the restaurant just across the piazza, was excellent – to medical services, refuse collection and shops. He issued them with sets of keys and the code for the Wi-Fi. An appointment had been arranged for them to meet the local bank manager the following day and to do this they could either travel there in Sophie's car or they could use the car that Uncle George had left here in the garage.

All in all, it sounded as though their uncle had thought of everything and Sophie was impressed – and relieved – that there was alternative transport available if her car were to give up the ghost entirely. In consequence her already strained emotions took another hit. After they had seen the lawyer out, Sophie sat down on a fine old chair in one corner of the hall and cried her eyes out all over again.

A matter of seconds later she felt a familiar nudge of a canine nose against her thigh, accompanied by a little whine of concern. She reached out to stroke the Labrador and glanced up to see her sister standing over to one side, tears running down her cheeks as well.

'He really was a lovely man, Soph.' The tender note in Rachel's voice did nothing to staunch the flow of tears down Sophie's face and she just dropped her head and cried until, finally, she could cry no more. She gave Jeeves a pat on the head and stood up, searching in her pocket for her tissue again. Finally surfacing, bleary-eyed, she turned towards her sister.

'I suppose I'd better bring the car in. How did you get up here?'

'By taxi from the station. I flew over from Orlando to Nice yesterday and took a train to Santa Rita this morning.'

'So you're living in the States?' This came as a bit of a surprise. Given that Rachel had been studying Spanish as well as English and had gone off to Puerto Rico, Sophie had always imagined her sister living in a Hispanic environment. Of course, thinking about it, she remembered that Spanish was widely spoken in Florida so maybe it wasn't so surprising after all.

Rachel nodded. 'Yes.' Her reply was curt and Sophie could see the tension on her face. Now that they were alone here, just the two of them, sooner or later they would have to sit down and talk but, for now, it didn't look as though Rachel was in a communicative mood, although she did manage a sensible suggestion. 'Why don't you go and fetch your car while I see if there's something here to drink?'

Leaving Jeeves with Rachel, Sophie went out, struggled to open the other half of the gates, and brought her car into the courtyard, pleasantly surprised that it started first time although the noisy clatter and the smell of burning were still a worry. She tried shutting the gates afterwards but only managed to get them roughly back together. Without some oil or grease, she got the feeling locking them properly was going to take a lot more strength than she could muster after two long days in the car. She grabbed her bags from the back seat and carried them up the steps and into the castle.

The heavy front door clunked shut behind her and she heard Rachel's voice echoing along a corridor. She found her in the large kitchen at the rear of the property. Although as their uncle had said in his letter it badly needed a makeover, the room was clean and comfortable in a nineteen-sixties way, with beige Formica worktops and starkly functional chocolate brown units with chrome handles. Although retro was supposedly back in style, she had a feeling this colour scheme wasn't, so she had to agree with her uncle's assessment that it needed replacing. Rachel was standing by the big old table with two mugs of tea in front of her.

'Somebody – presumably this Mrs Morandi – has stocked the fridge with more food than we'll be able to eat in a week. There's white wine and champagne in there if you prefer, but I thought as it's still the afternoon we might do better to start with tea. Besides, I'm feeling jet-lagged so I don't want to compound my problems with too much booze.'

'Tea's perfect, thanks.' Sophie glanced down at her dog stretched out on the floor at Rachel's feet. 'I'd better give Jeeves another drink. His bowl's in the car.'

'It's all right, I've already given him some water and he's drunk a fair bit.' Rachel pointed towards a bowl half-filled with water, surrounded by drops of water all over the tiled floor.

'Thanks, that was kind. Sorry, he's such a messy drinker.' Sophie was impressed. Steering clear of free alcohol, making tea and even thoughtful enough to give her dog a drink, this appeared to be a different Rachel from the one she had last known. She pulled out a chair and sat down, took a sip of hot tea and settled back, wondering what to use as a conversation starter.

Chapter 3

The conversation didn't have a chance to start. No sooner had Sophie sat down than Rachel picked up her own mug of tea and turned for the door.

'Like I said, I'm feeling zonked, so I'm going to stretch out on one of the sofas in the lounge and take a little nap.'

And that was that.

Sophie almost got up and followed her, eager to see the rest of the castle for herself, but she forced herself to remain seated. Rachel had been polite, but little more, and from her tone Sophie could tell she was still wary. She sat there, sipping her tea and wondering whether this was just a result of a guilty conscience or something else. After all, Rachel had gone off six years ago leaving her to look after their ailing mother without a backward glance. The only information she had gleaned so far was that Rachel had been living in the USA. Assuming they managed to cohabit for three months, half of the value of this wonderful old building would pass to her, but Sophie had no idea what her sister's plans would be after that. Would she stay in Europe or return to the USA?

She finished her tea and looked at her watch. It was gone half past five and she knew Jeeves deserved a decent walk in the fresh air after the long journey, so she decided to take the opportunity to kill two birds with one stone and check out the garden.

It rapidly became clear that there was far more than just a garden around the castle. As she walked out into the late afternoon air, the trees resounded to the calls of a multitude of little birds high in the branches and, beyond the trees, the land stretched onwards. The stone perimeter wall extended all the way along to the right, concealing them from the road, while the trees soon gave way to an open area of very arid lawn dotted with peach and apricot trees laden with fruit, beyond which was the unexpectedly large vineyard. The castle was situated on top of the ridge and the land was remarkably level here – and there was a lot of it. It took her almost ten minutes to reach the far end of the grounds where the stone wall turned to the left and finally stopped. The wall was replaced by new-looking wire fencing that formed a formidable barrier but allowed sweeping views over Santa Rita in the valley below.

Strolling back towards the castle, she came to a modern galvanised iron gate part way along the fence, and from the vehicle tracks in the gravel, it occurred to her this was how the gardener gained access to the property.

The estate – because that's what it was – was charming and very private, and after two full days cooped up in a car, Jeeves took full advantage, charging around and barking, begging for her to throw sticks and huge pine cones for him to retrieve and bring back to drop at her feet. She let him run about for as long as he wanted before he finally returned to her side and the two of them sat down – she on a bench and the dog stretched out in the dust at her feet.

A little while later she was just thinking about getting up again when she spotted a figure coming towards her. It was Rachel.

'Soph, you need to come and see this.' She sounded unexpectedly chirpy and Sophie jumped to her feet, as did Jeeves.

'I thought you'd gone for a lie down.'

'I did, but I couldn't sleep after all. It's a spooky old place so I came outside.'

Sophie followed her sister back until they could just about glimpse the rear of the castle through the trees once again. Here, off to one side, there were three stone outbuildings and it was in the first of these that she saw what it was that had excited her sister's attention. It was a large, sleek and no doubt expensive Mercedes saloon – presumably Uncle George's car. Sophie gawped at it in awe.

'Wow! You could fit my car in the boot.'

'It's gorgeous. And the lawyer said we could use it?' Rachel's eyes were just about bulging out of her head.

'That's what he said.' Sophie went over and peered in through the side window. It all looked amazingly luxurious with its leather-clad interior. 'It seems almost improper to think of Jeeves sitting on the back seat.'

'He's a good boy. I'm sure he'll behave.'

They were still ogling the car when a few minutes later they were surprised by a sudden short sharp woof from Jeeves and the sound of a male voice from behind them.

'Excuse me, ladies, but I thought I'd better come and introduce myself. My name's Dan.'

They both swung round in astonishment. The man was speaking in fluent English. He even had a soft American accent. More amazing was the fact that he was very good-looking and even more amazing was the fact that Sophie noticed. After her experiences with Claudio she had had very little interest in members of the other sex over the past twelve months. Such was her surprise, she actually took a step backwards, bumping into the wing mirror and banging her funny bone. Suppressing an expletive, she gave the man a welcoming smile, noticing out of the corner of her eye that her sister was also beaming at him.

'Hello, Dan. I'm Sophie Elliot, and this is Rachel. We're sisters.'

'I can see the family resemblance. You must be George's nieces. He often spoke about you.'

While he was speaking, Sophie took a better look at him. He was tall, with close-cropped fair hair and a stubbly chin. His shoulders were broad and he looked fit. He was wearing shorts and a faded T-shirt that bore the vestiges of a Harley Davidson logo on the front, and he looked very appealing. Sophie was almost annoyed at the unexpected ignition of a spark of attraction inside her. She soon discovered that she wasn't the only one to find him attractive.

'Hi, Dan, is that an East Coast accent I can hear?' Rachel was looking especially pleased to see him.

'It is. How did you work that out?' By this time Jeeves had also decided that the tall American was a friend and was standing up on his back legs, scrabbling at him with his paws while Dan fondled his ears. From the expression on Rachel's face she probably wouldn't have minded having her own ears – or more – fondled by him and Sophie saw her smile broaden even more.

'I recognise the accent because I live in the States. I've been living in Orlando for the past five years. Where's home for you?'

'Cambridge, Massachusetts, although I'm from New York originally.'

'So how come somebody from the United States has ended up here, Dan?' Sophie wondered if he was the gardener. And if he wasn't, how was it he was wandering about on private property?

'It's a bit complicated, sort of a busman's holiday, a mixture of work and leisure. I'm here on an extended summer vacation – it's like a mini sabbatical. I teach history at Harvard and I'm trying to finish writing a book. Nothing too exciting: a historical treatise on the influence of the so-called Saracen raids on the Mediterranean coastline in the Middle Ages.' He gave them a wink. 'It isn't likely to be a blockbuster. Anyway, George gave me a key to the gate back there and I've been keeping an eye on the castle since he passed away. I was walking up the track and I heard voices, so I thought I'd better check you weren't thieves about to drive off in the Merc.'

'Well, thank you very much. Is it you we have to thank for the beautiful flowerbeds?'

He shook his head. 'That's all down to Beppe. He does the garden. He comes in every Thursday.'

'So you knew Uncle George well?'

'We were good friends. I've known him for years. When he heard I was looking for somewhere to live along this part of the Ligurian coast for a few months, he told me about a house to rent just back along that way.' He waved in the direction from which he had come. 'He was a good guy and I was very sorry he died.' Looking back at them again he addressed himself to both of them. 'So how long are you staying?'

Rachel answered immediately. 'Till the end of September.'

Sophie saw what might have been interest on his face. 'That's pretty much the same as me. I arrived a month or

35

so ago and I'm planning on staying until early October before I have to go back to work. That should give us time to get acquainted.'

'And where did you say you lived, Dan?' Rachel was hanging on his every word.

He waved back towards the vineyard again. 'About a half mile that way. I'm in the stone house by the top hairpin bend. You can't miss it.' He glanced at his watch. 'I'd better get off. I'm sure I'll see you around.'

He headed back towards the side gate and both girls found themselves watching his retreating back. Sophie gave a tiny little internal sigh. With his broad shoulders and strong tanned legs, she couldn't deny that he did look good.

'Blimey, Soph, I think I'm in love… or at least lust.' Rachel kept her voice low but there was no hiding the feeling in her tone. 'What a hunk!'

For a moment, Sophie was reminded of all the times in their teens, and even in Rachel's first year at university when Sophie had been in her final year, when they had fallen out over random boyfriends. Time and time again Rachel, with her short skirts, cheeky grin and buoyant self-confidence had ended up the victor. Now they were almost ten years older, would history repeat itself? No sooner did the thought cross Sophie's mind than she did her best to dismiss it. First, he was American and he was going to disappear back to the States in the autumn and, second, she had already announced to the world in general – or at least to Chris and a few other close friends – that she had no interest in hooking up with another man any time soon. Most importantly, however, although she and her sister might have been lusting after Dan, he had given no sign of reciprocating their interest. Rather than respond, she decided to change the subject.

'I know it's still early, but I haven't eaten since breakfast and if I don't get something to eat soon I'll fall over. I think I'll treat myself to dinner in the restaurant across the piazza. Do you feel like coming? Hopefully they'll allow Jeeves in. I don't really want to leave him in a strange house all on his own straightaway. Apart from anything else, he'll probably bark the place down if he gets left behind.'

'I'll join you. I'm hungry too. Definitely a good idea.' Sophie was pleased to hear Rachel sounding perkier than before. Hopefully this was a good sign. 'I'm sure you'll be able to take Jeeves, although if you did have to leave him, inside those thick stone walls nobody's likely to be disturbed.'

'Apart from the resident ghosts, Rach.' Sophie reflected that this was the first time in six years that she had referred to her sister by the abbreviated form of her name she used to use.

'Don't even joke about ghosts. The place gives me the creeps enough as it is.' Rachel shuddered.

There was a welcome surprise in store for them as they came up past the side of the house. There, surrounded by a meticulously pruned hedge and protected by an enormous and clearly very ancient fig tree, was a swimming pool and, even more surprisingly, it was full of crystal clear, inviting water, ready for immediate use. Somebody must have readied it for them.

It was then that Sophie had a momentary lapse: instead of doing what she should have done – reaching for Jeeves's collar – she turned towards her sister to say something and that was all it took. In that split second, the water-loving Labrador set off at a gallop and flung himself bodily into the pool, sending up a plume of water as he disappeared beneath the surface, only to emerge seconds later with a broad canine smile on his face.

'Oh, God, Jeeves…!'

Sophie glanced across at her sister who erupted into fits of laughter as she watched Jeeves doggy-paddling happily around, snuffling to himself.

'Your face, Soph! It's a picture.'

'Bugger! You know what this means? We now have a smelly wet dog. Any self-respecting restaurant won't let us through the door I'm afraid.'

Sophie located the oldest towel she could find in the house and did her best to rub the worst of the water off the Labrador, but he was still very damp and decidedly whiffy as they went out of the gates and across the piazza to the Vecchio Ristoro. She was delighted to see that there were tables and chairs set up in front of the restaurant and, although it was fairly crowded, to her relief they were able to find a table to one side where her far from sweet-smelling dog wouldn't put anybody off their dinner.

There wasn't a written menu. The friendly elderly lady who came out to show them to their seats simply asked if they wanted the *menù gastronomico* or the *menù normale*. Sophie knew she was hungry, but she was also very conscious that she was short of cash. Until she discovered just what her uncle had meant by saying he had left them enough money to live in 'comfortable style', she opted for the normal menu just to be on the safe side, as did Rachel – and they didn't regret it. They didn't order any drinks, but a minute later the lady emerged carrying a carafe of red wine and a bottle of mineral water, along with a basket of lovely fresh-smelling ciabatta bread and a couple of packets of breadsticks. She deposited them on the table, gave a little bow and left them to it.

'Wine, Rach?' Sophie picked up the carafe.

'Definitely. I think I'm going to need a fair bit of Dutch courage before spending the night in there.' Rachel pointed towards the castle gates. 'I never thought I believed in ghosts, but now I'm not so sure. Let's face it, if they do exist, something tells me they'd live in a place like that.'

'It'll be fine.' Instinctively Sophie knew she needed to offer encouragement to her little sister. 'All you have to do is to think about our American neighbour and that'll stop you worrying.'

A smile spread across Rachel's face. 'You're right. I bet he'd come and protect us. Nothing beats a knight in shining armour… unless he takes it off, of course…' Her voice dissolved into a dreamy sigh.

Sophie was delighted to hear her sister sounding cheerful and decided this might be the right moment for them to start talking. She just needed to think how to break the ice. As a displacement activity, she picked up one of the little packets of breadsticks, tore off the top and slid them out onto the tablecloth. Two seconds later a damp dog's nose materialised at her side and plonked itself on her thigh. Hastily, she handed him a breadstick and saw him disappear under the table again. In the meantime, Rachel surprised her by launching into her tale without needing to be prompted.

'You probably want to know what I've been doing with myself for the past six years.'

Sophie took a big mouthful of wine and swallowed it without tasting it. 'I'd love to hear whatever you feel like telling me.' What she really wanted to know was why

Rachel had dropped out of the final year of her degree course at Exeter University.

'Do you remember Manuel?'

'Vaguely. Didn't I meet him at that Christmas party? Wasn't he the one with the pigtail?'

'Yes, that's him. He was at Exeter doing an English language course. He's from Puerto Rico and I decided to go off with him when he went back home.'

'But why? You were only a few months away from finishing your degree?'

'It's complicated, a combination of things. I'll tell you about it some other time.' Clearly this was not the time but Sophie didn't press her. The important thing for now was that her sister had started talking. 'I liked Manuel a lot, or at least I thought I did. We flew to Puerto Rico where he had told me he had a luxury yacht. The plan was to sail off into the sunset together and see the world.' From the downturn at the corners of her mouth, it was clear things hadn't gone according to plan.

'How much of the world did you see?'

'Not a lot. The luxury yacht turned out to be an ancient wooden thirty-footer held together by little more than faith and hope. We were only sailing for a couple of months altogether and I'd almost gone crazy, cooped up with him in the sticky heat, surrounded by sharks so we couldn't even go for a swim to cool down. Some luxury cruise it turned out to be! Somehow we managed to get as far as Georgetown in Guyana before the yacht gave up the ghost. Along with it went my relationship with Manuel.'

'So what did you do then?'

'With the last of my savings I bought myself a one-way ticket to Florida. By this time, I was broke, so I thought I'd find a job so as to save enough to get myself a plane ticket back to the UK. I got a job working illegally at first and then realised that I enjoyed living in the US. I worked for almost two years in a pizzeria in downtown Orlando before I finally managed to find myself a real job that paid a half decent wage, and applied for a Green Card.' She reached for her wineglass and took a sip. 'When mum died at the end of my first year in Florida, I was stuck. I'd been barely scraping by, just about managing to make ends meet, but I didn't have the money to fly home for the funeral. Besides, even if I had done, I would never have been allowed back into the US again. It's only now that I've got all my papers in order that I'm free to travel out and in.'

Sophie was about to respond when their antipasti arrived — and there was a lot to choose from. There were slices of huge tomatoes topped with pieces of succulent fresh soft mozzarella and basil leaves, drizzled with extra virgin olive oil. Alongside these were tiny fillets of anchovies and a cold seafood salad of baby octopus, mussels and clams. There was a wooden board loaded with different types of salami, from small spicy ones to large slices of what looked like mortadella laced with pistachio nuts. Unexpectedly there was also a piping-hot omelette whose bright yellow colour pointed to it having been made with real free range eggs — quite probably produced by the same hens she had heard when she first arrived. Sophie glanced across the table at her sister.

'Thank the Lord we didn't go for the *menù gastronomico*.'

It was excellent and as she ate, Sophie did a lot of thinking. She now knew where her sister had gone after leaving Exeter, but she still didn't know why she had taken this drastic step only a few months before graduating. No doubt Rachel would tell her more as they began to feel more comfortable together. However, this didn't alter the fact that their mother had received her terminal diagnosis only a few months after Rachel had left and yet she hadn't returned to see her. The story of being broke rang true but was unacceptable. One way or another, in Sophie's eyes, her sister should have begged, borrowed or stolen the money to fly home to be at her mother's side. There was no doubt that Uncle George would have happily flown her over, but presumably her stubborn pride had prevented her from asking.

Instead, the physical and emotional burden of supporting their mother right through her illness until her last days had been left to Sophie alone, and she knew it would be a long time before she could forgive her sister — if ever. Part of her felt ready to explode with all the pent-up frustration she had been storing up for the last six years but she managed to control herself. They had to sleep under the same roof for another ninety-one nights and it made no sense to antagonise her touchy sister, so she concentrated on her meal and tried not to think about it too hard.

The food helped a lot. The next courses were equally superb. First there was a local speciality called *farinata*. Sophie had never come across this before and had to ask what it was. It turned out to be thin yellow pancakes made from chickpea flour, served hot, torn roughly into odd-shaped chunks, and they tasted delicious. These were followed by a heap of char-grilled prawns and a mixed salad. Sophie feared she wouldn't have room for a little panna cotta at the end, but somehow managed, and it was divine. It was an exceptional meal and when the bill arrived, she was very pleasantly surprised to find that it hadn't cost much more than her pizza and salad in France the previous night. She was all set to pay the whole thing, in spite of her money worries, but Rachel insisted on paying her half and was amazed that, unlike in the States, they didn't have to add on a huge service charge.

They were sipping their little espresso coffees before heading back to the castle when they heard a familiar voice and looked up to see Harvard Dan emerge from the interior of the restaurant with a beautiful dark-haired woman at his side. When he recognised them, his face broke into a broad smile.

'Hi, again. Enjoy your meal?'

Choking back her surprise and a twinge of what might even have been disappointment at the sight of the other woman, Sophie answered.

'One of the best meals I've ever had. If I carry on like this for three months I'll need a crane to get me out of here.'

He gave them a little wave and bade them goodnight. As he and his lady friend strolled off, Sophie heard her sister's voice.

'Bugger!'

'Bugger, indeed.'

Chapter 4

Sophie slept remarkably well that night, but only after a shaky start. Somebody – presumably Signora Morandi – had prepared two rooms for them side-by-side at the rear of the castle on the first floor and to Sophie's surprise both rooms had en suite bathrooms which had quite obviously been created, or at least modernised, recently. The water was hot, the rooms immaculate, her huge king-size bed superbly comfortable and the towels and bed linen soft and luxurious. There was also ample space for her to put Jeeves's bed below the open window without fear of tripping over it. Altogether, it was like a top-class hotel – which allowed pets.

The trouble started twenty minutes after she turned the light out. She was lying there in the remarkably bright moonlight, mulling over the events of the day before drifting off to sleep, when she heard what sounded like shuffling footsteps outside in the corridor. She had closed her door just in case Jeeves decided to go for a midnight stroll, but she hadn't locked it and now she rather wished she had. She listened more closely and then suddenly heard a sinister creak of floorboards outside the door. Her eyes opened wide and she sat up in bed, all manner of scary thoughts rushing through her head. She, like her sister, had never believed in ghosts, but she found herself having serious doubts about that now here in this spooky location. The creak came again and she glanced across at Jeeves who was still fast asleep in his basket clearly illuminated by the moonlight. Slightly reassured by his lack of interest in supernatural phenomena, she climbed out of bed and tiptoed across to the door in her bare feet. After a few seconds' pause to summon up her courage, she turned the handle silently and pulled the door towards her so she could peer through the gap.

Her first reaction was one of relief as she saw nothing but shadows. Heartened by this she opened the door wider, stepping out into the corridor and looking around apprehensively. Then, to her horror, she was confronted by a vision and her hand shot to her mouth in disbelief. Illuminated by a shaft of moonlight, a figure in white appeared before her and she took a sudden step back, banging her bruised elbow against the door frame as she did so. This made her squeak with pain and the figure turned towards her.

It was Rachel in her nightie.

'For crying out loud, Rach, you frightened the crap out of me.' Nursing her aching elbow, Sophie reached back into her room with her fingers, feeling unsuccess-fully for the light switch. In spite of the pain, she felt an overwhelming sense of relief that the midnight apparition did not after all have a supernatural origin. She did her best to sound untroubled. 'What's the problem?'

'That creaking noise… did you hear it?'

Suddenly there was another creak – this time from the room behind Sophie and she glanced round to see Jeeves raise his head from his basket and gave a cursory thump of the tail at the sight of his mistress wandering about. The sound of the creaking wicker was one that Sophie recognised and with which she was familiar, but to her

46

sister it must have been the last straw. Rachel squealed and jumped back in concern – fortunately without banging her own elbow. Sophie was stunned into immobility for a few moments before being attacked by a fit of the giggles. As she stood there, shaking with laughter, she heard her sister's voice.

'It's not funny, Soph.' The old familiar petulant tone was all too recognisable.

'Not to you, maybe. Take a look – there's nothing here but a sleepy Labrador.'

'Yeah, well, we all make mistakes.' There was ample moonlight in the corridor for Sophie to see her sister's face. It was as pale as her nightie. 'I was scared, Soph. I was really, really scared.'

'Don't tell me you've suddenly decided you do believe in ghosts?'

'No, of course not. It's just… I was scared.' The petulance had been replaced by a childlike helplessness. 'It's a spooky old place and we're all alone.'

Sophie did her best to offer some reassurance – just as she had done so many times when they were growing up together. 'Don't worry, Rach, we've got Jeeves to protect us. You know what they say about animals and ghosts? If they don't feel there's anything untoward, we don't need to worry. To be honest, I was a bit scared myself, but he was snoring happily and he hasn't even bothered to get out of his basket.' Sensing a certain amount of residual fear still emanating from her sister, she made a suggestion. 'Would you like him to come and sleep in your bedroom? Or if you want to stay with me tonight, it's an enormous bed. There's bags of room.'

She saw her sister pull herself together and shake her head. 'I'll be fine, thanks. Goodnight.' And she returned to her room.

–

Next morning Sophie was woken at just before seven by a cold wet nose poking her bare arm. She opened her eyes and glanced down to see a pair of big brown eyes staring up at her from the floor.

'Good morning, Jeeves. Sleep well?'

She gave his nose a scratch and his long pink tongue reached for her fingers. She slipped out of bed, pulled on some clothes and let herself out, doing her best to keep Jeeves from making too much noise in the corridor as he bounced around happily in anticipation of his walk. Hopefully Rachel was still asleep after an untroubled night.

She went down to the kitchen and used the back door – a narrow but massively thick old wooden door studded with ancient square-headed nails – and locked it behind her, just in case. The key was about the size and weight of a banana and she reflected that back in the Middle Ages key rings had no doubt been a whole lot bigger and stronger than nowadays. Tucking it into the pocket of her shorts, she followed Jeeves out into the garden. She paused for a few moments beneath the pine trees, breathing in the scent of resin in the still comfortably cool morning air, and wondered which way to go. Of course there was ample space in the grounds for him to run to his heart's content, but she rather liked the idea of seeing a bit more of the village so she led him round to the front – carefully avoiding going round the side with the pool.

She heaved one of the gates open enough for them to be able to squeeze through, hoping that the grating noise wouldn't disturb the neighbours – not that there really were any close neighbours to speak of.

She and Jeeves walked across the square and into a narrow lane – little more than an alley really – where the only living thing they saw was a scrawny black and white cat that took one look at the big dog and leapt athletically about five or six times its own height onto a wall and disappeared. For his part, Jeeves appeared quite oblivious to it. The houses were made of stone, dating back centuries by the look of them, and no two were alike. Emerging from the narrow alley, Sophie started to see gardens with masses of scented bougainvillea, ranging in colour from deep purple to light pink, spreading luxuriantly over the walls, while palm trees punctuated the skyline. When the houses ended she was faced with a choice. The alley deteriorated into a rough track leading sharply downhill between an olive grove and a vineyard while a narrow path to the left promised to take them in the direction of the sea. She chose the path.

Before long they reached the same bench where she had first spotted her sister yesterday, and they continued on past it until the trees petered out and she was walking along the very crest of the ridge towards what looked like an old military installation situated directly above the sea far below. It was more exposed up here and the vegetation was now just sun-scorched grass and low scrub amid the rocky outcrops. As the view opened out on either side she could see for miles and miles in both directions. The sea was light blue at the shore and a deeper blue further out, and there was hardly a wave to be seen. The sky was cloudless and it felt good to be alive. Clearly, they hadn't named this place paradise for nothing.

She threw a stick for Jeeves to retrieve and let her mind roam. It looked as though relations with her sister were gradually on the mend and she began to feel a bit more confident that the two of them would be able to last out the full three months without scratching each other's eyes out. What would happen then? From what she had gathered, Rachel had given up her current job in order to come over here for the summer but Sophie assumed she would then want them to sell the castle so she could head back to the States with her half of the proceeds. That was only an assumption and it would be interesting to find out if there was anything or anyone calling her to return to Florida. As for Sophie herself, the short answer was that she didn't know.

After a degree in English at Exeter, followed by an MSc in Media and Communications at LSE in London, she had set her sights on a career in journalism, and the job offer that had sent her to Rome had appeared like manna from heaven at the time. Since the company had gone under and she had ended up unemployed, she had been having a lot of trouble trying to find another job. With newspapers going out of business left, right and centre, she had even been coming round to thinking that she should maybe try her hand at something completely different – the question, of course, was what? She felt comfortable being back in Italy so maybe she should try to capitalise on her fluency in the two languages to look for something over here if she couldn't find an online job in journalism. The two obvious careers were teaching English to Italians, or hospitality. Could she see herself as a teacher or could she see herself behind a reception desk for the rest of her life? It was a conundrum.

'Well, Jeeves, at least I've got three months to think it over.'

He sauntered up to her side, tail wagging lazily, licked her hand, and then trotted back into the bushes in search of a stick to carry home as a trophy. She watched him happily occupied without a care in the world apart from finding a stick and getting his food, and she had to admit it wasn't a bad life being a Labrador with all this open space in which to run around. And of course the castle grounds themselves were enormous and she wondered how much the place might be worth here in Italy. Pocketing a few hundred thousand or maybe even more would radically alter her situation. She gazed back in the direction of the village and realised that from here she could clearly make out the battlements of the castle and the trees surrounding it. There was no question it was a unique and surely desirable property. Might it be her financial salvation?

When she got back to the castle, it was to find that Signora Morandi had already arrived and was in the kitchen. She was doing something at the oven and turned as she heard the back door open. She was probably in her sixties, but agile-looking and, as she saw Sophie, her eyes lit up.

'*Buongiorno.*'

'*Buongiorno, Signora Morandi? Sono Sophie.*'

Signora Morandi beamed at her and continued in Italian as they shook hands. 'How splendid. You speak Italian. Signor George told me you and your sister spoke it, but I was afraid I might have to try to speak English to you. I'm afraid we would all have had a hard time if that had been the case.'

While they were talking Jeeves pushed past and trotted over to say hello. After a moment of apprehension, the signora must have realised he was friendly and she bent down to pet him. As she did so, Sophie remembered she had a confession to make.

'I have to apologise for messing up one of the towels last night. The dog got into the swimming pool just as we were going out to the restaurant and I had to try to dry him off. I looked for the oldest towel I could find and I was going to wash it today.'

'Don't you worry about that. Leave that to me. What a handsome dog. Is he yours? Did you bring him all the way from England?'

'He's even got a passport, although I'm sure he doesn't mind whether he's in England or in Italy. You can speak to him in any language and he'll understand as long as you're holding food.'

'Talking of food, have you had breakfast yet?' Seeing Sophie shake her head, she continued. 'I've just put some croissants in the oven to heat up. They're fresh this morning. Shall I make some coffee as well?'

'That sounds super, Signora Morandi. I'll go and see if my sister's awake.'

'Please call me Rita. Everybody does.' She smiled again. 'I'm the last of seven children and my parents must have run out of ideas by the time I arrived, so they named me after the town. I still live in Santa Rita now.'

'So you're the saint of Santa Rita.' Sophie went up to wake Rachel, reflecting that somebody who turned up with fresh croissants and offered to make breakfast was a worthy candidate for canonisation in her book.

She left Jeeves with his nose pointed at the oven door, nostrils flared, and went up to her room. As she went in, she could hear the sound of the shower running next door. She went into her own bathroom and took a shower herself, emerging clean and fresh ten minutes later to find Rachel waiting for her in the corridor.

'Hi, Soph. No dog?'

'He's downstairs in the kitchen. We've just been out for a walk along the headland. It's another gorgeous day and the views are amazing.'

'I'm sure…' Rachel looked a bit uncomfortable. 'Look, Soph, about last night, I've been a bit jet-lagged and I suppose I just wasn't thinking straight. Sorry.'

'No worries.' Sophie caught her sister's eye. 'Seriously. I was a bit freaked out myself, seeing as it was our first night in a spooky sort of place. The good news is that I slept well and neither Jeeves nor I were visited by any ghosts. All well with you?'

Rachel nodded. 'It took me a bit of time to drop off but then I slept almost all the way through.'

'Great. Coming down to the kitchen? Signora Morandi's arrived with hot croissants and she's making us breakfast as we speak. She answers to Rita, but you have to speak to her in Italian, if you can remember how.'

'Better than you might think. All the people in the pizzeria where I was working for the first couple of years spoke either Spanish or Italian and I got fairly fluent. I'm still good friends with most of them now so I often find myself speaking both languages.'

Back downstairs, Sophie found her dog stretched out under the table with a suspicious number of crumbs on the floor around him. Rita was quick to explain that she had given him half a bread roll as 'he looked hungry'. Sophie thanked her and added a caveat.

'Labradors in general, and this one in particular, are notoriously greedy, so don't be fooled. Given half a chance he'd eat until he explodes.'

Rachel introduced herself and soon the three of them were chatting freely. Sophie was impressed to hear that her sister's Italian was indeed fluent – albeit with an occasional Spanish word thrown in from time to time. Just as Signor Verdi had said, Rita was a goldmine of information on everything, from the best places to walk the dog, to the history of the castle, which was indeed medieval. By the time they had finished their breakfast they both knew a lot more about Paradiso and its surroundings.

Their appointment at the bank was at eleven o'clock down in the town so they left Jeeves in the kitchen with Rita and set out early, so as to check out the town and the beach. Sophie felt more comfortable taking her own car, but it was still making that same clatter and as they drove down the road that led into town, the smell of burning started up again. Rachel also noticed.

'That's a bit ominous. Hope it's not the brakes – this is a steep hill.'

At that moment they reached the first hairpin bend and their attention was drawn to a charming stone house set back from the road right at the apex of the corner. It was all on its own in a large garden among the trees and there could be no doubt about it. Sophie was about to comment when Rachel got there first.

'That must be Dan's house… I wonder if he's got that brunette with him.' Her voice was still wistful. Clearly she hadn't given up hope yet. To be honest, neither had Sophie, but she decided not to speculate out loud.

At the bottom of the hill, just as they were coming out onto the main road, Sophie spotted a garage on the left-hand side and made a quick decision. Pulling across the road, she drove onto the forecourt and was still getting out of the car when a tall man in overalls emerged from the workshop, wiping his hands on an oily rag.

'*Signora, buongiorno.*'

'Good morning, I wonder if you could take a look at my car. It's making a funny noise.'

He nodded. 'I could hear that. That's why I came out. It sounds to me as if you've blown your exhaust.'

'Is that bad?'

To her considerable relief, he shook his head. 'It'll probably need to be replaced, in part or completely, but it's not a major job.' He caught her eye and smiled. 'Or expense.'

'That's good to hear. Um… when might you have time to take a look at it?'

'If you can leave it with me for a couple of hours, I'll see what I can do this morning, even if it's only a temporary fix.'

'Fantastic, thanks. Is it far from here to the town centre and the beach?'

He shook his head. 'A quarter of an hour on foot at most. Just follow this road straight on down.'

Sophie thanked him profusely, left him the car, and she and Rachel set off along the road as instructed. Sure enough, in little over ten minutes they found themselves in the main street. This road ran parallel to the sea and was set back behind the first row of buildings by the beach. It was full of shops, many of them clothes shops and, as so often here in Italy, with at least three pharmacies. The good news was that they also spotted no fewer than four ice cream shops with a wide selection of flavours on offer. The nineteen seventies buildings flanking the main street weren't particularly attractive, but the selection of shops, bars and restaurants looked promising. After locating the bank, seeing as they still had half an hour, they carried on to the seafront. The main Via Aurelia – the old Roman road around the coast – ran parallel to the beach, separated from the fine expanse of sand by a raised promenade flanked by palm trees.

They strolled along the promenade, admiring the view. Although Rita had told them it would get even busier when August arrived, the beach was already packed with people bobbing about in the sea, children playing, and pedalos trailing slowly up and down. As was common all over Italy, the beach had been carved up into mostly private *bagni* where, for a price, holidaymakers could have the use of sunbeds, parasols, changing cabins, showers and even a beachside bar. They noted one called *Bagni Aurelia* which Rita had told them was run by her nephew and decided to come down here for a swim in the sea at some point – although with the luxury of their very own pool up at the castle, it hardly seemed necessary.

All in all it was a pleasant little seaside resort, complete with candy floss, ice creams, and shops selling buckets and spades, but without any of the antique charm of Paradiso. Sophie could see why Uncle George had chosen to live up there rather than down here. She swivelled her head round and could just make out the crenellated top of the castle among the roofs and trees on the hilltop and she resolved to explore the building fully later on when they got back home, as the view from the roof was bound to be exceptional.

At the bank they were ushered into the manager's office with unexpected deference. It was clear that Uncle George had been a valued client. Sophie knew from personal experience that bureaucracy in Italy, particularly in the banking system, was often protracted and infuriating. In consequence she was surprised and delighted to find that the formalities were quickly concluded, and the manager produced a little key which he handed across to them.

'This is your key to the safe deposit box. If you'd like to accompany me to the vault, your uncle wanted you to take a look at the contents.'

Down in the basement was a heavily armoured vault with a row of small lockers along one wall. Sophie inserted the key into number 337 while the manager inserted his own and they opened it together. The manager withdrew his key and stepped back discreetly.

'Please take your time. When you've finished, just close the door of the box again and it'll lock automatically. Don't forget to keep the key somewhere safe. If you need anything, press the button on the wall by the door. *Arrivederci.*'

They shook hands and he left. Rachel reached in, pulled out a slim tin box and opened it on a convenient tabletop. Inside were three envelopes. Two were thick and unmarked, the third was much slimmer and had both their names on it. Rachel opened this one first and read it out. It was dated February like the one Signor Bianchi had read out to them and it wasn't long.

> *Dear Sophie and Rachel*
> *By the time you read this I will be dead. They tell me the cancer is inoperable and I have only a few months left. I can't complain. I've had a good life and I'm pleased to say I don't have too many regrets, but prime among these is the fact that I*

will not see you two girls again. Still, I can at least provide for you.

Along with this note you will find an envelope for each of you with hopefully enough euros to keep you over the summer months. I do so hope you will be able to kiss and make up. I love you both dearly and it saddened me greatly to think of you separated for so long. If you want to do something to thank me, then all I ask is that you put aside your differences and become the loving sisters you used to be.

I send you my love and wish you both the happiest of lives. Thinking of you always.

Your uncle
George.

Rachel managed to get through it without losing her voice completely but she was reduced to barely a croak by the time she finished. Wiping away her own tears, Sophie reached for the remaining two envelopes and handed one to Rachel. She opened hers and was stunned to find fifteen thousand euros in green one hundred euro notes. A quick bit of mental arithmetic told her that this added up to more than a thousand euros a week from now until the end of September – certainly more than enough for her to live in extremely *comfortable style*. She glanced over at Rachel and saw her looking similarly staggered.

'Blimey, Rach, we're rich.'

'You aren't joking. How amazingly generous of him.' Rachel managed a little smile in spite of the tears in her eyes. 'Good old Uncle George.'

'Amen to that.'

Chapter 5

When they got back to the garage it was to find the car already waiting for them outside on the forecourt. The mechanic came out to explain what he had done.

'You're going to need a new exhaust and I'll order that if you give me the go-ahead. It should be here in a matter of two or three days. In the meantime I've done a quick repair with an exhaust bandage that should last a few weeks.' He went on to tell them how much the new exhaust would cost to buy and fit, and Sophie was pleasantly surprised – not least as she now had five thousand euros stuffed safely into the bottom of her bag. They had both decided to leave the bulk of the cash in the safe deposit box just in case, but five thousand each would surely last them for ages. The little silver key to the box in the bank vault was also safely stowed with the money in her bag and they would hide it somewhere secure when they got back to the castle. She thanked the man warmly and offered to pay for what he had done but he waved her money away and told her she could pay for it at the end. She gave him her phone number and he promised to let her know when the new part arrived.

The 'quick repair' had a magical effect and the car sounded completely different now as it positively purred up the hill to the castle. When they got there they were greeted warmly by Jeeves who, according to Rita, had behaved himself perfectly in their absence. While Rachel retired to her room to check her emails and Rita returned home to prepare lunch for her husband, Sophie and Jeeves went for another stroll around the grounds. As she was resting in the shade of a monkey-puzzle tree, watching the dog doing his best to dig a hole in the sun-baked ground, her phone rang and she saw from the caller ID that it was Chris.

'Hi, Chris. How's things?' She felt a familiar shot of pleasure at the sound of his voice.

'I'm fine but how about you? Did the trip go well? Did the car behave itself and did Jeeves behave himself? Come to think of it, did you behave yourself?'

Sophie told him all about her journey and described the castle and Paradiso in glowing terms, all the while thinking about the exact nature of her feelings for him. It was genuinely nice to hear his voice and to chat to him. She knew him so well and there was little doubt in her mind that he was a close friend, probably the best. She had been thinking about him a lot in the course of the journey down here. Because he had been going out with Claire, her flatmate at uni, she had always suppressed the attraction she felt for him, but might she want her best friend to morph into something more?

She was reminded of a scene from *When Harry Met Sally* when Billy Crystal tells Meg Ryan that men and women can never be just friends because sex always gets in the way. Was this true? Could she and Chris ever be more than just friends?

They had a good chat, but without any hint of anything other than friendship on his part, and when she got back to the house, she found Rachel at the kitchen table with her laptop.

'Nice walk, Soph?' There was no doubt she sounded more open today.

'Yes, thanks, and I just had a call from Chris.'

'I remember him. He used to go out with your flat-mate, didn't he?'

'Yes, but they split up around the same time I split up with my Italian man.'

'I've been wanting to ask you about your love life. I thought you might have been married by now. You were always looking for your one and only, weren't you?'

Sophie was pleasantly surprised to hear her sister speaking about such things. Apart from Rachel's brief description of the places she had visited and the jobs she had had after running away, she hadn't said much. She certainly hadn't mentioned her own love life, and her conversation had been limited to everyday practicalities – apart from a few lustful remarks about their new American friend. Hopefully this increased communication would help in thawing the strained relations between them.

Sophie managed a smile as she answered her sister. 'And I thought I'd found him.' She went on to relate the sad story of Claudio and her discovery of his multiple infidelities. 'Looking back on it, I feel such a fool.'

Rachel gave her a look that was full of sympathy and Sophie's spirits rose. 'It happens. So surely this opens the door for you to get together with Chris. You got on so well with him and I always thought he was very good-looking.'

'To be completely honest, I've just been wondering that myself. He's remained a friend, a very good friend. In fact he helped me pack my stuff last week.'

'And he hasn't hooked up with anyone else since his break-up?'

'Not so far as I know – and I'm sure he would have told me if he had.'

Rachel had a simple solution. 'Well, why don't you invite him to come and stay?'

'What, here?'

'Why not? There are loads of rooms and it'll be fun to have company. I remember him well and I remember I liked him a lot. It'll be great to see him again and that way you'll have all the time in the world to see how you feel about him – and how he feels about you.'

'I suppose I could...' Sophie wasn't used to her little sister telling her what to do and it felt a bit strange – even though her suggestion was eminently sensible.

'Go on, do it. After all, if you don't invite him this year, you never will, because by next year we'll have sold this place. We have to. Look what I've just found on the internet.'

Rachel turned her laptop so Sophie could see the screen. It was the website of a big international real estate company and the property on display looked vaguely similar to this one. It was described as a medieval castle on the Mediterranean coast near Genoa, probably not more than a hundred kilometres to the east of Paradiso, and the asking price was a phenomenal six million euros.

'And that one's a good bit smaller than this place and with nothing like as much land as this has.' Rachel looked up from the screen and let her eyes roam around the room. 'Blimey, Soph, we could be sitting on a fortune.'

'There's asking and there's getting.'

This had been one of their grandfather's favourite sayings and Sophie used it deliberately to urge caution. Mind you, she thought to herself, even at half that price and after no doubt paying a load of taxes to the government, it would make both of them very rich indeed. Seeing as her sister was sounding less confrontational, she risked a personal question or two.

'So what's your plan? What are you going to do if all goes well and we manage to sell the castle for a load of money? Are you going to head back to Florida? Is there somebody waiting for you over there?' She was moderately surprised to see Rachel shake her head. The one constant in Rachel's life in her late teens and early twenties had been boys – an ever-changing panoply of them.

'Nobody special. At least not now.' Her voice tailed off, unexpectedly sombre, and Sophie did a bit of digging.

'Not now, you say, but there *was* somebody…?'

'There was.' A long pause followed and Sophie was beginning to think she was about to be told to mind her own business when Rachel supplied a bit of clarification. 'It all fell apart just over a month ago.'

'Had you been together long?'

'Two and a half years.'

'Almost as long as me and Claudio. And why did it fall apart?'

Rachel gave a heartfelt sigh. 'I did something stupid.'

This sounded all too familiar and ominous but, before Sophie could speak, her sister added a few words of clarification – up to a point. 'But not what you think. Gabriel freaked out and I don't blame him.'

There was a finality in her tone that brooked no further questions – at least for now. Rachel subsided into silence once more, and this time she didn't pick up her tale again. Sophie hesitated before deciding to give her the chance to fill in the blanks when she felt like it. Instead, she returned to her other question.

'I'm sorry to hear that, Rach, but what about your plans for the future? Where would you like to live? If we sell the castle for that kind of money, you could choose anywhere in the world.'

She was pleased to see the light return to her sister's eyes.

'I honestly don't know for sure. I like Florida and I've got some good friends there; not so many back in England as we've lost touch over the years. For that matter, I've still got heaps of friends in Spain, near Toledo. I've known them since my year abroad while I was at uni and we've been corresponding regularly. But first things first, I really want to go back to Exeter and finish my degree.' She glanced up at Sophie. 'I've already been in touch and they've said yes. They've agreed that I can start back in October and just do the final year.'

'That sounds brilliant.' It really did. And what was even better was that Rachel appeared to be prepared to start talking a bit more freely at last. 'And then what?'

'Like I say, I haven't really made up my mind yet. I've enjoyed the job I've had for the past couple of years in the PR department of a big hotel chain. I think I'm good at what I do and they seem happy with me; in fact, they've told me they'll give me my job back any time I want. The chances of promotion are good there, but without a degree, any degree, I know I can only rise so far up the ladder.'

'So your plan is to go straight off to the UK in October, get your degree, and then maybe head back to America. Let's hope it all works out.'

'As long as you and I don't fall out this summer and screw up Uncle George's master plan.' Suddenly that harder note was back in Rachel's voice.

'You think we will?'

There was a pregnant pause before Rachel replied. 'It won't be my fault if we do.'

'Just so long as you don't do something stupid again.' Sophie had only been thinking out loud and she realised her mistake the moment she said it.

She saw a flash of irritation cross her sister's face. 'Neither of us is perfect, Soph. Doing stupid things isn't just my prerogative. Like I say, let's hope *we* don't screw up.' She laid a lot of emphasis on the pronoun. Sophie was quick to pour oil on potentially troubled waters.

'You're right, Rach; we're both going to have to work at it. Now, let's go and sign in while we remember. It would be annoying to fail before we've even started. Besides, I've been meaning to explore the castle properly. I've not been up to the roof yet, have you?'

'No, nor me. Sounds like a good idea.'

Rachel's prickly moment appeared to have passed and Sophie made a mental note to try to be more conciliatory in future. What was past was past and she would do well to remember that, if she and Rachel were to co-exist harmoniously for the next three months – if not longer. Besides, from what she had seen and heard so far, it really did appear as though this was a new, much more responsible incarnation of her sister.

Accompanied by Jeeves – not for fear of ghosts, Sophie kept telling herself – they set out on their exploratory mission, starting on the ground floor. The first thing they did as they walked around the living room, was to remove the spooky dust sheets from the remaining furniture and fold them into a neat pile. As a result the room looked a lot less forbidding, not least as this revealed a number of very un-ghostly twenty-first-century items, ranging from a pair of smart leather sofas to a massive TV. The shutters were permanently open now and sunlight filtered in to reveal the magnificent vaulted ceiling and a huge tapestry of a medieval hunting scene hanging on the far wall. It was a stunning room.

Beyond this were another couple of rooms, one of which had been transformed into a gym with a table-tennis table, a treadmill, a rowing machine and weights. Rachel studied them for a few moments before turning towards Sophie, looking and sounding much more like the old Rachel once more.

'No excuse for letting ourselves go, now that Uncle George's given us enough money to be able to eat at the Vecchio Ristoro twice a day every day from now till October.'

Sophie rolled her eyes. 'But what a way to go…'

Up on the first floor they found no fewer than six more bedrooms, all immaculate and all with en suite bathrooms. Certainly, Sophie reflected, if she were to decide to invite Chris to come and stay – and it was clear Rachel wouldn't object – there would be ample room for him. They went into Uncle George's study and she felt that same pang as his now obsolete belongings reminded her that she would never see him again. Doing her best to control her emotions, she and Rachel went over to the computer where they put their hands on the screen, one on top of the other, fingers entwined and pressing down as instructed. Sophie murmured a silent prayer that they would still be doing this in three months' time. Sure enough, the computer hummed into life, the red outline changed to green and a message flashed up, indicating that they had successfully logged their presence: day two… only ninety more to go.

On the floor above, little or nothing had been done and they both soon realised that the task of sorting through what Uncle George had referred to as bric-a-brac wouldn't be a quick one. There was all manner of junk strewn about willy-nilly in three large, low-ceilinged rooms. They spotted everything from piles of old newspapers and magazines now yellowed with age, maybe even going back to the Fascist period, to fascinating objects like an intricate and beautifully handmade wooden birdcage, three ancient fishing rods, and a number of metal items maybe linked either to agriculture or the Spanish Inquisition, but whose original purpose was now impossible – and probably inadvisable – to guess. A narrow wooden staircase led up from the top landing to a low doorway, the hefty door secured by two massive bolts. With the aid of her shoulder, Rachel heaved it open and they emerged, blinking, into the midday sunlight, high up on the roof of the castle.

The view, as Sophie had expected, was incredible. From here they could see the coast curling away to the east and to the west for miles and miles, and the wide expanse of clear blue sea towards the distant horizon was dotted with yachts, fishing boats and even what looked like a cruise liner. Behind them, rows of tree-covered hills and mountains formed the Ligurian Apennines, a solid barrier between Liguria, where they now found themselves, and the rest of northern Italy, resulting in the clement micro-climate to be found along this bit of coastline.

'Wow, what a view.' Sophie went across to the battlements and leant over to look down, hastily ducking back as she saw just how far they were from the ground. 'I pity any besieging army trying to take this place.'

She glanced around the roof. A pair of massive chimneys emerged over on the far side and she remembered that these were another of the tasks on Uncle George's to-do list. Rachel sat down on a gnarled old wooden bench and Sophie went over to join her, patting Jeeves's head as he came and settled down between the two of them, panting in the heat.

'I mustn't let Jeeves stay out in the direct sunlight for too long. Elementary physics tells us that dark objects retain heat more than light ones.'

They sat there in silence for a few minutes, feeling the burning heat of the sun on their faces. Jeeves wasn't the only one who would soon need to head for the shade. It was Rachel who broke the silence.

'So what are you going to do for the next three months, Soph? A bit of a holiday's all well and good but you'll get bored before long, won't you?'

'I'm still working, so that'll give me quite a bit to do. Come to think of it, today's Wednesday, isn't it? I've got a deadline to hand in a piece tomorrow at noon and I haven't done a thing since last Friday.'

'Does that mean you're still writing?'

Sophie nodded.

'What sort of stuff? I thought you said you'd lost your job in Rome.'

'That's right. Ever since then I've been writing short stories for a couple of magazines. It doesn't pay brilliantly, but they each publish one every couple of weeks, so it adds up and it's been paying the rent while I look for another job – so far without success.'

'Although thanks to Uncle George's cash, you hardly need to bother now, don't you?'

The same thoughts had been going through Sophie's head as well since their visit to the bank and Rachel's discovery of the possible value of the castle, but she was naturally cautious. Until she and Rachel had managed to cohabit for the full period and the castle had sold, she knew it would be unwise to stop looking for a permanent job or give up the story writing, which she rather enjoyed.

'I'll keep going with the writing. I mean, even if you and I were to suddenly become millionaires...' She looked across at her sister and grinned. 'Sounds amazing, doesn't it? Anyway, even if we end up with loads of money, we're still going to need something to do or we'll be bored stiff. After all, you've got things mapped out for yourself career-wise. I need to do the same.'

'These short stories, what are they? Love stories?'

'Women's fiction, although I throw in a bit of heartache – you know, people dying or going off – just to keep them guessing.'

'You always had so much more imagination than me. I tell you what you should do: you should write a book, a romance. Haven't you always wanted to?'

'It's definitely something I've often thought about. The thing about writing is that unless you're J. K. Rowling or Dan Brown, it's hard to make a living at it. What was that movie where the guy says "The only kind of writing that makes money is ransom notes"? He knew a thing or two.'

'But now you've been handed a free pass, or at least a lifeline for the next three months, why don't you give writing a try.'

'I might well do that. And what about you, Rach? How are you going to fill your time this summer?'

'I thought I'd have a little chat to the gardener tomorrow. Didn't Dan say he comes in on Thursdays?

Maybe he'd let me help him. I'd love to learn all about vines. Depending where I end up, it would be fun to grow my own grapes and even make my own wine. Apart from that, there's a huge reading list I've got to work my way through before I restart my degree. All in all I reckon we'll both manage to avoid getting bored. Besides, we are in Paradiso after all. Have you ever heard of people being bored in paradise?'

'From what I remember of Genesis, it has happened before. Be careful if you decide to pick an apple off a tree to keep well away from the snake.'

'Ah, but I'd need an Adam first and so far I haven't got one of those.' Rachel shot Sophie a grin. 'Although I wouldn't mind sharing an apple with our American neighbour.'

Neither would Sophie, but she didn't comment. What was great, however, was to hear her sister sounding more like the sister she knew and loved. Could it be things were gradually returning to normality between them after the great rift? Still, she reminded herself, she had yet to learn exactly what it was that had tipped Rachel over the edge. Had it been work pressure in her final year, some yet unnamed man, or something else?

She didn't have time for conjecture as Jeeves got up, shook himself, and made his way over to the shade of the chimneys. Sophie stood up in her turn. 'I'd better take Jeeves back inside. It's mad dogs and Englishmen time.' She looked at her watch. 'It's gone two o'clock. After last night's meal I thought I'd never eat again for as long as I lived, but I now realise I could manage a sandwich or something. Coming down?'

Back in the cool of the kitchen, Sophie checked out the contents of the fridge. Rachel hadn't been joking last night. It was absolutely jam-packed. As well as food, there were bottles of wine, including a 1998 Dom Perignon champagne that was no doubt worth a small fortune. Together they pulled out lettuce, tomatoes, cheese and salami and made themselves excellent sandwiches with the fresh bread brought earlier by Rita. Sophie was eating her sandwich and sipping cold mineral water – they had both decided to avoid drinking wine at lunchtime – when she noticed a narrow door in the corner that she hadn't spotted before.

'I wonder where that leads.'

'Down to the dungeons or the torture chamber I expect.'

'Rachel, don't! Besides, wasn't it you who was wandering around the corridors last night looking terrified?'

'All right, all right, I'm sure there aren't any dungeons. I tell you what – maybe there's a wine cellar down there.'

After finishing her meal, Sophie gave Jeeves his lunch, and while he was occupied vacuuming up his food in record-breaking time, she went over to the little door. She turned the key in the lock and it opened easily, fortunately without any spine-chilling creaking. She was delighted to see a light switch and she flicked it on to reveal a stone staircase leading downwards. She glanced back at Rachel who was fiddling with the coffee machine.

'I'll go and take a look. Wish me luck.'

Rachel had been right with her second guess. Sophie found herself not in a dungeon but in a low-ceilinged room with racks of bottles along one wall as well as half a dozen huge round glass bottles in wicker cases even taller than Jeeves, like much larger versions of the old Chianti flasks, and by the look of them they too were full of wine. There was nothing scary down here apart from some dusty cobwebs, one of them inhabited by a sinister-looking striped black and yellow spider the size of a plum. At the far end was a sloping ramp leading up to hefty wooden doors at ceiling height, which presumably opened into the courtyard outside, as there was no way all this wine could have been brought in through the kitchen and the narrow door. Sophie resolved to make her next mission to explore the outside of the castle as closely as she had done the inside. In the meantime one thing was clear – if she and Rachel felt like drowning their sorrows, there was more than enough wine here to keep them permanently plastered.

After giving her sister the good news – and a warning to avoid Stripy the spider – she drank the remarkably good espresso Rachel had managed to conjure from the machine and then took Jeeves out for a walk in the garden. She wandered through the trees, hugging the shade, turning over in her head what Rachel had said about writing a book. In fact, it was something she had often considered but had never had the time or the financial security to try. It was ironic, given her recent bad experience with Claudio, but the fact was that the genre that attracted her most was romance. All she needed was a story.

That afternoon she retired to the relative cool of the dining room and sat down at the head of the huge table with her dog at her feet and worked on the short story she was due to hand in tomorrow. This one was a salutary tale of infidelity and revenge set in a little West Country village. She managed to write almost all of it before having to stop as she couldn't think of a suitable way of finishing it off. The villain of the piece, a flashy used-car salesman called Monty, needed to get his comeuppance, but short of pushing him into a passing combine harvester, she couldn't think of anything suitably bad, but not too bad. Death would be a rather too extreme penalty for his dalliance with flighty barmaid Maisie, but it needed to be something that would resonate with the readers. Shelving the question for now, she glanced at her watch and saw that it was already gone five. The sun was shining brightly outside and even in here it was now quite warm so she decided to go for a swim. She had no idea whether it would be all right for Jeeves to join her in the pool, so she resolved to risk it for today but to query it with the gardener tomorrow.

She went up to her room and changed into a bikini, pulling her shorts and top back on over it just in case she met someone. She called out to Rachel but there was no response and her bedroom door was wide open. Down in the kitchen there was no sign of her there either, so she and Jeeves went out of the back door and made their way around to the pool, only to discover that Rachel had had the same idea.

And so had somebody else.

Sophie emerged through the little wooden gate, hanging onto her dog's collar for grim death, just in time to see the trim, suntanned body of a certain Harvard professor dive into the water from the springboard while her sister, wearing a fairly skimpy bikini, stood looking on adoringly and clapped enthusiastically as he surfaced. A cohort of cheerleaders couldn't have done better.

'Hi Soph, got your story finished?' Rachel turned towards her with a big satisfied smile on her face. 'I went for a walk and happened to meet Dan so I asked him if he'd like to come for a swim.'

Sophie wondered whether her sister's walk might have deliberately been in the general direction – or even right up to the front door – of Dan's house, if not his bedroom, but as he hauled himself out of the water and came over to shake her hand, she had to admit that it had been a good idea. He looked somehow taller without clothes and there was no missing the fact that he had a lovely, well-honed body. As he stood in front of her she couldn't help following the little streams of water with her eyes as they ran down his strong chest, across his ribbed stomach and beyond, before dripping onto the ground at her feet. Yes, he certainly was a good-looking man. She shook his hand, doing her best to avoid the little seismic shock this aroused in her.

'Hi, Dan. Good to see you again.' By this time Jeeves had temporarily forgotten about the pool and was jumping up to be petted by his new American friend.

'Hi, Sophie. What's this about a story? Are you a famous author?'

'No, I'm really a journalist but I'm out of a job at the moment, so I'm keeping the wolf from the door by writing stories for a couple of magazines.'

'But she's thinking of writing a book.' Rachel was quick to mention the conversation they had had earlier. 'She's going to become the next Barbara Cartland.'

Rachel rolled her eyes. 'I wish… but I'm just thinking about it right now. Not like you, Dan, you're actually writing a book. How's your magnum opus coming along?'

His face creased into a smile. 'Well, I have a beginning and an end. All I need now is a middle lasting about fifty or sixty thousand words.'

'Sounds not too different from the problem I've got with mine. It's the ending I need. I'm trying to think of a suitable punishment for an adulterer in a little English village, present day. Killing him off's a bit extreme.'

'How about public humiliation? That's what they would have done in the Middle Ages. I know, what about tipping him into the river... or even better, into a heap of manure? That should do it.'

'Brilliant, Dan, manure it is. Maybe you should take up writing romance novels yourself.'

'I'd be useless at romance. I'm a man, remember?'

How could I forget? Sophie studiously kept her eyes off his body. 'Men can and do write romance. You should give it a try.'

She walked across to a row of half a dozen sunbeds and dropped her towel onto one. Accepting the inevitable, she let go of Jeeves's collar and watched as he launched himself into the water. While the others were busy laughing at his antics, Sophie slipped out of her shorts and her top and gave a surreptitious glance down to check that everything was in place before going to the shallow end and walking down the tiled steps into the blissfully cool water.

She swam around lazily for some time, cooling down and secretly watching Dan performing some stylish dives while her sister drooled over him. For his part, he looked happy but didn't demonstrate any sort of romantic interest in either of them – in fact he seemed decidedly more affectionate towards Jeeves. In the pool, the Labrador was in his element and, seeing his head was now level with his mistress's, he became boisterously affectionate and almost drowned her in the process.

Finally refreshed, she persuaded her dog to relinquish the water and to follow her out of the pool. She sat down on the sunbed and as she did so Rachel came up with a very sensible suggestion.

'Fancy a drink, Soph? I'll go and get a bottle of wine and three glasses, shall I?'

After Rachel had gone off, Dan padded over and sat down on the edge of the low stone wall beside Sophie's sunbed, reaching down to scratch Jeeves's tummy as the dog lay sprawled on his back on the paving stones grunting happily to himself.

'He's a lovely dog, Sophie. Have you had him long?'

'Just over a year. He's still a youngster.'

'Does that mean you work from home? You said you're a journalist, didn't you?'

'I was a journalist in Rome for four years until the company folded. Now I'm working from home and looking for a new job, but I'm seriously considering a career change, though I don't really know to what. I enjoyed living in Italy and I'm wondering about staying on and maybe doing something like teaching English as a foreign language.'

Dan straightened his legs and stretched. As he did so, Jeeves on the ground did the exact same thing and Sophie almost laughed out loud at the scene.

'Teaching's not a bad life.' He gave a little shake of the head. 'As long as you don't have to teach kids – at least that's the way I see it. My students are all adults – theoretically – and I certainly enjoy what I do.'

'Lecturing at Harvard's impressive. Congratulations. You must be good at your job.'

'I hope so. The main thing is that I'm lucky to have found a job doing what I love most. I've always been totally hooked on history.'

They chatted more about history and his current writing project and she enjoyed his company. It was refreshing to find a man who was both good-looking and intelligent. He was friendly and chatty but there was no getting away from the fact that his interest in her – or, indeed, her little sister – didn't appear to go any further than simple friendship. She had no idea whether this was because he was already in a relationship – he wasn't wearing a wedding ring, but that meant nothing these days – but, whatever the reason, it was probably for the best. Apart from the fact that she was maybe starting to have similar feelings for Chris, now that she had just about made peace with her sister the last thing Sophie needed was a pitched battle with Rachel about some man.

The three of them sat and chatted, sipping the very drinkable white wine Rachel had found in the fridge. This was in an unmarked bottle and Dan told them it was in all probability from the castle's own vines.

'Check it out with Beppe when he comes in tomorrow. He's responsible for the vines. He makes mostly red but there's also some white.'

By the time Dan collected his things and left, Sophie felt she knew him a lot better and she liked him a lot. After he had left, she glanced across at Rachel.

'Nice guy.'

'Very nice guy. Pity he's already taken.'

'You reckon?'

Rachel shrugged. 'It's inevitable. A Harvard professor who looks like that – and with a body like that – must have women queuing up for him halfway across the States. No, I think we've just found ourselves a friend, but nothing more.'

Sophie nodded in resignation. But maybe it was for the best.

Chapter 6

Beppe arrived early next morning – so early in fact that when Sophie emerged for Jeeves's walk in an unkempt state, just wearing a hastily donned pair of shorts under the old T-shirt that served as a pyjama top, she was surprised and a bit embarrassed to bump into the gardener just outside the back door. Jeeves trotted over to say hello while Sophie, conscious that she wasn't wearing very much at all, crossed her arms across her chest and gave him a cheery smile that belied her discomfiture.

'Good morning. You must be Beppe. I'm Sophie. George was my uncle.'

'Good morning, Sophie. I am indeed Beppe and you're even more beautiful than your uncle told me.' He was probably around the same age as Rita, well into his sixties, his bald head as brown as a nut, and he had one of the most infectious grins Sophie had ever seen. In spite of his gushing flattery and her dishevelled state, she couldn't help smiling back at him.

'Beppe, you need to get your eyes tested. I've just rolled out of bed and I know how scruffy I look.' Cautiously she removed one arm from her chest and shook his hand. 'But thank you for the compliment all the same.'

'And you're here with your equally beautiful sister, I believe?'

'She's still asleep but I'm sure she'll thank you for the compliment too. In fact you'll be seeing her soon. She's always been keen on gardening and she wants you to tell her all there is to know about vines, grapes and wine-making.'

He was still grinning. 'That could take some time. Hopefully she has a year or two to spare.'

While Jeeves went off to cock his leg on a convenient tree, Sophie and Beppe chatted and she soon realised that he must have known Uncle George very well indeed as it was clear that her uncle had often spoken about her and Rachel. She explained how their father had died while they were still young and that Uncle George had always been there for them. Beppe nodded his head in sympathy.

'Yes, George told me. So sad. That's why George took such an interest in you. He loved you both very dearly and the rift between you two sisters over the last few years was hard for him.'

Sophie reflected that Uncle George and Beppe really had been close if he knew this. 'It was hard on me, too, Beppe. Still, we're starting to make up now and I'm sure it won't be long before we're back to being proper sisters again just like before.'

'Very good, very good. Now, is there anything I can help you with? You know about the peaches and the apricots, don't you? If you don't start eating them they'll rot. And the figs on the big tree by the main gates are ready now and are excellent. Just watch out for the wasps. They love them. Is there anything you need done or shall I get on with my own work? I'm here all day.'

'Just one thing, Beppe, I don't suppose you've got any oil or grease, have you? I really need to do something about the front gates and the lock. They're terribly stiff.'

'Leave it to me. I never use that entrance and nobody'd been in or out that way for well over a year. I'll see to it.'

'Thank you so much.' Another thought suddenly occurred to her. 'Would you happen to know if it's all right for my dog to swim in the pool? It isn't going to be bad for him or for the pump or anything, is it?'

He stopped to think for a few moments. 'Dog hair probably isn't too good for the filters, but I don't think they're too expensive to change and George left me more than enough petty cash to take care of that. I'd be more worried about the dog. I'm not sure if the chemicals we put in the water might be harmful to him in the long run. Next time you go down into Santa Rita, why don't you ask Gianni? He knows all about that sort of thing. It was his cousin's firm who installed the pool here three or four years ago.'

'Thank you, I will. And where can I find this Gianni?'

'When you reach the bottom of the hill and head for the seafront, you'll see his garage on the left. You can't miss it.'

Realisation dawned. 'I met him only yesterday. He fixed a problem with my car.'

Beppe nodded sagely. 'Gianni can fix anything. I know him well so I can ask him if you prefer.'

'Don't worry. I need to take the car back to him one of these days for a new exhaust so I'll ask then. Thank you, Beppe.'

She and Jeeves went down as far as the vineyard, and as she walked, Sophie made plans for the day. The weather forecast last night had indicated that rain was on the way tonight or tomorrow so she resolved to give Jeeves a good long walk today and decided to follow Rita's advice and head away from the sea for a change. The hills here ran down to the sea like fingers, separated one from the other by valleys like the one where Santa Rita lay, and Paradiso was on top of one of these finger-like ridges. Rita had told her to walk back along the ridge as it slowly started to climb in the direction of the distant wooded mass of the mountains above the coast. There was a good path leading to the next village and a way of coming back again by a slightly different route. But first, Sophie reminded herself, she had to finish the short story and send it off. Sight of a huge compost heap reminded her of Dan's manure suggestion and she allowed herself a few minutes to think about him in particular, but also about her own situation in general as far as men were concerned.

Dan was a nice guy but she agreed with her sister that he was almost certainly not available, and it seemed clear he wasn't interested – for whatever reason. And then there was Chris. She was beginning to come to terms with the fact that she really might be starting to think of him in a romantic way, and she was coming round to agreeing with Rachel's idea of inviting him over. Apart from anything else, he was such a good friend and he had been such a help to her that he deserved a treat, even if it turned out he didn't feel the same way about her. And surely an all-expenses paid summer holiday in a medieval castle on the Ligurian coast wasn't to be sniffed at. She would contact him to make the offer and see what he said.

The interesting thing, of course, was the fact that it was only since arriving here in Paradiso that she had started considering the prospect of another relationship after the emotional shipwreck brought about by Claudio. A full year had passed, so maybe it was time to move on. She couldn't continue to live a monastic life forever. The thought cheered her. Could it be she had finally managed to get some sort of closure? Perhaps coming back here to Italy had been the jolt she had needed to move on.

Back in the kitchen she found Rita had once again brought fresh bread and croissants. First things first, Sophie tried to give her money to pay for these, but it transpired that Uncle George had left money for household expenses as well as garden expenses and there was no need. Murmuring a silent thank you to her incredibly organised and generous uncle, she went upstairs to take a shower and put on some clothes. She was just emerging from her room a bit later when she met Rachel on the landing.

'Hi, Rach. I didn't hear you wandering about last night so can I presume you've got over your fear of ghosts or whatever it was?'

'Absolutely. And I slept almost right through last night. Have you already been out?'

'To take Jeeves for his walk, but I must try to remember to wear a bra on Thursdays. Beppe starts early.'

Over breakfast, she told Rachel of her plan to go for a long walk and asked if she wanted to come too. Rachel declined, saying she wanted to spend time with Beppe in the garden, so Sophie left her to it. An hour or two later, once the used-car salesman had been dumped in the manure and the story sent off to the publishers, she loaded a big bottle of water and a couple of fresh apricots into a little backpack and set off with Jeeves.

It was very hot by now and she could feel the increased moisture in the air. The sight of clouds beginning to build on the horizon indicated that the rain predicted for tonight was almost certainly on its way. After a few hundred metres on the road, she turned off onto the track Rita had told her about and she was able to let Jeeves off the lead. At first the track led through a pine forest which provided welcome shade but this soon gave way to low scrub and she came out into the full force of the sun. Fortunately, for the very first time, there was now a little breeze that brought some welcome relief.

After walking for half an hour or so she came to a little ruined chapel and stopped for a rest in the shade of its dilapidated walls. The timbers supporting the roof had long since rotted away and there was more vegetation inside than architectural gems. She tipped some of her water into the plastic bowl she had brought specially for that purpose and Jeeves gulped it down gratefully, tail wagging. She took a couple of photos of the chapel and then sat down on what once upon a time might have been a horse trough. She was sitting there, sipping from her bottle and wiping the sweat from her brow, when her phone rang. The caller ID told her it was Mariarosa, her best friend from when she had lived in Rome. Mariarosa worked for the big media company where Sophie's employers had rented an office and was one of the few people to have met Claudio and to be aware of the acrimonious conclusion to their relationship.

'*Ciao, Mariarosa. Come stai, cara?*'

'I'm fine thanks, Sophie. So how are things in Paradise castle?' Sophie had told her all about her uncle's generous bequest. 'Does it have a ghost?'

'No ghost, thank goodness, although it's a spooky old place. I'm getting used to it now and it's really lovely. There's even a pool.'

As they chatted Sophie let her eyes range over the panorama before her. Beyond the trees she could see the roof of the castle highlighted against the deep blue of the sea, with the lighter blue of the sky beyond, now flecked with cotton wool clouds. The air was alive with the sound of bees collecting nectar from the colourful wild flowers at her feet and her canine companion was staring up at her with adoring eyes. She stretched her legs and leant back against the warm stone wall of the chapel, reflecting that this really was a little piece of paradise.

However, her idyll was about to be shattered as Mariarosa came to the main reason for her call.

'Listen, Sophie, I've put my foot in it. I was out for a drink with the girls from work and they were asking if I'd heard from you. I was telling them how you'd inherited a castle and how happy I was you'd landed on your feet after everything that happened to you last year. They were all ever so happy for you. But then who should appear but Claudio of all people, throwing his money around and generally behaving like a big-headed pain in the butt? After what he did to you I refused to talk to him so I left, but it now emerges that Carla, one of the new girls, got talking to him and must have told him that you're back in Italy.'

Sophie did her best to reassure her. 'It could be worse. Don't worry, Mariarosa. So he knows I'm back; Italy's a big country.'

'Yes... but... you see, I've always thought Paradiso was such an unusual, romantic name that I mentioned it to the girls and Carla told him.'

'Ah...' Sophie let her breath escape slowly, trying to suppress her irritation. As the seconds ticked away she knew she had to say something to try to defuse the situation. 'It's all right, Mariarosa, it's not as if he's going to do anything about it. After the way he behaved, even a moron like Claudio can be under no illusion that I never want to see him again. Surely even he can't be stupid enough to think there's any point in trying to get in touch. Don't worry, it'll be fine.'

They carried on chatting but once the call ended and Sophie finally returned the phone to her pocket, she kept wondering whether he really might be that stupid. One thing was for sure – the last person on earth she wanted to see was Claudio.

After another hour's walk in the hot sun, she finally reached the next village and was delighted to find a bar with tables in the shade, a drinking bowl full of fresh water for Jeeves, and a fine selection of homemade ice cream for her. A wonderful mixture of kiwi, lemon and strawberry ice cream and a bottle of sparkling mineral water went a long way towards cooling and calming her down. She was living in a castle after all, designed to repel assault from far more formidable foes than Claudio. She glanced down at the dog, stretched out on the cool cobbles at her feet, untroubled by such thoughts. Sometimes the idea of a life built solely around walks, food and snoozing had definite attraction.

When she got home again, feeling hot and sticky and quite weary, the sky was already starting to cover over and the humidity in the air was palpable. The first thing she did was to slip into her bikini and then she and Jeeves headed for the pool. She found her sister there sunbathing topless and the thought did occur to her that this might have been in the hope of another visit from their American neighbour, but such was not the case today.

'Hi Soph, good walk?'

'Great, thanks. I'll tell you about it when I've had a good soak in the pool. I'm sweltering.'

Some time later, she climbed back out of the pool and stood under the poolside shower with Jeeves to wash the chemicals out of her hair and his fur, deciding she had better go down to Santa Rita in the morning to ask Gianni the mechanic about any possible detrimental effects of the chlorine on her dog. Not that Jeeves looked too bothered – he was soon rolling around on his back, legs in the air, growling ferociously at some imaginary prey. Dabbing herself dry, she sat down on the lounger alongside her sister and told her about the lovely walk and the not-so-lovely revelation from Mariarosa. Rachel snorted and told her not to worry.

'From what you told me about the break-up, Soph, Claudio must have got the message that you never want to see him again. Don't give it a thought. You won't hear a thing from him.'

Sophie's phone beeped and she checked it apprehensively just in case there might be a message from Claudio, but instead she saw it was from Gianni the mechanic telling her the new exhaust had arrived and to drop off the car at the garage any time she wanted. She replied, thanking him and saying she would be down the following morning. After pressing *Send*, she turned to her sister.

'I'm taking the car in tomorrow morning. Fancy coming down with me for a bit of retail therapy? I'm going to need another bikini and you might want to do the same – and remember, young lady, you're supposed to wear both bits.' She tempered the admonition with a smile.

Rachel smiled back and Sophie was delighted to see her looking so relaxed. 'Yes, big sister. You sound just like mum. It's all right, I won't show you up. I knew nobody was coming this afternoon. I saw Dan when I was out for a walk this morning and he told me he was going to be hard at it all afternoon.'

'What's he working on?' An image of Dan, stripped to his waist, muscles rippling and running with sweat, digging a hole in the ground came to mind and, in spite of her nascent feelings for Chris, she suppressed a sigh.

'His book... or so he said.' Rachel actually did sigh out loud. 'He really is such a hunk.'

Sophie couldn't disagree. Of course, she had never seen Chris with his shirt off so maybe there was a similar treat in store for her there if he were to come over to the castle to visit her. She settled back onto the sunbed and breathed deeply, feeling pleasantly relaxed. Her relaxation didn't last long as her sister's voice shook her out of her somnolent state.

'By the way, Soph, I've invited a few people to come and stay.'

Sophie raised her head and stared at her disbelievingly. 'You've already invited them? Wouldn't it have been a nice idea to run it by me first?' Quite clearly the old self-centred Rachel hadn't gone away with the passing of the years after all.

'Well, I thought seeing as you've invited Chris, you wouldn't mind... It's only fair.'

'First, I haven't invited Chris – which, by the way, was your idea in the first place – and there's a big difference between inviting one person we both know and a load of strangers.'

'Not a load of them, I promise. And they're very nice. They're those friends of mine from Toledo I told you about. I did a bit of phoning around and one thing led to another.'

Sophie gave a resigned nod. 'So how many have you invited? Two, three, four?'

Rachel had the decency to look a little sheepish. 'I'm not completely sure but maybe seven or eight... certainly no more than ten.'

'Ten...!' Sophie could feel her temper rising and she deliberately took her time before replying. 'And when is this invasion going to happen? Please don't say tomorrow.'

Rachel shook her head violently. 'No, of course not. In a few weeks, I expect. Probably some time in August.'

'You expect?' Once again, Sophie had to struggle to resist the temptation to grab her little sister and shake some sense into her. 'And how many days are they going to be staying, or don't you know that either?' From the expression on Rachel's face it was clear that she didn't have a clue, so Sophie decided to lay down the law. 'Remember what Benjamin Franklin said, "Guests, like fish, begin to smell after three days." Got that?'

'But they're coming all the way from Spain...' Rachel's expression hardened. 'Besides, half this place is mine and if I want to invite people, I can. Why can't you stop being the same old bossy big sister calling all the shots?'

Sophie had had enough. 'Whatever... I'm going in to wash my hair. I'll see you later.' She had just stood up and collected her towel when another thought occurred to her. 'And we both need to sign in on the computer or you won't have a castle to invite them to.'

Chapter 7

Next morning Sophie didn't want to get up. She had been woken just after midnight by the sound of a torrential downpour which had continued for most of the night, occasionally punctuated by claps of thunder and bright flashes of lightning which had worried Jeeves to the extent that she had even had to get up a couple of times to sit beside his basket and calm him as the storm passed overhead. In consequence she hadn't slept a lot, and when he started nudging her with his nose around seven o'clock she would happily have rolled over and gone back to sleep again. Instead, accepting the inevitable, she kicked the covers aside and got up. The good news was that it was a whole lot cooler in the room after the overnight rain and the temperature outside, while not cold by any stretch of the imagination, was definitely refreshing.

She and Jeeves let themselves out of the front gates, which now opened smoothly and without protest, and murmuring a sincere thank you to Beppe and his oil can, she headed along the track towards the sea. This time they carried on along a narrow path as far as the military-looking construction festooned with a mass of wires and aerials right on the headland overlooking the beach far below. The rain had turned parts of the path into a quagmire and by the time they got to the end, Sophie's trainers were soaked and muddy and Jeeves's legs were those of a chocolate Labrador while the upper part of his body remained black.

She sat down on a low wall and ran her fingers through her hair. Although it was freshly washed, she could feel it was getting very scruffy. Maybe with Uncle George's money she might treat herself to a visit to a hair salon. She knew her friends back in London, including Chris, had been on at her for months about her not looking after herself properly since the break-up with Claudio, but she simply hadn't been bothered. Maybe now was the time to start again. Thought of Chris made her take out her phone and send him a short message telling him how great Paradiso was and asking if he felt like coming over. As she pressed *Send* she knew she would be very happy to see him again – whatever her intentions towards him or his towards her.

Dinner the previous night had been subdued, although the quality of the cured ham and handmade *agnolotti* they found in the fridge had been excellent. Rachel had spent the evening sulking, while Sophie had been left wondering if she had maybe been too hard on her impulsive sister. She now sat and continued with that train of thought. After the death of their father when Sophie was just seven, she had always looked out for her little sister, doing her best to help her mother who had often struggled to cope. Time and time again, however, Rachel had repaid her efforts with indifference, tantrums or worse. At university, when Sophie had been studying hard for her finals, she had also had to put up with continuous demands for help from Rachel in completing her first year English assignments. The problem, as Sophie knew well, wasn't a lack of intelligence, it was a lack of application to her studies. For Rachel, her social life had always come first.

Sophie dreaded to think what this gang of Spaniards was going to be like. Noisy, no doubt. Hopefully the castle walls were thick enough to avoid disturbing the rest of the village too badly, but she had a sinking feeling that she herself wouldn't get much sleep while they were here. Of course, she told herself, it was only fair and right for Rachel to invite friends to stay, but she shouldn't have done it off her own bat without consultation. Sophie had tried to make that point time and time again over dinner, but Rachel had remained grumpy and monosyllabic and had disappeared off to the lounge to watch a movie from Uncle George's huge collection as soon as the meal was over. Sophie cleared away the dishes and hoped that her sister's moment of pique would pass; otherwise day four of their time together promised to be grim.

Back at the castle, Sophie found a hose and tap by the back door and managed to wash the worst of the mud off her shoes and her dog. Hearing the noise, Rita came to the door, took one look at Jeeves and went off to get his towel – now lovingly washed and ironed. Sophie made sure he was reasonably dry before setting her shoes on a ledge in the sun to dry and following him into the kitchen barefoot. To her surprise, she found Rachel already sitting at the table, sipping a cappuccino.

'Hi, Soph. What happened to your shoes?'

She even produced a smile and Sophie felt a wave of relief. That had so often been the way with Rachel's tantrums and moods – although ferocious at the time, they soon passed.

'The rain last night turned the ground into mud.'

'Still, it's exactly what the garden needed. Beppe told me it was going to rain and he was right.'

'How did it go with him? Do you know all about vines now?'

'I haven't even scratched the surface. There's a hell of a lot to know, especially when it comes to pruning and, of course, making the wine. Anyway, that's one less thing for you to worry about. You can cross keeping an eye on the grape harvest off Uncle George's list of tasks for us. Leave that to me.'

This was all sounding very promising and Sophie was delighted. 'Terrific, Rach. Thanks.'

'Oh yes and the wine to the church, I'm on that as well. Next Thursday Beppe and I are going to deliver a *damigiana* – that's the name for the big fifty-litre glass containers – of red to the priest.'

'Is that for his personal consumption or as communion wine?'

'I have no idea, but it's good stuff. Beppe and I tasted it yesterday and it's really good. I brought a couple of bottles up and they're in the fridge. He tells me it's okay to keep them in the fridge in this hot weather.'

'That's what we're drinking tonight, then. So, are you still up for a visit to the shops this morning? We should buy some food – we can't keep relying on Rita to supply us – and I wouldn't mind getting my hair done.'

'I got mine done just last week before I left Florida, but I never say no to a bit of shopping.'

They left Jeeves in Rita's care and drove down to the garage just after nine. Sophie had quizzed her about hair salons and as a result had phoned to make an appointment for ten thirty. It would be good to tidy herself up a bit. She might even buy some new clothes – something she hadn't done for over a year. Did this mean she was over Claudio and ready to move on? The precise direction in which she would move on was still unknown, but this seemed like a positive first step. Thought of Claudio, however, reminded her of Mariarosa's call yesterday and she experienced a sense of impending doom at the thought of a potential visit from him. She did her best to chase him from her mind, but it wasn't easy.

As she handed the keys over to Gianni at the garage, she told him where they were living and asked him about pool chemicals and Labradors. He didn't seem too worried.

'I can't see they could harm your dog – after all if the water's safe for little kids, it should be safe for a fur coat – but I'll ask my cousin, Dario. He installed the pool up at the castle so he knows all about it. His workshop's in Albenga, but he travels all along the coast. Next time he's in the area I'll get him to call in at the castle and test the water for you. That way you'll know for sure.'

Down in the town centre, Sophie and Rachel spent an enjoyable hour working their way through the numerous clothes shops along the main street and Sophie emerged not only with a new bikini but also a couple of new tops and a light and, by her standards, very short summer dress that Rachel bullied her into buying. As ten thirty approached, she left her sister browsing the shops and headed off to the salon. The young stylist – a good-looking man with a pony tail and a diamond earring, whose mother turned out to be a bosom buddy of Rita's – gave her a long, searching look and suggested radical action.

'You have beautiful long hair – and I love the colour – but don't you think it might be time for a serious trim?

For the health of your hair, it really needs to be cut back a bit.'

In for a penny, in for a pound, Sophie agreed and sat back, hoping for the best. She had always had long hair but she was aware that it had been getting out of hand – mainly because she hadn't been bothered doing anything about it. While the man, Romeo, got to work, they chatted and he proved to be as good a source of information about Santa Rita and its surroundings as Rita herself, but with the added benefit of being half the housekeeper's age. He told Sophie where along the coast the nightclubs were, which were the chic bars and the best restaurants for atmosphere as well as food. He also told her about the social highlight of the year, the beach festival scheduled for *Ferragosto* – the fifteenth of August.

'Until you've tried dancing in sand, you've never danced. Promise me you'll come along.'

Sophie promised.

When she emerged from the salon, she felt very self-conscious at first. He had probably only taken three or four inches off her hair but it felt completely different. Thinking about it, for the last six months or more she had only ever worn it tied back in a simple ponytail, as much to keep it out of her face as anything else. Now it was hanging loose, just grazing her shoulders, and it felt good, but she knew it would take a bit of getting used to. When she met up with Rachel in a cafe as arranged, she was relieved to get her sister's seal of approval.

'You look great, Soph, really great.'

Sophie ordered an Americano and they chatted and it soon emerged that Rachel had been on the phone to Toledo.

'There are eight of them coming – two couples and four individuals. I've met almost all of them and I'm sure you'll like them.' Sophie saw her shoot an apprehensive glance across the table. 'Is it all right with you if they stay for a week? I promise if they're a nuisance or if you don't get on with them I'll send them packing earlier – just say the word. And I'm sorry I didn't check with you first.'

There was a big difference between three days of potentially smelly fish and a whole week but her sister's apology was welcome so Sophie swallowed any further objections and nodded her agreement. 'And when are they coming?'

'The middle of August, if that's okay.'

Sophie bowed to the unavoidable. At least that was still well over a month away. 'That's fine, Rach. That way we've got time to get everything ready for them.'

At that moment, Rachel suddenly jumped to her feet and started waving frantically. 'Dan, Dan, over here.'

The tall American had appeared on the far side of the street and, seeing them, came across to join them.

'Hi, ladies. You're both looking good today.' He paused to get a better view of Sophie. As he did so, she felt a distinct tremor run down her back and her stomach tense. 'Sophie, you're looking *very* good. It's your hair, isn't it?'

She nodded mutely, feeling the colour rush to her cheeks. Either not noticing or diplomatically pretending not to notice, Dan glanced over at Rachel, and Sophie saw him realise he might have put his foot in it. He hastily proved that his diplomatic skills extended to both sisters. 'Not that you don't look gorgeous as always, Rachel.'

She didn't blush, but then she had been receiving compliments on her looks all her life. 'Thanks, Dan, and Sophie does look good, doesn't she? Feel like joining us?'

He pulled out a chair and waved to a passing waitress. '*Un espresso, per favore.*'

Doing her best to sound unflustered, Sophie gave Dan a welcoming smile.

'Thanks for the compliment. I badly needed a haircut – the stylist told me my split ends had developed their own split ends – so I took the plunge. What's new with you? How's the book coming along?'

'Slowly. I've been going on a number of research trips so as to get some real on-the-ground proof of some of the ideas I've been formulating. You know, visiting places along the coast which were already around back in the Middle Ages, to see what traces, if any, are still left.' He leant back as the waitress placed a little cup of coffee in front of him and gave her a murmured, '*Grazie*'.

'What sorts of places? Santa Rita and all this modern development certainly wasn't here way back then.'

'No, although your castle was, of course. It dates back to the fourteenth century. I've been to a number of similar medieval castles and townships along the coast, or just inland, between here and the French border, and I still have a few to go. I've even been up to a little village called Seborga which – believe it or not – actually declared independence from Italy in 1963, claiming it's an autonomous principality. To be honest, I think that one's more a publicity stunt to attract tourists, but it shows just how isolated some of these little hilltop communities could be. For each place of significance I then need to write up my notes, and this gradually fleshes out the text. Closer to home, I've just read that there are the remains of a little thirteenth-century chapel a couple of kilometres back along the ridge as you head inland from Paradiso. I must go and take a look some time.'

This sounded familiar to Sophie. 'I think I might know the one you mean. Hang on.' She pulled out her phone and clicked on the photos she had taken yesterday. 'Is this it?'

He reached over and grasped her hand along with the phone. His touch sent another little spark racing through her and she hastily picked up her coffee with her free hand and sipped it in an attempt to take her mind off the sensation. In the meantime his attention was completely trained on the screen.

'Yes, that's it all right. Would you know your way back to it?'

She nodded. 'No problem. I can lead you there any time you like. I walked up there with Jeeves.'

'I tell you what; let's exchange phone numbers. Next time you're thinking of heading in that direction, just give me a shout.'

'Any time you want. Why don't you call me when you want to go there? One day's much like any other for me at the moment.'

He punched in his number on her phone while she did the same on his. Just as he was about to hand hers back it bleeped and he glanced at the screen.

'You have a message from somebody called Chris.'

'Chris is Sophie's boyfriend.' There was a note of triumph in Rachel's voice and Sophie ground her teeth and hastened to explain.

'He's an old friend. He used to go out with one of my friends.'

'And now he's going to go out with Sophie. He's coming to stay.' Then just to make sure that Dan could be in no doubt, she added, 'Lucky old Sophie.'

Maybe sensing the tension in the atmosphere, Dan swallowed his espresso in one and stood up. 'Anyway, I have to go. I'll see you girls around. Bye.' He headed inside to the cash desk.

'So what does Chris say, Soph?' Rachel's tone was butter-wouldn't-melt-in-her-mouth innocent. 'Is he coming over?'

Repressing her irritation, Sophie read the message out loud to her sister.

> Hi Soph. I'm going to be in Milan in a couple of weeks' time for a meeting. Could I come and see you for the weekend maybe? x

'That sounds good. The sooner the better.' Rachel was sounding encouraging. 'What does he do?'

'He did History of Art at uni and now works for a big auction house and travels all over the place. I expect he's coming over to eye up a valuable painting or jewellery or something.'

'Let's hope he brings some free samples. Who knows? Maybe he'll bring you a nice antique engagement ring with a whopping great big diamond on it.' Seeing the expression on Sophie's face, she relented. 'Anyway, it's probably a good thing if he's just coming for a couple of days initially. If things don't work out, he'll soon be off, and if you and he do get it together he can come back for a longer stay later on.'

Chapter 8

That evening at just after six, Sophie was roused from her laptop by the sound of a bell closely followed by a woof from Jeeves who jumped to his feet and charged out of the room. It took her a moment or two to work out that this had to be the front doorbell so she followed the dog into the entrance hall, heaved the heavy door open and looked out. The doorstep was empty but of course the main gates were locked. Presumably somebody had rung the bell outside in the square. She picked up her keys and went out to see who it was.

She was about to open the gate when she had a sudden thought that it might be Claudio casually dropping in to renew his acquaintance with her, and she almost slammed it shut again. Still, taking a deep breath, she pulled it open and was relieved to see an unfamiliar face. He was a good-looking man with dark hair and a closely trimmed beard and he looked friendly.

'Good evening, can I help you?'

'Good evening, my name's Dario Fornero. My cousin Gianni told me you had a problem with the pool.'

'Oh, thank you very much for coming but it isn't so much a problem as a query.' She beckoned him in and explained about Jeeves and the water and she saw him nod. As if following the conversation Jeeves nudged him with his nose and got a pat on the head in return.

'Gianni mentioned that to me. It should be fine but what I would recommend is to line your skimmer basket with a skimmer sock.' He must have noticed the blank expression on her face. 'Don't worry. It's simple. I've brought a pack with me and it'll only take a few moments to fit one. Shall I show you how?'

They walked round to the pool and found Rachel, thankfully wearing both parts of her bikini this evening. Hanging onto Jeeves's collar with one hand to prevent him from leaping into the water, Sophie introduced Dario to Rachel and couldn't miss the look he gave her sister. Clearly he liked what he saw. He opened the pool house door and squatted down to fiddle with something and Rachel gave Sophie a wink.

'I'm beginning to see why they call this place paradise, Soph. Another hunk!' Evidently she approved.

'If you'd like to come over here, I'll show you how to fit it.' Dario waved to them to join him. They did as instructed and watched as he demonstrated how easy it was. 'Check it every week or two. If you see a lot of dog hair caught in the sock, just peel it off and replace it, okay?' Seeing them nod, he reached into his bag again. 'Seeing as I'm here, I'll just check the pH level of the water, but it looks and smells fine to me.' He produced a little piece of apparatus and dipped it in the water. Pulling it out, he checked the result and smiled at them. 'Perfect. No need to alter anything. Your pool's fine and your dog's quite okay to swim as much as he likes – as are you.'

No sooner had Dario stopped talking than Jeeves looked up at Sophie as much as to say 'You heard'. She released her grip on him and as he flung himself into the water she turned to Dario and asked how much they owed him. He shook his head and waved her offer away.

'No charge. You're very welcome.'

'The least we can do it to offer you a glass of wine.' Rachel made the suggestion and Sophie decided it was her turn to act as wine waiter tonight.

'We've got red, white or champagne. You choose, Dario.'

'If it's no trouble, a glass of red would be great.'

Sophie left them to it and returned to the kitchen, reflecting that Dario appeared to be as efficient and generous as his cousin, who had given her car back to her earlier sounding as smooth and quiet as if it were new – and hadn't charged her the earth. Remembering what Rachel had told her, she found several unmarked bottles of red in the fridge and carried one back out to the pool along with three glasses and a tub of the intensely flavoured local *Taggiasche* black olives. Dario was sitting on the edge of a sunbed directly opposite Rachel and didn't appear able to keep his eyes off her. Sophie set down the tray and poured the wine before taking a seat a tactful distance away from the two of them. Dario managed to tear his eyes off her sister's body long enough to give Sophie a glance and raise his glass.

'Cheers, and thank you.'

'Thank *you*, Dario.' Rachel reached over and clinked her glass against his. '*Cin cin.*'

Sophie planned to drink her wine and leave her sister with the handsome Italian – if that was what she wanted. She took a big mouthful and had to agree that Beppe's red wine made with the castle's very own grapes was excellent.

'Are you ladies planning on staying here long?'

Dario politely managed to include Sophie in the conversation although his eyes were still on Rachel, who didn't seem to mind in the slightest. Sophie left it to her sister to explain that they would be here until the end of September. After a few minutes, Sophie swallowed the last of her wine, stood up, thanked him again and excused herself. Rachel gave her a little wink as she did so. As Jeeves was still wet Sophie took him for a walk around the garden so that he could drip dry himself before going back inside.

When they reached the far end of the vineyard, she sat on a conveniently sited bench and looked out through the fence, down across the olive groves and vineyards towards Santa Rita. Even from this distance she could see that the promenade was still packed. No doubt it would get even busier in a few weeks' time when the main holiday month of August started, but up here, Paradiso was living up to its name. As if to emphasise the point, a beautiful orange and black butterfly almost the width of her hand fluttered past and landed on Jeeves's head. He was stretched out on the dusty ground, eyes closed, looking as if he had just run a marathon, and blissfully unaware of his temporary guest. The butterfly sat there for a few seconds, wings pulsing in the sunlight, before deciding that there were more fragrant places to take a rest and flitting off again.

Sophie started thinking about the idea of writing a book, and a story began to develop in her head. Here she was in a medieval castle, so what better place to set the story? The Middle Ages were a fascinating time and, she reminded herself, she had the added bonus of having a medievalist living just down the road, who would no doubt be able to help her get her facts straight. What did they eat and drink seven hundred years ago? What clothes did they wear? Did they have Labradors? What did they do without television? Did they really have chastity belts? She realised she would have to spend quite a lot of time with

Dan in order to get to the bottom of all these queries and the idea of seeing more of him had considerable appeal – particularly if Rachel had found herself a man in the shape of the handsome Italian pool guy. Of course, that left the question of Chris unanswered, but there would be time to worry about that the weekend after next when he came to stay.

As for the plot of her book, she rather liked the idea of a story of two sisters, both countesses or duchesses or princesses – she had better add medieval aristocratic titles to her list of queries for Dan – who lived here in the castle. The girls' father was away on the Crusades – when were the Crusades please, Dan? – and they had been left in the not-so-tender hands of their stepmother. The story could involve different suitors, rivalries and jealousies as well as a shot of heartache and a few hints of something steamy. There could be a masked ball, a couple of banquets and maybe a wild horseback ride across the mountains to escape an attack by Saracen pirates. She sat there and let her mind tick over, and by the time she stood up again, the nucleus of a story had started to take shape.

Back inside the castle there was no sign of Rachel so Sophie threw together a salad laced with gorgonzola, walnuts and pieces of speck, the lovely smoked ham from the Alps. She accompanied it with a glass of red from another bottle in the fridge and switched on the TV in the corner of the room to watch the news. She had just finished her meal and was feeding Jeeves when the back door opened and Rachel reappeared. Jeeves didn't look up – dinner time was far too important for that – but his tail did wag a little bit harder.

'Hi, Soph, sorry I'm late for dinner.'

'No worries, there's plenty of salad left over. Has your guest gone?'

Rachel winked at her. 'Yes, for today…'

'But tomorrow…?'

'Tomorrow he's taking me out for dinner and then, in a few days' time when he can get away, he said he's going to take me out on his yacht.'

'Just remember what happened last time you were on a yacht – it sank.'

'It didn't actually sink like in a Titanic kind of way. It just sort of died in the harbour. When we went to bed at night it was fine. When we woke up next morning there was a foot of water in the cabin which just kept getting deeper and deeper until there was only the mast left sticking out of the water.'

'Well, just be careful.'

'Yes, big sister.' In spite of the jibe, Rachel looked happy.

'And if you bring him home, remember my room's next door to yours. I wouldn't want you to make so much noise you frighten Jeeves.'

'Yes, big sister.' Rachel was still smiling as she poured herself a glass of red and sat down. 'But I have no intention of leaping into anything with Dario – at least not until I know him a lot better. He seems like fun so why not, but you don't need to worry about me bringing him or any other random men home.' She pulled out a chair and sat down. 'So when're you going to go for that walk with Dan, you know, to his little chapel in the hills?'

'I've given him my number. I'll wait for him to call or, if I don't hear in a few days, I'll call him. After all, I don't want to sound too eager.'

'Why not? If you like him – and you do – you should be brave and make the first move. Besides, a walk to an old ruin isn't quite in the same league as dragging him upstairs to your bed.'

'Yes, but… there's Chris, to consider. I'm not some sort of femme fatale juggling suitors and breaking hearts, you know.' She very nearly added 'like you used to be' but stopped herself in time.

'Look on it as seeing how the land lies. Maybe Dan'll tell you he's married with five kids. It wouldn't hurt to find that out before things get serious. And, after all, you have no idea whether Chris feels the same way about you yet anyway. Go for a walk with Dan and see what you can find out. Wasn't it Sun Tzu who said that sometimes a mere scrap of intelligence could be mightier than a thousand men?'

Sophie was impressed that her sister remembered the legendary author of *The Art of War*, but it didn't really help her much. The way her luck had been going over the last twelve months, it would most probably turn out that both men were unavailable. Still, as Rachel had said, it wouldn't hurt to find out more about the handsome American.

Chapter 9

A couple of days later Sophie was delighted to get a call from Dan asking if she felt like showing him the way to the chapel. She agreed immediately and they met up at ten thirty the morning after. He was wearing his usual shorts and trainers but today, instead of a T-shirt he had on a faded pink polo shirt that showed off his suntanned arms to advantage – and Sophie had always had a thing for men's forearms. For her part, she was also wearing shorts and a white top that bared her shoulders, although the effect was somewhat spoiled as she had to smother herself in factor fifty sun cream to avoid getting sunburnt. In consequence there was a lingering odour of coconut about her and she was quick to explain. He clearly approved.

'A very sensible precaution. Besides, I've always liked coconut.'

As they walked up through the pinewoods, she told him about her idea of a romantic novel set in the Middle Ages, and as she had hoped, he had answers to all her questions – although she did stop short of asking him about chastity belts. The most startling takeaway from his precis of medieval habits was that there had been a very different attitude towards hygiene back then.

'For many people, washing was a once-a-month thing – at most – and they only fully immersed themselves in water if they fell in a river.'

'Even princesses?'

'Maybe *they* did bathe a bit more often than normal women, but you can be sure that most of the knights in shining armour were crawling with lice underneath the armour.'

'Ugh... Maybe I won't set the book in that era after all.'

'There is such a thing as poetic licence. I doubt if your readers are likely to question the minutiae of your characters' habits. After all, very few people watching movies about Robin Hood would stop to think what might be going on beneath Robin's tights.'

'Speak for yourself.' Sophie giggled mischievously. It was fun being with him and she got the impression he was enjoying his time with her too. When they emerged from the trees into the full force of the sun, the track became narrower and they had to walk in single file. Needless to say, Jeeves went first and so Sophie followed him with Dan behind. From time to time the path widened and she slowed so they could talk, but it was only about generalities until they reached the remains of the little chapel. Here, after making a minute study of the ruins and taking a load of photos, Dan sat down beside her in the shade and they continued to talk. After a few moments he asked her a direct question.

'When's your boyfriend coming to stay?'

Sophie was taking a sip of water just as he asked the question. As a result she spluttered so badly, it went down the wrong way and she dissolved into a fit of coughing. Once she had recovered her breath, she wiped her eyes and did her best to set the record straight.

'Sorry about that. Went down the wrong way. I'm not sure when Chris's coming; I'm waiting to hear. He said in a couple of weeks so I imagine it'll be towards the end of the month, but he's not my boyfriend.' She went on to explain how she had known him and Claire for almost ten years now and how her friendship with him had continued even after he and Claire had split up.

'I see, so why did Rachel call him your boyfriend then?' Dan immediately corrected himself. 'I'm sorry, that's no business of mine. I'm afraid I ask too many questions. Curiosity's a bad habit of mine. Forget I spoke.'

Sophie had regained control of her vocal chords by now so she resolved to tough it out. 'It's all right; I don't mind at all. It's no big secret. I was in a fairly serious relationship up until last year and now Rachel's trying to get me married off. She thinks I need to find myself another man pronto.'

'And you aren't interested?' His tone was studiously neutral with no hint of anything other than natural curiosity.

'I honestly don't know. He's a lovely guy but I'm scared stiff I might frighten him off if I let myself develop feelings for him that he doesn't share. We'll see what happens when he gets here but, anyway, I'm fine as I am. Let's just say, with a few notable exceptions, the male of the species isn't too high on my list of favourites at the moment. Give me a Labrador any day.'

'On behalf of the males of the species I apologise for whatever that man did. Men do stupid things, I'm afraid.'

Sophie reflected on what little her sister had told her about the demise of her own relationship in the US, although she still had no idea of the exact circumstances leading to the break-up. 'Not just men. Women also do stupid stuff, but in this case it was all down to him although, thinking back, I was probably far too trusting, pretty naïve, really.' She gave him a quick, sanitised version of the circumstances that had caused her to dump Claudio.

'I'm sorry. It must have been tough but don't blame yourself. Trusting people's a good thing. He's the one in the wrong here.' His voice was soft and sympathetic and she decided to throw the question back on him.

'And what about you, Dan? Was that your wife or partner we saw you with last week at the restaurant?'

He shook his head. 'No, Gina's just a friend, and a colleague. She's from the University of Genoa and she's been helping me with my research.'

'So nobody's waiting for you back in Boston?'

There was a pause before he replied. 'I honestly don't know.'

She waited for him to elaborate but she waited in vain. In the end she gave him a gentle prompt. 'So that means there might be.'

'I suppose so.' A long pause. 'To tell the truth, listening to you talking about your friend Chris, it sounded all too familiar. The situation I'm in's a bit like yours... in fact I suppose it's very much like yours. My best friend back in the States is a girl called Jennifer. Sorry, I should say a woman called Jennifer, but I've known her since high school and old habits die hard, although she's the same age as me.' He caught Sophie's eye for a second and smiled. 'And I'm thirty-four and definitely no longer a teenage boy.'

She smiled back, although her brain was turning over what he had just said. 'You don't look a day over thirty-three and a half.'

'You're too kind. Anyway, Jen and I've been best buds for almost twenty years but it's only now, since I've been over here on my own, that I realise how much I miss her. And after what you've just told me, I'm beginning to wonder if there's maybe more to it than just simple friendship.'

'And neither of you have married or got into serious relationships?'

'Neither of us. Of course I've had girlfriends and she's had boyfriends, but none of them stuck. In my defence I've been working hard over the last few years to get my PhD and to start making a name for myself in the field, but the fact is that I've never really met the right girl – apart from Jen.'

Sophie rested back against the rough wall of the ruined chapel and did her best to marshal her thoughts. It sounded as though he was dead right. From what he had said, his relationship with Jennifer sounded remarkably similar to her own relationship with Chris. On the one hand this was reassuring. It made her realise that her relationship with Chris maybe wasn't so abnormal after all – friends could become more than friends. On the other hand, it was disappointing to think that this handsome, intelligent American was probably already involved with somebody else, even if he didn't quite realise it yet. Mind you, she reminded herself, hadn't she just told him she wasn't interested in finding herself a new man?

They sat in silence for a few minutes, each lost in their own thoughts, until Jeeves stood up and came over to prod her bare knees with his nose, rousing her from her reflections. She turned towards Dan.

'If you've seen all you need to see here, what would you like to do? If you want a longer walk there's a little village with a bar about an hour that way, or would you prefer to head back to Paradiso?'

She saw him glance at his watch. 'If you like I've got some food in the fridge at home. Would you maybe feel like coming to my place for lunch?'

That sounded like a great idea. 'I'd love that, Dan, thank you, and I'm quite relieved you don't want to do the longer walk. I admit I don't really fancy a two-hour trek in this heat. It's even hotter today than it has been, I think I might melt.'

They walked back together, chatting sporadically but mostly just in silence, one behind the other on the narrow path. When they got to the house he was renting she was impressed by what she saw. It was delightful. It was clearly very old – nothing like as old as the castle, but certainly a couple of centuries or more. There wasn't a pool, but there was a covered veranda at the rear with a stunning view over the well-maintained gardens into the valley below. A hint of a breeze did a good job of cooling her down as she took a seat in the shade with her dog sprawled at her feet, tongue hanging out.

After setting a bottle of cold mineral water and glasses on the table and a bowl of water on the old terracotta tiled floor in front of Jeeves, Dan disappeared back into the house again. Jeeves wasted no time in drinking half the water in the bowl, splashing much of it onto the floor around him as usual. Sophie did the same with her glass of water, but less messily. Dan reappeared shortly after, carrying a tray laden with food. As he unloaded it onto the table, he gave her a running commentary.

'The ham's from the farmer halfway down the hill, as are the little round goat's cheeses. The figs are from the garden here, and so are the tomatoes and the lettuce. And the bread...' – he paused for effect – '... is my own creation.'

'Wow, a baker as well. A man of many talents.'

'Wait until you taste it. Jen showed me how to do it but it's only the second time I've tried, and the first lot was almost inedible. And the wine, of course, is from the castle. I stock up every now and then from Beppe. Did he tell you about keeping it in the fridge at this time of year, even though it's red? The purists might turn their noses up at the thought, but he's dead right.' He filled two glasses and passed one across to her.

'He certainly did and I quite agree. Cheers.' She clinked her glass against his and sat back, enjoying the shade, the view and the company. In a way, knowing that there already was a woman in his life made it easier to relax in his company. He was such a nice guy and she was delighted to be his friend – and that was going to have to be that.

Dan's homemade bread turned out to be more than edible, as were the other very simple ingredients of what became an excellent meal. They chatted over their food and he told her more about his work and his plans for the future. It was clear he was firmly wedded to his work at Harvard and she reflected that it was just as well he had got this Jennifer woman waiting for him. There could be no doubt that he would move back to Boston in the autumn. If somehow Sophie and he got together, it would be fraught with problems. Unless she were to find herself a job in the US – which was highly unlikely – any relationship with him would be destined for disaster. So she ate her food, drank her wine, and enjoyed the conversation, but she knew in her bones that friendship was all that was developing here.

At the end of the meal, he made a proposal – but not of a romantic nature.

'You know I was saying I need to start making a few research trips? Well, I was thinking about beginning later this week or early next with a visit to Albenga.' Seeing the expression on her face, he explained. 'It's only twenty minutes or so along the coast to the east. It's a lot bigger than Santa Rita but it still has a medieval, partially walled, centre with some towers and a load of other old buildings. I've read about it but I haven't been there yet. If you feel like coming, and Rachel as well if she's interested, I'd enjoy your company and it might be nice for you to see another town.'

'That sounds great. I'd enjoy that and I'll mention it to Rachel as well. I'm sure she'll be delighted to come too.'

'I've rented a little car here so we can go in that. It's a bit small but the three of us should just about be able to squeeze in.'

Sophie had an idea. 'Uncle George's Mercedes is up at the castle. Why don't we take that? Apparently it's insured for anybody to drive.'

'If Rachel's coming, that would be great, thanks. My little Fiat really is tiny. By the way, where did you say she was today? Didn't she feel like a walk?'

'She's doing stuff in the garden. Ever since Beppe came in, she's been hard at it. Gardening has always interested her. She spends her days out there among the plants, with a bit of swimming and sunbathing thrown in, and most of her evenings working for her return to university in October. Maybe she told you she left before finishing her degree and now she wants to remedy that.' A thought occurred to her. 'Talk of swimming reminds me of something I've been meaning to say – if Rachel hasn't already said it – any time you feel like coming over for a swim, you've got the key to the back gate, so just come.'

'Thanks, Sophie, that's very kind. To be totally honest, George told me the exact same thing the last time I saw him and I was swimming regularly before you arrived, but I stopped as soon as you set up home here. It didn't feel right.'

'Seriously, Dan, any time.' She paused and fought to suppress a smile. 'But, depending upon your attitude towards such things, it might be wise to whistle as you approach the pool as Rachel has a habit of sunbathing topless and I wouldn't want to shock you.'

He threw his head back and laughed. 'I don't shock that easy, but I'll make sure I whistle from now on.'

It occurred to Sophie that here she was, behaving like the big sister again. When all was said and done, what Rachel decided to wear or not to wear was her own affair, and she made another mental note to try to treat her sister as a grown-up.

Chapter 10

Over the rest of the week Rachel – whose dinner with Dario had gone very well – continued to work in the garden. Sophie was determined to get on with selecting the replacement kitchen, feeling sure that this would take time to order and have fitted. To this end, she and Rachel drove to Alassio on the Wednesday to visit a kitchen showroom recommended by Rita and Beppe. They picked out some lovely glossy white units accompanied by grey granite worktops and the designer arranged to call round early the following week to take all the measurements, assuring them it would all be fitted well before the end of September. Sophie crossed her fingers. This was one of her uncle's main stipulations in addition to signing in every day, which she and Rachel had been doing religiously. Things between her and Rachel appeared to be well on the way to getting back on an even keel again, not least because Sophie was making a conscious effort to be a bit less Big Sister with her. After years in that role it wasn't easy, but she knew it was something on which she had to work if they were to co-exist peaceably.

On Thursday, Rachel and Beppe hauled a fifty-four litre *damigiana* of wine out of the cellar and onto a trolley and trundled it across the piazza to the priest's house. She returned at lunchtime with bright red cheeks.

'We had to taste it with him, after all.'

'And he approved?'

'From the speed with which it went down his throat, he definitely liked it. If he keeps up at that rate, I have a feeling we might have to offer him another fifty litres long before we leave.'

Sophie wasn't surprised to see her disappear up to her room for a snooze in the afternoon. As for herself, she concentrated on her romance novel, spending a considerable amount of time browsing the internet for suitable names that would have been around seven hundred years ago. It was very unlikely that Elvis, Kylie or Kanye would have been in circulation back then. After a lot of dithering, she settled on Beatrice and Constance for the two medieval princesses. She kept on planning her book over the following days and discussing it with Rachel who came up with a number of sensible suggestions. On Friday morning, she actually sat down to start writing and got as far as opening a new Word document on the laptop. That was when her problems started.

She spent almost an hour sitting staring at the blank screen, racking her brains, before giving in and typing *Title to be Decided* at the top of the page and moving on to the first paragraph. One thing she remembered from Creative Writing lectures had been the vital importance of the first page, if not the very first line. And so she spent another hour making multiple stabs at producing a suitably punchy first line before deleting each attempt and trying again until she felt like screaming in sheer frustration. It was almost a relief when she heard Jeeves rise to his feet and come over to prod her with his nose.

'Want to go out?' His tail wagged lazily. 'You realise you're interrupting me in full flight, don't you?' The tail wagged a bit harder. 'Well, all right, we'll go, but it's all your fault if this never makes it onto the bestsellers' list.'

It was almost lunchtime but there was no sign of Rachel in the house. Sophie found her in the front garden, dead-heading the roses. Beside her was a basket almost full of pink, red, and white petals, many burnt dry by the sun. Sophie breathed deeply. The scent all around was heavenly and the numerous bees buzzing among the blooms showed that they shared her opinion. Rachel looked up as she felt Jeeves's nose in the small of her back.

'Hello, dog, going for a walk?' She swung round and ruffled his ears before switching her attention. 'Hi, Soph, how's the world-famous author getting on? How many thousand words have you written?'

Sophie held up her fingers in a zero sign and was about to elaborate when her phone started ringing. She pulled it out and glanced down at the screen.

'Oh, crap.'

'Who is it, Soph?' Sophie's expression must have given it away. 'Don't tell me... your ex from Rome?'

Sophie nodded. 'Claudio.' She gazed blankly at the phone without moving until, after about another dozen rings, it fell silent.

'You're not going to talk to him? If it was me, I'd tell him to take a flying leap... only not as politely.'

'I'd be wasting my breath. He's impervious to criticism. According to Mariarosa he claims he still can't understand why I left him. He says he didn't do anything wrong.' Sophie felt the anger building again. 'If you don't count sleeping with half the women in Rome, then he didn't.'

'And what will you do if he suddenly pitches up here?'

Sophie shuddered. 'Barricade myself in the castle and pour boiling oil down on him from the battlements.'

Rachel winked at her. 'You want to put that in your book. That would give it a bit of oomph.'

Just then her phone beeped to indicate the arrival of a message and the sisters exchanged glances. No prizes for guessing who the sender was. Sophie reached for the *Delete* button but hesitated as Rachel interrupted her.

'If I were you, I'd at least read the message. What if it says he's standing in the piazza right now?'

'Oh, God...' Sophie turned her back to the sun so she could read the message in her own shadow. It was short and unwelcome. She read it with disbelief before passing it over to her sister as she struggled not to scream out loud.

> Ciao, Sophie. Long time no speak. I hear you're back in Italy, in Paradiso. I'm coming north in a few weeks' time and I'll look you up. I miss you. Un bacione. Claudio.

'*Un bacione...?*' Rachel sounded flabbergasted. 'You're right about him having a thick skin. Fancy sending you a *big kiss* after what he did! I say get that oil on the boil and wait for him to show up. Pity there aren't any cannons lying around here as well.'

Sophie pressed *Delete*, but still stood there, staring stupidly down at her phone. Rachel was right. It beggared belief. How could he possibly think there might be any point in trying to re-establish contact after his behaviour and their rancorous break-up? She was still standing there helplessly when her sister came up with a theory that made a lot of sense.

'Of course, he now knows you're about to inherit a castle. He must realise that this will make you a very rich woman and I reckon he wants some of it. He's obviously determined to try to woo you back so he can get his grubby little hands on your inheritance.'

At least her sister's choice of vocabulary brought a weak smile to Sophie's face. 'Nobody woos anybody these days, Rach, but I must use the word in my book – if I ever get started. One thing's for sure, the last person on earth I'd like to see on my doorstep with a bunch of flowers in his hands – which, by the way, would be immaculately manicured, not grubby – is Claudio.' Snapping out of her daze, she slipped the phone back in her pocket and glanced down at Jeeves who was being unusually patient.

'Right, you want your walk, don't you?' He wagged his tail and she glanced over at her sister. 'I won't be long, Rach. See you for lunch.'

By the time she and Jeeves got back she had simmered down, but the prospect of Claudio darkening her doorstep in a few weeks' time was genuinely unpleasant and most unwelcome. Much as it went against her nature and her wishes to reply to him, she decided she had better spell it out once and for all. While Rachel pulled food out of the fridge for lunch, she picked up her phone and started writing.

> Claudio, believe me when I tell you that I never want to see you again. Forget me and do not bother me again. If you come here I'll call the police.

She read it out to her sister who nodded approvingly. 'And you could maybe add that he should never ever try to contact you again, or else.'

Sophie added the warning and pressed *Send*.

'Here, Soph, a glass of cold red is called for. I know it's lunchtime but it'll help you forget about Claudio and it might get your creative juices flowing this afternoon. Don't forget, there's a long history of writers drinking themselves to death. You don't need to go that far, but a little drop won't hurt.' She filled both glasses and clinked hers against Sophie's. 'Cheers. Here's to a big vat of boiling oil. I'll help you tip it on him.'

The glass hadn't even reached Sophie's lips when she heard a beep from her pocket. She set it down and pulled the phone back out of her pocket. She almost threw it across the room as she read his latest message.

> I know you don't mean that, carissima. We love each other. C

She was so angry, she was genuinely speechless, and she just passed the phone mutely across to Rachel who read it and snorted. 'What planet does this guy live on? *Carissima*, indeed! It's a pity Jeeves isn't a Rottweiler. This guy needs something big and hairy to bite him – where it hurts.'

'I told you he really fancies himself, but even I'm gobsmacked. I genuinely think he's gone crazy.'

'Not crazy; greedy. All he can think about is the money.'

Sophie sent him another message. It grated to waste time on him again but it had to be done.

> Leave me alone. Never contact me again.

And she pressed *Send*.

–

Sophie ended up having two glasses of wine with her lunch and, as a result, decided she had to go up to her room for a snooze in the afternoon. Jeeves stretched out on the cool terracotta floor beside the bed and was snoring within minutes. She woke an hour later and lay there for a little while, still trying to think of a suitable opening line for her novel, but finding her head filled with thoughts of Claudio. It was hard to imagine that she had once truly believed she wanted to spend the rest of her life with him. Looking back on it now, she realised she had been blown away by his larger-than-life personality, his smouldering good looks and his ability to charm her with the sort of romantic words she had never heard from a man before. Compared to the series of fairly average British university student boyfriends she had had in Exeter, the handsome Roman had appeared like Cupid himself, a vision of romance and love.

Of course, with the benefit of hindsight, she now realised that the fact he was such a smooth talker meant that he had had a lot of practice – and had continued to hone his art on other women all the way through his relationship with her. How could she have been so blind, so stupid? Well, she told herself firmly, she would never make that mistake again, with him or any other man. And if Claudio were brazen enough to turn up here in Paradiso, she would set him straight in no uncertain terms, with or without the aid of a cauldron of boiling oil. Snorting to herself, she stretched and sat up. Hearing movement, Jeeves also got up and prodded her with his nose.

'It's all right for you, Jeeves. You have no such worries.' The vet had seen to that. 'But I'm counting on you to defend me if you see Claudio.' Although she felt sure the best she could hope for would be that he would lick Claudio to death.

Seeing as it was still swelteringly hot, she slipped into her bikini and headed for the pool. By now the word 'pool' was firmly lodged in her dog's vocabulary and he bounced along at her side, raring to go. As soon as she opened the back door he disappeared at a gallop. When she reached the pool she found him already happily splashing about in the water while Rachel was sitting in the shade with a newspaper.

'Hi, Soph. Been writing?'

'Sleeping mainly. Remind me not to drink wine at lunchtime again. What about you?'

'I've been reading and snoozing. It's so wonderful not to have anything urgent to do. In spite of living in Florida, I haven't had a real lazy holiday for years.'

Sophie perched on the end of her sunbed. 'That reminds me, when you see Beppe next Thursday, would you ask him for names of builders to sort out the things on Uncle George's list? Signor Verdi strikes me as a very pernickety sort of character so we need to make sure we fulfil all of the stipulations – not just the residence requirement. And as you're looking after the vineyard and wine side of things, I'll make a start on sorting through the stuff on the top floor one of these days.'

'On that subject, have you seen this?' Rachel was holding a copy of the local newspaper. She folded it over and handed it to Sophie, tapping the bottom of the page with a finger. 'Check out the advert. I've seen a couple of posters in the piazza too.'

Sophie read the banner advert carefully. It was advertising an antiques fair to be held here in the square at Paradiso on the last Sunday in August. Sophie handed the paper back and nodded.

'Great idea. Anything that's saleable I'll put to one side and we can set up a stall in front of the gates that day and hopefully shift the lot.' A thought occurred to her. 'Not sure what we do with the proceeds, though. I'd better run it past Signor Verdi just to be on the safe side.' She set down her towel and stood up. 'And now I'm going to join my dog in the pool.'

Chapter 11

Sophie spent a quiet weekend writing two more short stories and working on her book – or, rather, making multiple attempts to begin it but without success. Rachel went out sailing on Saturday with Dario, returning at almost midnight, but she didn't invite him in. Sophie was impressed to see her sister carrying out her plan of taking things slow. After her own experience with Claudio, she was still feeling distinctly mistrustful of Italian men, if not all men – although she was honest enough to acknowledge that this was probably an unfair and biased opinion – and she approved of Rachel's cautious approach. This indicated considerable maturity on her part and a change from the impulsive Rachel of old. As for Sophie herself, now that Dan was safely out of the equation, there remained the question of Chris.

She would hopefully be able to sort out her head – and her heart – a bit better when he came to visit. Trying to think of somebody who had been such a close, supportive friend in a different light was especially hard without having him alongside her, and she was quite apprehensive about what was likely to transpire when he came over. To add to her anxiety was the possible looming arrival of her Roman ex. She had always considered herself to be a fairly pragmatic person and having big unknowns like these in her life was disturbing and even a bit annoying but, as Rachel never ceased reminding her, it made life interesting.

On Sunday afternoon Dan appeared at the kitchen door, saying he had come for a swim, and received a rapturous welcome from Jeeves. The two of them headed off for the pool and Sophie went upstairs to change before joining them there. Outside, it was still searingly hot, even though at this time of day the trees shielded the pool from the direct rays of the sun. In spite of this, the poolside thermometer told her it was thirty-five degrees. She unwrapped her towel from around her body and sank gratefully into the cool water where she was immediately leapt on by Jeeves. She had intended to keep her hair dry but as that was now a forlorn hope she threw a tennis ball down to the other end of the pool for the dog, lay back and floated with her head and her hair in the water. It felt just perfect.

Later on Rachel arrived with a bottle of cold white wine and three glasses, and they sat and chatted until the mosquitoes began to circle and they decided to head back inside. As ever, Dan was charming and friendly, but nothing more, confirming Sophie's impression that theirs was purely friendship. He even brought up the subject of Chris, asking if she now knew exactly when he was coming, and the cheerful smile remained on his face throughout. They invited him to stay for dinner but he declined, saying he had to prepare for his next research trip and they arranged to accompany him to Albenga the next day.

He arrived as agreed at ten o'clock next morning and Sophie was relieved when he offered to drive the Mercedes. Apart from feeling as if it was twice the size of her own car, it was automatic, and she had never driven one of these before. Rachel on the other hand had driven exclusively automatics for the past few years in the States, but she sounded equally happy to let him drive. She immediately bagged the front passenger seat, but Sophie didn't mind. She had put Jeeves's towel down to protect the leather of the rear seat alongside her and she wanted to make sure he behaved himself.

As a plan it wasn't a great success. This was the first time the dog had found himself sitting on a car seat beside his mistress and she was soon involved in an ongoing struggle to turf him off her lap. Still, it made the journey slip by very quickly and by the time she had finally persuaded him to get off her and settle down, they were already turning off the motorway after what had only been a fifteen minute drive.

The outskirts of Albenga weren't immediately promising. The road in from the *autostrada* ran along the bank of a wide riverbed now almost completely dried up, with a sprawl of modern commercial buildings along the other side of the road. There were certainly no traces of anything medieval and Dan must have sensed her scepticism.

'Look up ahead. See those towers? That's the old town.'

He navigated his way into the centre where they managed to find a parking space after a bit of a hunt. Evidently Albenga was popular this morning. They walked from the car to the gates of the old city and Sophie's first impression of it was, frankly, as fairly scruffy with posters peeling off the walls and modern road signs and adverts all over the place. However, once through the old gateway all that changed. They found themselves in a narrow stone-paved street, flanked on both sides by cafes, restaurants and shops – many of them selling designer clothes – and the feel of the place changed dramatically for the better. This area was for pedestrians only and there was no shortage of people milling around. Lots of the shops had displays outside on the roadside and Sophie kept a strict eye on Jeeves in case he should take it into his head to cock his leg against a basket of fruit or a display of pricey mohair jumpers.

About a hundred yards down this street Dan led them off to the left and they suddenly found themselves well and truly in the Middle Ages. The road became much narrower and the buildings on both sides became distinctly older, with brick arches, columns and intricate stone-work. The brickwork was a weathered deep red, while the plastered walls were predominantly sun-bleached pink, giving the whole place a delightful summery feel.

'Look up.' Dan pointed upwards and Sophie followed the direction of his finger. 'Check out the windows.'

Sure enough, many of the windows above them looked old and very elaborate, most of them set into stone arches. Sophie was reminded of a photo she had seen of Juliet's house in Verona and it was easy to imagine medieval ladies in wimples leaning out to exchange greetings with passers-by mounted on horses. She made a mental note to include a trip to Albenga in her novel – assuming she ever managed to get beyond the first line.

A few paces further on they emerged into a little square with three very ancient tall, slim red brick towers rising up from the sides, a lovely old church at one end and the town hall diagonally opposite. The remarkably small cathedral, constructed with horizontal lines of alternating grey and white stone, was just a few yards further along and all of a sudden they felt as if they had stepped back in time.

'What do you think of Albenga?' Dan had his phone out, taking a succession of photos. 'From the outskirts I wasn't expecting anything as good as this.'

'It's lovely.' Rachel had no hesitation, but then revealed that her reasons for this statement weren't necessarily architectural or historical. 'Now if you don't mind, I spotted a dress back there in one of the shops that I'd like to take a closer look at.'

'Of course.' Dan looked around and pointed to a cafe at the end of the square with tables and parasols outside on the paving slabs. 'I want to take a look inside some of the buildings – like the cathedral for example – so why don't we meet up here at, say, half past twelve?'

'Fine by me. See you.' And Rachel was off.

Sophie stayed with Dan – as much for his company as for the history – and enjoyed listening to his expert commentary on the places they visited. In particular, she loved the feel of the twelfth-century cathedral. According to Dan this had been built on the site of a much older original church. They took it in turns to go inside, as one of them had to wait outside with Jeeves. At first sight the inside was quite plain – until she remembered Dan's advice and looked up. She was astonished to see the whole expanse of the vaulted ceiling had been entirely covered in medieval frescos. Alongside the cathedral was another even older building, the Baptistery, whose origins apparently went right back to the fifth century. All in all, Albenga was a fine old historic site, but still very much a thriving twenty-first century commercial town.

Rachel was waiting for them at the bar with a carrier bag full of purchases beside her. In view of the time, Dan suggested heading straight to a restaurant for lunch. This turned out to be a tiny little place called *Da Puppo* and it was packed out. They managed to get the last free table, squashed in the far corner of the side room with Jeeves under their feet and Dan explained that he had first come here a few weeks back on Beppe's recommendation and he had loved it.

'It's just such an authentic eating house. You can't book tables; you have to queue up. Lunchtime's supposed to be quieter than in the evening, but we only just got in, didn't we? I shudder to think how busy it must get at night. As you can see, it's very basic, there are no fancy tablecloths or uniformed staff, but the food's delightful and – although I shouldn't tell you this as this is my treat today – it's really cheap.'

'There's no need for you to pay, Dan. It should be on me. I owe you lunch, remember?' Sophie was the first to object and her sister chimed in straight after.

'That's not fair, Dan. You realise if you insist on paying, then you'll have to let us buy or make you dinner one of these days to say thank you.'

'Fine by me. I look forward to it.'

The meal was indeed excellent. The menu was only in Italian and included a number of regional dishes that had Sophie searching on her phone for translations. What a non-Italian-speaking tourist would have made of it was hard to tell and a quick glance around the room confirmed Sophie's initial impression that their fellow guests were almost all Italians – always a good sign. The other two chose *farinata*, the local chickpea crêpe speciality, as a starter but Sophie wasn't especially hungry so she went for a simple salad followed by a skewer of grilled prawns and squid. Accompanied by a glass of cold white wine it was a super lunch.

While they ate, Sophie related the latest developments with Claudio and his text messages. Dan looked sympathetic.

'The man's clearly an imbecile with the thick skin of a rhinoceros. I'm going to Rome tomorrow for a week or so. Tell me what he looks like and if I run into him I'll push him in the Tiber.'

Sophie chuckled at the thought. 'Thanks for the offer, but I've got half a dozen people I know there who'd be only too happy to do the same, but physical violence isn't the way forward. No, I'll just have to hope that he comes to his senses and really does forget about me.'

'You'd be pretty hard to forget.'

There was real warmth in Dan's voice and Sophie caught a surreptitious wink from her sister. She gave Dan a little smile.

'Thanks, Dan. It's good to know I've got you on my side.'

'Always.'

At that moment she felt her phone vibrate and saw that it was a call from Chris. 'Hi, Chris, how's things?'

'Hi, Sophie, I'm fine thanks. Listen, I'm sorry it's taken me so long to get back to you with a definite date. It's now confirmed that I have to be in Milan on Thursday next week. Would it work for you if I came down on the Friday afternoon and left again on Sunday morning?'

'Of course, it'll be great to see you anytime. It's a pity you can't come for longer, but maybe you'll be able to come back again another time.'

'As far as I can work out, there's a train from Milan that gets me down to Santa Rita just after six. Would that be okay?'

'That would be great. I'll be waiting for you at the station. Call me if you run into problems.'

They chatted for a few minutes before he hung up and she glanced across at Rachel.

'Chris – he's coming on Friday, I mean a week on Friday.'

Rachel gave her another, broader wink. 'Exciting...' Sophie saw her shoot a mischievous grin over towards Dan. 'The weekend after next's going to be interesting.'

Chapter 12

The next few days passed quickly. When Sophie wasn't out with Jeeves or agonising over the blank page that so far constituted the entirety of her attempt at a novel, she spent much of the time up on the top floor, sifting through the piles of stuff. She started by clearing one of the rooms completely so she could use it to store anything she felt might be worth keeping to be sold at the antiques fair. Things she deemed unsuitable for sale, she carried downstairs and soon a sizeable pile of unwanted rubbish was accumulating outside the back door. Rachel checked with Beppe to see what they should do with it all as there was far too much stuff for the normal bins and he advised them to let it mount up until it was all there and then he would rent or borrow a van and take it to the municipal dump.

The collection of things worth keeping grew at an alarming rate. Sophie found a set of fine-looking dining chairs upholstered in what looked like velvet. They were a bit worn, but still serviceable. There was a child's train set still in its box and from the picture on the cover, it was quite old. In fact there were several boxes of children's toys and Sophie wondered idly who their owners had been. There was a hefty wooden chest full of old magazines which was far too heavy for her to move, so she left it where it was and carried on piling up the smaller stuff. It certainly looked as though there would be no shortage of items to put on display at the antiques fair at the end of next month.

She contacted Signor Verdi about what to do with the proceeds of the sale and he assured her that Uncle George had already considered that. In his usual organised way, their uncle had specified that she and Rachel could split and keep any money they raised from the sale of items in the house. When she passed this news on to her sister, she suddenly found her only too happy to join in, no doubt hoping to happen upon an old master or a jewellery box crammed with gems. Alas, they found no paintings and no jewellery, although they did come across a couple of rather moth-eaten mink coats. It was clear that whoever had lived here prior to Uncle George had been wealthy, although, Sophie reminded herself, you didn't normally find too many poor people living in a castle worth millions of euros.

As for her novel, she finally had a breakthrough moment one evening. She and Rachel had decided to treat themselves to dinner at the Vecchio Ristoro and it was as they reached the end of another excellent meal – this time including guinea fowl roasted in the oven with fennel and sweet potatoes – that the idea came to her. They were sitting at the same table as before, tucked to one side overlooking the castle gates, when she suddenly came up with the title.

'*Behind the Castle Gates.*'

'Sorry, what, Soph?'

'That's what I'm going to call my novel. As a title, don't you think it sets the scene and hints at mystery? I can see the cover now – a forbidding-looking pair of gates with a medieval castle just visible behind.'

'Forbidding-looking? I thought you were writing romance.'

Sophie paused for thought. 'I've changed my mind. I think I'm going to write a mystery, with some romance of course, but a bit darker, maybe even with a supernatural element thrown in. And I reckon I'll make it part-modern, part-medieval.'

'I like the idea.' Rachel winked at her. 'So how about two modern-day sisters who inherit a castle and discover the secret history of what happened there way back in the mists of time?'

Sophie shook her head slowly. 'I'm not sure – a bit too close for comfort, maybe?'

'Well, instead of the two sisters, why not make it two or three cousins who barely know each other being forced to do what we're doing? That could work.'

Sophie turned the idea over in her head and found she liked it. A lot. 'That's brilliant. So it can be the story of them getting to know each other, as well as discovering the history of the place.'

Rachel reached over and tapped the back of Sophie's hand. 'I suppose that's what you and I are doing really – getting to know each other again after six years.'

'On that note, there's something I've been wanting to ask you for days now.' Seeing her sister still looking relaxed, Sophie took the plunge. 'You've told me where you went and what you did after dropping out of uni, but you haven't told me why. Why dump everything just a matter of months before graduating? I've never been able to get my head round that. Why, Rach?' She sat back and reached for her half-empty wine glass. The smile had faded from her sister's face by now and Sophie had to wait over a minute for the reply – and when it came it packed a punch.

'If I'm being totally honest, there were a number of reasons, but the main one was you.'

'Me?' Sophie almost spilled her wine. 'What did I do? I wasn't even in Exeter then. I was working in London.'

'You may not have been, but your ghost was.'

'My ghost?' Sophie felt herself struggling to understand.

'Do you remember Doctor Grantham in the English department?'

'The twentieth-century literature guy? Yes, I remember him. I always thought he was a bit full of himself. Fancied himself as God's gift to academia.'

'He remembered you well – very well in fact – and he never stopped rubbing your name in my face.'

'What do you mean? Why *my* name?'

'Because you were Miss Bloody Perfect, that's why.' There was a more bitter note in Rachel's voice now as she stared down at her hands on the table top. 'You're the one who got the First-Class Honours degree; you won all the prizes; you were the star of the English Department. And it was always like that all the way through school as well. As for me – and Doctor Grantham spelt it out brutally clearly to me on numerous occasions – I was just a poor imitation of you.' Sophie saw her look up from her knuckles and couldn't miss the tears in her eyes. 'There comes a time when always being treated as second best gets just too much to bear. It was when he told me my Christmas assignment was superficial and unimaginative and how you would never have handed in something so poor, that I just flipped. I told him where he could shove his assignment and I went out and got hammered along with Pablo – my Puerto Rican friend. The next day I packed my bags and we left.'

Sophie was flabbergasted. Of all the explanations she had been expecting, she hadn't thought for a moment that she herself might have been responsible, however inadvertently. She reached across and caught hold of Rachel's hands in both of hers.

'Rach, I don't know what to say. Doctor Grantham had no right to bring me into it, but I had no idea you felt so badly about living in my shadow. In fact, with you being so popular and getting the best boyfriends, I always felt it was the other way round. I can honestly say I've been living in *your* shadow for years, since we were teenagers – sensible Sophie, the teacher's pet, the swot, that was me, while you were the one everybody wanted to be with. But, please believe me, if I'd thought for a minute that I was affecting you like that, I'd have done something about it.'

Rachel turned her hands so as to grip Sophie's fingers gently in hers. 'What could you have done, Soph? It's just that you're brighter than me.' Before Sophie could object, she modified her statement. 'All right, it's not necessarily a matter of intelligence. Maybe it's not that I'm thick. Looking back on it now I can see that the fault was my own. I just didn't have the same attitude to work as you did. I mean, I didn't skip lectures or anything, but I always found a million reasons for not doing any more than the bare minimum.'

After a pause for breath, followed by a mouthful of wine, Rachel continued.

'I went skiing in Austria with a bunch of friends in January that year and I copied the Christmas assignment almost word-for-word off the internet the day I got home, just hours before the deadline. I still object to what Doctor Grantham said, but there's no question I did deserve a very low mark. The trouble was that by that time everything had been mounting up and it was the last straw. I just couldn't handle it any more and I knew I had to get away – or so I thought. If it helps, I very soon regretted it. I was crying my eyes out before the plane had even taken off from Heathrow. You know that feeling when you know you've screwed everything up and it's all your fault?' She produced a little smile. 'Of course you don't, because you don't make those sorts of mistakes, but, believe me, it hurt.'

'Of course I do. I've made all sorts of mistakes – starting with Claudio for instance. But you should just have got straight back on another plane and come home again…'

Even as she said it, Sophie knew that this would have been an impossible ask for her sister, whose pride simply wouldn't have tolerated it. To have slunk back like that would have been an admission of defeat. But the good news was that she now appeared to have got her life back on track. Sophie reached for the carafe and emptied the remains of the wine into their glasses.

'Well, I'm terribly, terribly sorry for my part in what happened. If only I'd known… Look, let's drink to the fact that you've got yourself sorted out now – and a damn sight better than me, for that matter. At least you have a clear trajectory to follow while I'm still floundering about, trying to work out what I want to do.' She leant forward and clinked her glass against Rachel's. 'Cheers, Rach. Here's to the future, not the past.'

'The future.' Rachel took a sip of wine and wiped her eyes before looking up again with renewed optimism.

'And it's looking amazingly bright for both of us, thanks to Uncle George.'

Sophie raised her glass again.

'Here's to Uncle George.'

Chapter 13

Next morning Sophie gave Jeeves a longish walk first thing and then left him with Rita while she and Rachel headed for the beach for a swim in the sea and to check the place out. Although it was still relatively early when they got down to Santa Rita, it was already heaving with people. Italian schools were now on holiday and there were holidaymakers all over the place. Sophie had taken her little car rather than the big Mercedes but even so it took two or three tours of the streets behind the seafront before they found a parking space. Goodness only knew how much busier it would become as August arrived and so many Italian companies and businesses closed down for some or all of the month. They made their way through the side streets to the promenade and walked along until they spotted the sign for *Bagni Aurelia*.

They descended a flight of steps to the sandy beach where a cheerful suntanned man, Rita's nephew, greeted them and showed them to their *ombrellone* – literally big umbrella. This blue and white striped parasol had two sunbeds laid out neatly beneath it side-by-side, arranged directly perpendicular to the sea, the sand around them meticulously raked. This place wasn't cheap, but it did offer a lot of amenities. The beach was maybe ten feet or so below the level of the promenade and changing rooms had been created underneath the walkway. Sophie and

Rachel had their own lockable changing room and the use of hot showers and even a washing line to hang their wet costumes to dry. It was all very organised, but maybe a bit too regimented for Sophie's liking, although she had to admit that being able to change without scrabbling about under a towel was a real bonus.

They left their street clothes in the changing room and set off down the beach to the sea. In fact, as soon as they came out of the shelter of the forest of parasols, the sand was so blisteringly hot they hopped as quickly as possible down to the water's edge and splashed in gratefully.

'Blimey, Soph, that sand's scorching.'

'The water's great though. It feels a bit cooler than our pool, but that might just be after the hot beach.'

Together they waded out into the remarkably clean and clear water. The beach shelved gradually and they walked some way before it was deep enough to duck down and swim. The sea was flat calm and there were virtually no waves to disturb the glassy surface. Looking back at the beach, they could see it was made up of a series of sunbed encampments, each laid out with mathematical precision and each with its own set of colours. The *spiagge libere*, tiny 'public' areas of sand between each *bagno*, were packed with those unable, or unwilling, to undertake the considerable investment necessary to rent one of the coloured parasols. The water's edge was a mixture of children splashing about while matronly ladies and paunchy elderly gentlemen strolled slowly up and down in the shallows and vendors of all nationalities, carrying everything from sarongs to counterfeit watches and hand-carved African figurines, plied their trade.

By this time Sophie and Rachel had acclimatised to the temperature and it was delightful to float lazily about, the salty water so much more buoyant than their pool. Sophie was bobbing gently in the water when she heard Rachel's voice and glanced across to see her face looking suddenly serious.

'Soph, will you tell me about mum, please?'

Sophie's state of lazy relaxation changed abruptly. She had been trying to find the right time to bring up this subject but had kept putting it off. Now it had come.

'You mean about her illness and her death?'

'Yes. I feel so terribly guilty for not coming home to see her before she died, but I was in a bad place... in my head. Tell me, was it awful?'

Sophie felt a whole lot closer to her sister now, but she couldn't help the host of dreadful memories that came bubbling up inside her head.

'It *was* awful. Maybe not so bad towards the end – at least for mum, as she was drugged up – but for me it was ten months of hell. I had to put my life on hold and give up my studies for a whole year so I could look after her. Thank goodness I was able to do that. If I'd been working, I could have lost my job. Of course, by the time I went back to uni again, all my friends had moved on. As for mum, the thing she couldn't understand was why you didn't come to see her.' She glanced over at Rachel again and was not surprised to see tears running down her sister's cheeks. 'Couldn't you have borrowed the money or something?'

Rachel nodded. 'I know. That's what I should have done but it was so complicated. Like I said, I was working illegally and if I'd left the country they'd never have let me back in but, truth be told, I was afraid of what mum would say. Mum and I always had a bit of a love–hate relationship. We both know you were always her favourite.'

Sophie was about to object but she stopped herself. While she had no doubt that their mum had loved both daughters, there was no getting away from the fact that her firstborn, the sensible, boring, hardworking one, had always been uppermost in her mind, if not her affections. Looking back on it now, it was so clear and so unfair, but at the time she had just accepted it as the natural order. Taking her silence for agreement, Rachel continued.

'So if I'd come home I was afraid I'd have burned my bridges, or boats, or whatever it is you burn, as far as working in the States was concerned, and I knew what she would have said: "Look at you, ruining your life, wasting your time, while your sister's such a success." She never was one to mince her words when she thought I'd screwed up. I know she had every right to tell me off, but it didn't stop it hurting.' She ducked her face into the water to wash away the tears. When she emerged, she reached over and caught hold of one of Sophie's hands. 'I'm really, really sorry, Soph. I should have come home and I know that now. In fact, I knew that then, but I was too pigheaded to accept it. Above all, I'm sorry that you had to do everything. I should have been there for you and for her, and the guilt I still feel will be with me forever.'

Sophie clung onto her hand as she felt the tears spring to her own eyes. Hindsight is a wonderful thing and she could understand everything her sister had told her. She did her best to reassure her.

'Mum had her problems, Rach, we both know that. It can't have been easy bringing up two children all on her own and there's no getting away from the fact that you weren't the easiest, at least when you were in your teens.' She caught her sister's eye to show there was no sting intended in her words. 'After you'd left, she asked after you at first but then she became so introspective she wasn't really interested in much apart from herself and the cancer. By the end, she barely knew who I was and I'm sure she hardly noticed your absence. For me it was tough and, yes, I would have liked your help but I managed, and it all worked out. Just try to forget about it and use the experience to help you in the future.'

Rachel pulled Sophie to her and they hugged. After that, by tacit agreement, they didn't speak about it any further but Sophie felt the air had finally been cleared and she knew she could now move on. They had lost their mum, but she had got her sister back at last.

Around mid-morning, they showered to remove the salt that had dried on their bodies and changed out of their swimming things. After that they set out on a walking tour of the town. Apart from modern shops, cafes and restaurants, there wasn't much to see until they came to a steep flight of old stone steps leading sharply upwards towards a church built almost into the near vertical cliff face. The church itself was obviously not terribly old but the panel outside informed them that although this building had been constructed in the late nineteenth century, it had been built to replace a much earlier medieval church which had been destroyed by a powerful earthquake in 1887. Inside it was all fairly bland but there was an ancient baptismal font, probably salvaged from the old church, carved out of pink marble. The carvings appeared to show boats and armed figures who might even have been wearing turbans or similar headdresses, and Sophie took a few photos and resolved to mention it to Dan, in case it was a reference to his marauding Saracen pirates.

Above the church was the old part of town and they climbed yet more steps, squeezing between ancient houses, mostly white, cream or faded pink in colour, until they emerged above the rooftops and had a clear view down across the town and the beach to the headland beyond. There wasn't a cloud in the sky and the sea was an almost unbelievable cerulean blue, with strange whitish swirls where currents moved the waters. A flotilla of little sailing boats with red sails, a massive multi-million dollar yacht and a faded green fishing boat added extra touches of colour to the scene, while the cluster of pink roofs of Paradiso, above them amid the trees, looked almost magical. Sophie breathed deeply – not just because of the hundred steps they had just climbed.

'It's a gorgeous area, isn't it? I can see why Uncle George loved it.'

'I was thinking the same thing. Although I'm looking forward to the financial security the proceeds of the sale of the castle will provide, it'll be sad to lose the connection with Paradiso.'

'How's this for an idea? Let's see how much we get for the castle but maybe we might have enough left over to buy ourselves a little piece of paradise of our own, somewhere we could come for holidays or just to chill out.'

'I think that's a great idea. And when you become a famous writer I can imagine you up there at your typewriter, Jeeves at your feet, looking out over this view as you plan your next bestseller while Chris, stripped to the waist and oiled, gently fans you with a palm frond.'

Sophie couldn't help laughing. 'We live in hope – although the only oil that interests me at the moment is the oil I'd like to pour onto my former boyfriend if he's stupid enough to turn up at the door.'

Before returning to Paradiso, they went to a big super-market on the outskirts of town and bought a load of provisions in readiness for Chris's arrival on Friday. Thought of him once again raised the question in Sophie's head of just what sort of relationship she had, and might have, with him. Pleased as she was at the thought of seeing her best friend again, she was feeling unusually nervous at the prospect.

Chapter 14

Chris's train was bang on time on Friday evening. At Rachel's insistence, Sophie took her courage in both hands and drove down in the Mercedes, dropping Rachel and Jeeves at a bar overlooking the beach first, but when she got to the station she couldn't find a parking space for the big vehicle. In consequence she was sitting in the car in a no-waiting area, checking her mirrors for traffic wardens, when she saw him emerge from the station building. She jumped out and waved.

'Chris, over here!'

His face split into a broad smile and he waved back as he came across the road to meet her. She threw her arms around his neck and gave him a warm hug, kissing him on the cheeks, really glad to see him. He was looking very smart – and uncomfortably hot – in a dark suit, collar and tie.

'Blimey, Soph, what's with the car?'

She affected an air of disinterest which quite obviously didn't fool him one bit. 'What, this heap of junk? Just something I found lying around the castle.'

'How the other half lives, eh? You'll soon be too posh to even talk to plebs like me.'

'I'll never be posh and I'll never stop talking to you, Chris. You know that.'

She locked his bag in the boot and as she drove him to the bar to meet up with Rachel and Jeeves she gave him a quick run-down of events so far. Although it was almost half past six, the streets and promenade were still packed with noisy people and she reassured him that up on top of the hill in Paradiso it would be a whole lot quieter. He nodded approvingly.

'Do you realise that in less than three months I'll no longer be eligible for a Club 18-30 holiday? We old folk need a nice quiet holiday destination.'

'That means you've still got three months to go wild.' She grinned across at him. He had always been sensible and grounded, and she had never seen him do anything particularly wild. Not that she minded – she wasn't that sort of person either. That had always been her sister's preserve. She turned onto the road that ran alongside the beach and, to her amazement, discovered no fewer than three free parking spaces right outside the bar. She gave a surreptitious sigh of relief. She had been dreading trying to squeeze the big vehicle into a narrow space with Chris watching.

Rachel was sitting at a table on the higher deck, overlooking the beach and the bay. She spotted them and waved and, as she did so, Sophie saw a big black head emerge from under the table, tail wagging as he recognised who it was.

'Chris, you remember Rachel, don't you?'

Chris went over and extended his hand, but Rachel caught hold of his shoulders and pulled him down so she could kiss him on the cheeks. Sophie smiled as she saw him blush.

'Chris, hi, long time no see.'

'Hi, Rachel, of course I remember you. You're looking great.'

And Sophie agreed that she did. With her tanned face and limbs and the new short skirt she had bought in Albenga earlier in the week, she looked gorgeous, and Sophie felt sure Dario would like what he saw when he met up with them here at seven as arranged. Things had been going well between Rachel and her Italian man and the plan for tonight was for her to go straight off for dinner with Dario and leave Sophie alone with Chris.

'And you look as handsome as ever, Jeeves.' Chris bent down and made a fuss of the dog. 'Been behaving yourself?' For a moment it almost looked as if the Labrador nodded.

'You're look as if you're boiling, Chris. Take off your jacket and tie.' Rachel reached over to help him. 'You're at the seaside now. You could roll your trouser legs up and tie a knotted handkerchief on your head as well if you like. Has Sophie told you we've got a pool up at the castle? You can have a swim when you get up there if you fancy it.'

She shot a surreptitious wink across the table towards Sophie who almost blushed. Clearly, Rachel was determined to get Chris out of his clothes as soon as possible. Sophie, while not averse to a swim herself or, indeed, to seeing Chris in his swimming things, was definitely going to take things a whole lot more slowly, not least because she still hadn't completely made up her mind about the whole best friend to boyfriend thing. Could that happen? Did she really think of him that way? She had certainly felt a flash of strong affection for him as he had emerged from the station, but the exact nature of this affection was hard to judge. For now, she told herself firmly, she was very pleased to see him and that was all that counted.

Dario arrived punctually at seven and, after exchanging greetings with Sophie and Chris, took Rachel off for dinner. Sophie and Chris carried on chatting, catching up on what had happened over the past weeks since they had last seen each other, before she glanced at her watch.

'I was going to cook you dinner tonight but then I thought you might prefer a real Italian meal.'

'Anything, Soph, really.'

'There's a super restaurant up at Paradiso and I thought we could eat there – but before you say anything, this weekend's on me to say thank you for all you've done for me.'

Needless to say he objected to letting her pay but she was adamant and insisted, telling him this was something she really wanted to do and now that she was living rent-free, she had the means to do it. Reluctantly he gave in and they set off back up the hill. He was clearly very struck by the panoramic views as they climbed higher and when she saw the expression of awe on his face as they crunched to a halt on the gravel outside the castle, she almost laughed. His eyes were almost bulging out of their sockets.

'Blimey, what a place!' He climbed out of the car and just stood there, staring in amazement. 'I tried looking it up on Google Earth but the aerial shot doesn't do it justice. Wow, it looks like the kind of place a princess should live in.'

'Funny you should say that. It's actually going to be the place where two princesses used to live.' He retrieved his bag and she led him up the steps and in through the front door, telling him more about her plan to write a novel and, as always, he was immediately very supportive.

'Brilliant idea. How many times have I said that's what you should do? And what a location for a story!'

She showed him to his room and left him to change into something lighter while she and Jeeves went for a quick walk in the garden. By the time she returned to the back door, she found Chris, now wearing shorts and a T-shirt, poking about in the pile of rubbish she had brought down from the top floor. She couldn't help noticing that he had rather nice forearms as well as strong leg muscles and this only served to increase her feeling of attraction towards him.

'How come you've suddenly developed an all-consuming interest in trash, Chris? Thinking of a career change to recycling operative?'

'Trash? Some of this stuff's amazing. Look at this.' He was holding a dusty, worm-eaten wooden case containing a dozen old vinyl LPs that she had had no hesitation in consigning to the bin. 'I'd need to check current values, but some of these records are almost certainly worth anything upwards of a hundred pounds each.' He pulled one out and wiped it reverently against the leg of his shorts. 'Look at this: Pink Floyd's *The Piper at the Gates of Dawn*. We sold a copy of that last year in one of our specialist music auctions and I seem to remember it went for almost two hundred pounds.' He looked up in awe. 'Wow, if you've got any more of these, you're sitting on a goldmine.'

Sophie was equally amazed. 'To be honest, I don't really know what we've got. Part of our instructions have been to clear the junk out of the top floor rooms and I've barely started.'

'If you like I could take a look. In fact, I'd love to take a look.'

'Thanks, but that would make this a bit of a busman's holiday for you.'

'No worries. Really, I'd love it. The chance to root around in the attic of an old castle is the sort of thing people in my profession dream about.' He shot a grin across at her. 'All right, I know my dreams are boring.'

'Well, if you're sure, you can take a look tomorrow. For tonight, you're mine and I'm taking you out for a really good dinner.'

This time she deliberately chose the *menù gastronomico* for both of them and it was predictably outstanding – although far, far more than she could possibly eat. To go with it she ordered a bottle of Grignolino, an excellent, slightly effervescent light red wine from nearby Piedmont, as a special treat. As well as the familiar antipasti, including the omelette, this menu also included a platter of fresh seafood ranging from mussels to scallops, with a heap of dressed crabmeat in the middle. This was followed by no fewer than four different types of pasta – not as alternatives, but served one after the other – and ended with a T-bone steak whose aroma had Jeeves salivating under the table. By the time the selection of desserts arrived, Sophie knew she was on the point of exploding. She was also finally approaching the moment she had been dreading when she would attempt to find out if Chris might consider her as more than a friend and vice versa.

However, before she could launch into some sort of tentative declaration, she heard an American voice at her shoulder.

'Hi, Sophie, *buon appetito.*'

She looked up, finding herself feeling almost embarrassed. Until Dan had told her about his best friend in the US, she had felt attracted to him and here she was now with another man. Hastily doing her best to swallow her embarrassment – and a burp – she greeted him.

'Hi, Dan, back from Rome?'

'I've literally just climbed out of the car now. I'm hoping I'm still in time to get something to eat from these guys.' No sooner had he spoken than the elderly lady – whose name Sophie now knew to be Carmela – appeared and confirmed that she would grill him a steak.

'Can I introduce my good friend, Chris, from England? Chris, this is Dan. He's living just up the road and he knew my uncle.'

'Hi, Dan. It's good to meet an American. This means I don't have to try to speak Italian.' He gave Dan a smile and held out his hand.

The two men chatted amiably as Sophie debated what to do. Should she ask Dan to sit down with them, even though he already knew that Chris was here supposedly so she could see whether she fancied him as more than a friend and vice versa, or should she take the easy way out and let the American eat alone? She quickly realised that she only had one option. Dan had become a good friend and of course she had to ask him to join them. Her talk to Chris would have to be postponed – for now. She waited for a break in the men's conversation before indicating the empty chairs at their table.

'Sit down, Dan, and join us. To be honest, we've just about finished, but I could do with a coffee and it's always good to catch up. How was Rome?'

He pulled out a chair and sat down. Seconds later Carmela arrived with his cutlery, napkin and glass. As Sophie ordered two coffees, Chris picked up their wine bottle and held it out towards Dan.

'There's a drop of Grignolino left if you feel like it.'

Dan shook his head. 'Thanks, but I'll just drink water tonight. I've been eating out a lot in Rome over the past week and I need to detox.'

'Was that a business trip?'

'Research. I had to take a short trip down to Sicily and then I've been picking brains at Rome University – la Sapienza.'

Sophie was quick to explain. 'Dan's a lecturer in Medieval History at Harvard. He's over here on a sabbatical.'

'Fascinating.' Chris sounded genuinely interested. 'Listen, Dan, I wonder if I could ask you something, but only if you can spare the time. Are you going to be around tomorrow? I'm only here for two nights but there's something you could help me with if you have a moment. I'd be extremely grateful.'

'I'll be here, and I'm happy to help. What's the problem?'

Chris told him how he worked for an auction house and had been in Milan to value a private collection of paintings that would be coming on the market in a couple of months. 'The thing is, I'm struggling to identify one of the paintings. It's a portrait of an austere-looking old man and he looks familiar, but I've drawn a blank. It isn't signed but from the style and the materials it looks to me as if it has to date back to around about the fifteenth or early sixteenth century. If I could work out who the man is, that would be a major step forward. I wonder if a medievalist might be able to shed some light on who he is. I've got photos of the portrait on my iPad.'

'Sounds fascinating. I'll call in at the castle tomorrow. Say, mid-morning if it suits?' Dan glanced across at Sophie. 'Now, if you'll excuse me, I really must go and wash up

before my steak arrives. I've been on the road for hours.'
And he left.

Chris caught Sophie's eye and threw her into confusion. 'Dan's a good-looking chap, and bright with it. Are you considering him as a replacement for your Roman boyfriend by any chance?'

Sophie shook her head. 'No, he's just a friend.' For a moment she almost launched into speaking to him about their own relationship but the sight of Dan emerging from the front door of the restaurant stopped her in her tracks – that was a conversation for when she managed to get Chris alone.

–

Sophie and Chris were in the lounge, sitting on a sofa side-by-side – a chaste distance apart – watching one of Uncle George's old black and white movies when she heard the front door slam. She had been trying to think of a way of opening up about the way her feelings for him were changing but kept chickening out. After all, she repeatedly reminded herself, she had once managed to convince herself that Claudio was her one and only, and look where that had got her? Even so, she was on the point of taking her courage in both hands when the sound of the door made her shelve any such plans for now. Jeeves raised his head, clearly debated for a moment whether he should bark, but then decided he was far too tired and lowered his head to the floor again with a thud. Seconds later the lounge door was flung open and Rachel stomped in. You didn't need to be an expert in body language to see that she was furious.

'Hi, Rach, what's up?'

Her sister came to a halt in front of them and Sophie saw her take a deep breath in an attempt to calm herself – which didn't work. 'What's up is that he's married, that's what!' She almost had smoke coming out of her ears. 'He's bloody well married.'

'Dario?'

'Yes, of course, bloody Dario...' Sophie saw her stop in mid flow and make a real effort. 'Sorry, Soph, I shouldn't take it out on you.'

She dropped her bag onto an armchair and slumped down beside it. By this time Jeeves had worked out that support from him was needed, so he pulled himself to his feet and trotted over to rest his nose on Rachel's knee, his tail wagging slowly. She stroked him gently as she continued – this time in a calmer voice.

'So we're sitting in this really nice little restaurant on the hill, looking down over Alassio, and suddenly this woman marches in and starts screaming. I didn't understand everything she said but the message was crystal clear: Dario's her husband and I would do well to get the hell out of there, pronto, before she stuck a fork in me. Which is what I did. I legged it down the hill to a taxi stand and got a lift back here.' She wiped her forehead with her hand. 'What a mess!'

'How awful for you.' Sophie got up and went over to perch on the arm of the chair alongside her. 'And he seemed like such a nice guy.'

Rachel nodded. 'Yes, he was a nice enough guy, although nothing was ever going to happen between the two of us. It's not the fact that I can't see him again that bothers me; it's being lied to.' She glanced up. 'I wish I'd slapped him before storming off. I feel really sorry for that poor woman. Fancy discovering your husband with another woman. It's awful. To be honest, I'm surprised she didn't stab me with a fork.'

Perching on the arm of Rachel's chair Sophie caught hold of her sister's hand and gave it a squeeze. 'What was it I was saying about Italian men? Don't worry, sweetie, you weren't to know.'

'If it helps, Rachel, it isn't just Italians, and it isn't just men.'

Both sisters looked up in surprise at the sound of Chris's voice.

'Something similar happened to me a year ago, not long after splitting up with Claire.' In response to their inquisitive gazes, he elaborated. 'I met a woman at a trade fair in Dusseldorf. I took her out for dinner, one thing led to another and she invited me back to her apartment. Luckily I had to stop in the lobby to take a call so she went up in the lift ahead of me. When I got up to her door I found her waiting outside, looking scared stiff, with the news that her husband had unexpectedly arrived home from a trip and so I'd better make myself scarce. I still have nightmares about what would have happened if I hadn't stopped to take that call or if he'd come home half an hour later.'

'And you had no idea?' Sophie was fascinated. This was the first time Chris had mentioned other women to her.

'Nope. No ring, no mention, nothing.' He gave Rachel an encouraging look. 'So it can happen to anyone. Just put it down to experience and move on.'

'And that's what you've done?' Now she had got him on the subject of other women, Sophie was keen to keep him talking.

He shrugged his shoulders. 'Well, I've put it behind me, but I don't seem to have moved on much.'

Sophie was pleased to see that these revelations from Chris were having a positive effect on Rachel. She was sounding much less angry and decidedly curious now. Sophie looked on with interest as her sister picked up the questioning. 'So what does that mean? Isn't there a woman in your life at the moment?'

'Not really.'

Rachel pounced on his choice of vocabulary. 'What does "not really" mean? Is there someone or isn't there?'

He actually blushed. 'I don't think so. There's a girl, a woman, but somehow I don't think anything's ever going to happen there.'

Sophie exchanged surreptitious glances with her sister. Of course it was inevitable a good-looking man like Chris would have found himself somebody, although maybe if he hadn't actually hooked up with this woman yet...

Rachel interrupted her train of thought. 'So, no girl-friend, eh?' She winked at Sophie before returning her attention to Chris. 'You need to do something about that.'

He shook his head. 'I'm fine, Rachel. My job keeps me very busy and I'm often on the road. With a lifestyle like mine, it's hard to keep a relationship going. It'll happen when it happens but, for now, I'm fine.'

Rachel was still sounding upbeat. 'So that means all three of us are currently unattached. I tell you what, why don't we go clubbing tomorrow night? Didn't you say the guy in the hair salon told you the best places to go?'

Sophie choked back a giggle as she saw the look of terror on Chris's face. She couldn't remember ever having seen him on the dance floor – indeed, this had been one of Claire's few grumbles about him. She was quick to reassure him.

'I'm not so keen on going dancing, but Romeo the hairdresser did tell me about a rather nice-sounding little cafe over on the next hill. Apparently that's where all the beautiful people go and they make a house cocktail that's amazing.'

The relief on Chris's face was all too obvious and he shot her a grateful glance. 'Sounds much more like my kind of thing. Besides, what's the point of my going to a night club if I don't speak enough Italian to ask a girl to dance?'

Sophie caught her sister's eye and gave a shrug of the shoulders. The intention had been to get him dancing with *her*, not with some random Italian woman. Clearly he wasn't following the script – or more probably he had no idea there was a script to follow.

Chapter 15

When Sophie got back with Jeeves from their early morning walk, she was surprised to find Chris already outside the back door, sifting through the junk pile. Next to him were half a dozen objects ranging from a gruesome-looking rusty metal poker to a moth-eaten top hat in a battered velvet case, all of which he had salvaged from the heap. Over breakfast he told her all about the items he had identified and she could feel his enthusiasm. Like a bloodhound on the trail, he was in his element. Rita didn't come in on Saturdays so there were no warm croissants, but Sophie had planned ahead and there was more than enough to choose from, including a fruit tart she had made the previous day topped with apricots from their own trees. She was delighted to see him pick up a piece, taste it, murmur appreciatively, and then return to his favourite subject.

'At a conservative estimate, the few bits and pieces I've rescued from your junk pile should bring in several hundred pounds, maybe a whole lot more. Add in the LPs I saw last night, you must be nudging the thousand pound mark and that's just the stuff you were slinging out. If you like I can take the LPs back with me. We've got a music memorabilia sale coming up at the end of August. When can I see the rest of it?'

By eight o'clock he was already on the top floor up to his armpits in dust, working his way through the room where she had put the items she had deemed worthy of keeping to be sold at the antiques fair. When she showed him the two remaining rooms still dotted with boxes, he was like a little kid in a candy store. She helped as much as she could but it was clear he wanted to take a good look at everything by himself so she ended up standing at the doorway, keeping up a desultory conversation as she watched him happily ferreting about. She would dearly have liked to ask him more about the woman he had mentioned with whom nothing was going to happen but the opportunity didn't present itself. As for embarking upon some sort of meaningful dialogue about the exact nature of their own relationship, now was definitely not the time. He was clearly totally absorbed by his antiques hunt.

She took a closer look at him as he sorted through the objects and almost for the first time she realised two things: he really was a good-looking man – well, she had always known that, but she now realised that the sensation currently coursing through her body was none other than desire. From the breadth of his shoulders and the strong muscles in his legs and arms, it was obvious that he must have been working out recently. Back in the days when he and Claire had been together, he had never, to her knowledge, done more than play squash – albeit at a high standard – but such had been her gloom and despondency over the past year after the Claudio debacle that she had failed to see that he had slimmed down and toughened up noticeably since splitting from Claire. Never having seen him with his shirt off, she suddenly found herself wondering what he would look like in his swimming shorts and this also came as a shock to the system. This appeared to be the confirmation that she really did fancy him. But whether he fancied her remained unknown, although by the sound of what he had said last night, she wasn't going to be first on his list.

After a while she went down to the kitchen and found Rachel in there having breakfast.

'Where's Chris?'

'Upstairs.'

For an instant she caught a spark in her sister's eyes. Rachel had disappeared off to bed last night, leaving Sophie and Chris to watch the end of the movie together.

'So does that mean you and he…?'

'No, it doesn't. He's been on his hands and knees amidst all the junk on the top floor since eight o'clock. You know when Jeeves is rooting around in the dry leaves for his tennis ball, tail wagging? Well, that gives you an idea of the scene.'

'At least it gave you a chance to take a good look at his butt.' Rachel gave her an encouraging smile. 'Any developments since I last saw you?'

Sophie shook her head. 'Nope, but I keep thinking about that thing he said.'

'About fancying some other woman?'

'Yes.'

'And you have no idea who he might have meant?'

'None at all.'

'Has it occurred to you he might have meant you?'

'Me?' Sophie hadn't thought of that. 'But he said nothing could ever happen…'

'Which is what he would say if he was talking about his best friend, isn't it?'

Sophie's brain cleared. 'But then that thing about asking some random girl, not me, to dance? No, he can't have been thinking of me, I'm sure.'

'All right, if you say so, but I'm still not sure. Assuming he didn't mean you, he said he didn't think he had a chance with this woman, so the coast's still clear for you.'

'I don't know...' In fact, Sophie reckoned she did. Last night when they were sitting alone at the TV would surely have given him a chance at least to hint at something, and he hadn't taken it. 'No, I think I'm on a hiding to nothing with him. Anyway, I'd better go back up and see how he's getting on.'

By the time Rachel called up to them an hour or so later with the news that Dan had arrived and there was coffee in the kitchen, Sophie was feeling uncomfortably hot and Chris was dripping with sweat. There was no aircon up here and the heat of the sun was radiating through from the roof above. Even so, she almost had to drag him away from his treasure hunt. Again to her amazement, she found that gripping his arm and tugging his sweaty body towards her aroused feelings in her that were very different from the way she used to think of him.

'It's time you took a break, Chris.' She glanced at her watch and saw that it was almost eleven o'clock. He had been hard at it for three solid hours. 'Besides, Dan's here and you wanted to ask him something, didn't you? Come down and have a coffee and a rest. You deserve it.'

Downstairs Dan was sitting at the kitchen table with Rachel and, by the sound of it, she had been relating the sorry saga of what had happened to her the previous night with Dario's wife. He looked up as Sophie and Chris came in and shook his head in disbelief. 'What's wrong with some guys? Rachel's just been telling me her tale of woe.'

Sophie just rolled her eyes and shrugged helplessly while Chris sat down beside Dan and opened his laptop. Sophie and Rachel crowded round behind the two men and stared down at the image on the screen. As Chris had said, it was the portrait of a serious-looking elderly man in elaborate robes wearing a distinctive cap with an unusual blunt point sticking up at the rear.

'Mind if I take a closer look?' Dan sounded fascinated.

'Help yourself, please.'

Dan studied the painting very carefully, enlarging parts of the scene and dwelling in particular on the hat. In the end he sat back and gave his verdict.

'Well, I think I can definitely tell you *what* he is, although I'm not sure of his name – yet. That hat he's wearing is the traditional head covering of a *Doge* of Venice.'

'Of course, I should have known that.' Chris's voice was a mixture of excitement and annoyance at himself. He glanced momentarily over his shoulder at the two sisters. '*Doge* is what the Venetians called the ruler of their republic, and now that you say it, Dan, it's so obvious. Of course I've seen that hat before. What an idiot!'

Dan gave him a grin and returned his attention to the screen. 'Don't beat yourself up, there were a hell of a lot of hats going round way back then. Anyway, I'm going to take a guess and say he might be the one of most famous of them all: Francesco Foscari. Mind if I check something?'

He clicked on a search engine and in a remarkably short space of time came up with visual proof in the shape of a painting by a Venetian artist called Bastiani. There could be no mistake. The likeness was unmistakable.

'Got him.' He punched the air triumphantly. 'That's our man: Francesco Foscari, one of the best-known of all the doges. This one was painted in 1457, so I imagine your painting's roughly the same age. This won't necessarily help you find the name of the artist, but at least you now know who the subject is.'

Chris reached over and high-fived the American. 'That's terrific, Dan, thank you so much. I'll mark it up as School of Venice by an unknown artist, late fifteenth century, and describe it as a portrait of Foscari, just like you've said.' He held out his hand towards Dan and shook it more formally. 'Really, thanks a lot. Listen, professional advice of this calibre from an expert like yourself is something we're happy to pay for, and pay handsomely. If you don't mind us using your name in the description, please let me have your bank details and I'll see something appropriate lands in your account to say thank you.'

They sat and chatted for half an hour or so. Dan appeared very interested to hear of the carved font in the little church down in Santa Rita and to see the photos Sophie had taken. Because it was a fairly recent church, he had ignored it so far, but he would definitely be checking it out now.

After a while, Rachel revealed that she had made plans for the day. 'I called Dan while you two were up on the top floor and told him to bring his swimming things. I've prepared a light salad lunch with a few bits and pieces. It's all in the fridge and I thought we could maybe go for a swim first and then eat outside at the table under the shade of the big fig tree by the pool. How does that sound to everybody?'

That sounded excellent and Sophie was soon sitting by the pool in the presence of two attractive men with well-honed bodies, realising that she couldn't fault Rachel's logic. Chris without a shirt on was a very pleasant surprise and she felt that same little stirring of lust she had felt back upstairs. Clearly he didn't spend all his time sitting at a desk. It then immediately occurred to her that this was the very first time he had ever seen her in a bikini and she wondered what sort of impression she might be making on him. To avoid any further conjecture, she decided to join her dog in the pool. A few seconds later the others followed suit.

By the time she emerged from the pool and stretched out on her towel to dry she was feeling less self-conscious. From behind the protection of her sunglasses she watched the others do the same and had to admit that the sensation of finding herself sandwiched – in the most innocent possible way – between these two men was rather nice. She felt pleasantly relaxed, lying here in the shade, with hardly a sound to disturb her – apart from the constant buzzing of bees as they laboured among the blooms all around them. She was almost drifting off to sleep when her sister's voice roused her.

'Here, Soph, Dan brought a bottle of fizz. Will you open it and see that everybody gets some?' Sophie looked up to see her sister set a tray down on the table beneath the fig tree.

Dan reached for the bottle. 'Let me do that.'

Sophie stood up. 'Thanks, Dan. I'll go and help Rachel bring out the food.'

'I'll come with you.' Chris jumped to his feet and together they headed round to the kitchen. They collected the rest of the food and drink and carried it back to the poolside with Jeeves bouncing along at their sides, nostrils flared. By this time Dan had already filled four glasses with Prosecco which he distributed.

'Cheers, and thanks for the lunch invite.'

Sophie was very impressed by lunch. Rachel must have gone down to Santa Rita in the car that morning while she and Chris had been upstairs. She had bought lovely fresh focaccia bread as well as hand-carved ham and fennel-flavoured *finocchiona* salami. Along with the meats, she had made a huge salad containing at least three types of lettuce, fresh tomatoes from the garden, quails' eggs and mozzarella cheese. To accompany the ham there were wonderful, sweet fresh figs from the garden. A bowl of white flesh peaches, again home-grown, completed the meal. To drink there was cold red as well as white wine, along with mineral water. Altogether it was a real feast and Jeeves clearly shared that view as he stationed himself under the table and wandered hopefully from person to person, nudging them with his cold wet nose. But, fore-warned by Sophie, they refused to give in to his pleading eyes – although she did see the occasional bread stick disappearing under the table, mainly from Rachel.

It was a tasty meal and Sophie thoroughly enjoyed the company – not just the two men but her sister as well. She was delighted she and Rachel appeared to have returned to the uncomplicated relationship they had once had, and she could honestly say that her misgivings about the two of them being able to cohabit had proved unfounded – at least for now. How the arrival of the Spanish contingent in a few weeks' time would affect the dynamic remained to be seen but, for the moment, peace had very definitely broken out.

As for the men, it was hard not to make comparisons. Both were intelligent and successful in their own fields. In purely physical terms, Dan would probably have won a handsomest man contest, but it would have been a close-run thing. Both were tall and had blue eyes – something

Sophie had always liked – and both had friendly faces. Most importantly, both had the ability to make her laugh, and a good sense of humour had always been high on her list of desirable male attributes.

There was just one complication – she heard Chris telling Dan that they were going to a special bar for a cocktail this evening and inviting him along to make up a foursome. Although mathematically neat and tidy, this effectively ruled out any chance Sophie might have had of getting Chris on his own this evening so she could work on analysing her feelings towards him more precisely. When Chris headed back to his beloved antiques and Dan disappeared along the path towards his house, she gave a long sigh of frustration, turned round, and let herself fall backwards into the pool, closely followed by her dog. When she surfaced and dissuaded Jeeves from licking her face, she saw her sister crouching at the water's edge with a broad grin on her face.

'Nothing's easy, is it, Soph?'

–

That evening at the cafe Sophie and Rachel insisted on paying as they were celebrating. Among all the bits and pieces on the top floor, Chris had discovered a real treasure. Rolled up in a dusty blanket and tucked away in the far corner of the furthest room, he had come upon a sinister-looking weapon. It was a very old, very heavy, stubby musket, embossed and engraved with animal figures, including a vicious-looking snake and a remarkably friendly lion, and it was in excellent condition. Although it was a Saturday, Chris immediately phoned a colleague from their Milan office in order to discuss it with her, and the result was a 'cautious' estimate in excess of ten thousand euros, possibly more. The lady from the auction house indicated her willingness to come down on Wednesday to inspect it in person with a view to putting it into their autumn antiques sale and Sophie immediately agreed.

In consequence, the mood of the evening was buoyant. The bar recommended by Romeo, the hair stylist, was in a village on the other side of the valley, which didn't look dissimilar to Paradiso – but without the castle. It was reached up a steep, winding road and was perched on top of a wooded headland above the sea. From there you could even see Paradiso itself on the opposite hilltop above Santa Rita. The bar was in the main square, the chairs and tables set on the paving slabs sheltered from the evening sun by the tall stone buildings all around but, unlike Paradiso, the place was humming with life. Motorbikes and scooters were parked right in front of the bar and vehicles kept arriving and departing – mostly with a screech of tyres – almost without a break, spewing out a never-ending stream of noisy people.

Sophie and the others were fortunate to arrive just as one group got up and left and so were able to grab a table. The average age of those around them was probably five or ten years younger than they were and Sophie might have been feeling a bit out of her depth if it hadn't been for the boost she had received from Chris with his great news about the musket. He, on the other hand, was clearly feeling his age.

'Blimey, guys, what a racket! Do you think people live in these houses? I just hope the bar closes at a reasonable time or they aren't going to get much sleep.'

Rachel grinned at him. 'Listen to you, Chris. You sound like an old man.'

'Compared to most of the people around here, I feel it.' He glanced across at Sophie. 'I can't tell you how happy I am we aren't going clubbing.'

She was quick to reassure him. 'Me, too. I don't know why, but I feel quite tired today. I think I'm going to be happy with a quick drink, something to eat and early to bed.'

And this looked likely to be not only on her own, but also without getting any nearer to any sort of closure as far as things between her and Chris were concerned, unless she could find a way of getting him on his own between now and then. It was frustrating in the extreme. Certainly, this weekend wasn't turning into the sort of cathartic moment in her relationship with him that she might have hoped.

When the cocktails appeared, accompanied by a dish of salted biscuits which immediately had the dog looking up, tail wagging hopefully, she sat back and did her best to look on the bright side. So what? She was comfortable, she was surrounded by friends and she had her other best friend – the four-legged one – sitting at her side with his head on her lap. Paradiso might be on top of the next hill, but this place was pretty good all the same – give or take a bit of noise. As for Chris, time would tell. She wasn't in a hurry after all.

Was she?

The cocktails proved to be rather less amazing than Romeo had indicated – more like a colourful exotic fruit salad with the addition of a whole lot of vodka. Dan had once more volunteered to drive the Mercedes and opted for the non-alcoholic version. Sophie tasted his glass and secretly preferred it. By the time she had finished hers, she wasn't feeling any less tired – very much the opposite in fact. Nevertheless, she and Rachel insisted on buying dinner for everyone and they asked Chris to choose what he wanted. His answer came back immediately.

'I still don't think it's fair for you girls to pay but, if you insist, I'd really like a pizza.' He smiled across at Sophie. 'I know it sounds a bit boring but I love pizza and there's nothing to beat a real Italian one.' He caught Dan's eye. 'All right, you Americans have some good pizza houses over there too, but don't forget that it all started here in Italy.'

The pizzeria they went to – on Dan's recommendation – was as good as any Sophie had been to before. When she received her massive thin crust *Quattro Stagioni*, she felt sure she wouldn't be able to eat even half of it. It was so big it was overflowing off the plate onto the tablecloth. To her surprise, however, she managed almost all of it and had to agree that it was excellent. She even found room for a small lemon sorbet afterwards but then called it a day and felt sure she wouldn't eat for a week.

On their way back up to the castle, they could see the lights of the towns along the coast flickering in the distance. It was still warm out but now that the sun had gone down the temperature was a bit more bearable. Dan drove up the hill slowly with the windows open and the scent of pine tree resin filled the car. When they got home he kissed Sophie and Rachel on the cheeks, thanking them for the meal, before shaking Chris's hand.

'I'd better get off. I have a Zoom session coming up with my head of department and he never remembers the time difference. Chris, good to meet you. Will I see you again? Are you planning on coming back over?'

Sophie waited with interest for his answer. She had already mentioned that he was very welcome, but no date had been fixed.

'Good to meet you, too, Dan, and thanks again for your help with the *Doge* painting. I'd love to come back. I'll check with my line manager and take a look at my schedule for the rest of the summer and see what I can arrange. I'm going to be tied up in August but I think September's looking a bit clearer. It would be great to come back and see everyone again.' As he spoke, his eyes met Sophie's and held them for a second or two. She took this as a positive sign and struggled not to blush.

Once Dan had departed, Rachel diplomatically told them she had to rush inside to check her emails while Sophie announced she was taking Jeeves for his walk. She hoped Chris would take the hint – she wasn't going to have many more chances to get him on his own before he left next morning. To her relief, he immediately offered to come with her. They went out through the front gates and set off along the path towards the headland. By now the stars were beginning to shed enough light to make it quite easy for them to see where they were going. When they emerged from the trees and the track widened, Sophie went across to him and caught hold of his arm with both of her hands, appreciating the solid feel of his biceps as she did so.

'Thanks for coming to see us, Chris. I hope you've enjoyed yourself.'

'It's been great, Soph. I love the castle and I love Paradiso. I'm so pleased things seem to be working out between you and Rachel.'

'And will you come back again, for longer? We're here at least until the end of September.'

There was a momentary pause. 'If you'd like me to.' He sounded quite tentative.

She had no hesitation. 'I'd love you to. You are my closest friend, after all.'

'And I'll always be your friend; you know that.' He leant across and deposited a tiny little peck on her cheek before stepping back. 'I'll do my best to come back to see you here in September – but no more of you two paying for everything. Fifty-fifty, right?'

'We can argue about that when you get here. I just hope you can make it.'

'I'll do my best. Of course, by that time you and Dan may be madly in love and you won't want to be bothered with me.'

This time there was no stopping her cheeks from flushing and was thankful it was night-time. 'I'll always want to see you, Chris. Besides, nothing's going to happen between me and Dan. He's a good friend. That's all.'

'Sort of like me, then.'

'Something like that.' She repressed the overwhelming urge to scream in frustrated annoyance, this time at herself, but it was a struggle. Surely this would have been the moment for her to give him at least a bit of encouragement but, oh no, sensible Sophie, the teacher's pet, had done it again. She had been waiting so long for him to make the first move, she had missed the opportunity to give her own input to resolve the dilemma.

She could still feel his touch on her cheek as they turned and walked back to the castle. It had felt good, but there was no getting away from the fact that this had been a potentially romantic moment and all that had emerged from him, and from her, had been gestures of friendship but nothing more.

Chapter 16

On Wednesday Sophie drove down to the station at twelve o'clock to collect the antique weapons expert from Milan. Chris had told her this was a dark-haired woman in her early thirties who would be carrying a brown briefcase, but he had omitted to say that she was extremely beautiful. She was wearing a stylish two-piece grey suit over a white blouse but didn't look in the least bit hot – even though Sophie was boiling in just shorts and a T-shirt. This woman also had the enviable ability that had always eluded Sophie of walking confidently and steadily even though she was wearing shoes with three-inch heels. Sophie went up to her and held out her hand.

'Signora Lombardi? I'm Sophie Elliot.' She addressed the lady in Italian but the answer came back in fluent American-accented English.

'Miss Elliot, hi, it's a pleasure to meet you.' Signora Lombardi extended a slim, manicured hand, her fingers adorned with cherry red nail varnish to match her lipstick, and gave Sophie's a firm, business-like shake. Sophie gave her a welcoming smile and was pleased – and relieved – to receive a very cordial smile in return.

'Please call me Sophie. Did you have a good journey?'

'Fine, thank you and do call me Paola.' The woman was looking more relaxed now. 'I had a long video call with Chris yesterday and he's told me all about your remarkable piece of good fortune in inheriting what sounds like a magnificent property full of all sorts of treasures.'

Sophie accompanied her across to the Mercedes – thankful she hadn't brought her own little car with its lingering doggie smell and intrusive black hairs floating about everywhere – and they conversed politely on the drive up the hill to the castle. She went in through the rear gates and parked round the back from where she led Paola in through the kitchen door. Rita had already left for the day, but Rachel was in there preparing lunch under the unblinking scrutiny of the Labrador. Even so, as Paola walked in, the dog abandoned the lovely foodie smells to come over and greet the new arrival. Sophie wasn't surprised. He had always had an eye for the ladies. This particular lady obviously took an immediate liking to Jeeves and bent down to pet him, thus going up in Sophie's estimation.

After introducing Rachel to her, Sophie wasted no time in taking her through and showing her the musket which was lying on its old blanket on the dining room table. Paola gave it a thorough investigation – without damaging her nails – before setting it back down again and turning towards Sophie with a look of satisfaction on her face.

'It's a stunning piece. It's what's known as a Miquelet rifle and to find one in such good condition is rare, particularly one of such high quality. It's old – maybe even late sixteenth century. The breech, lockplate and sideplate have been engraved by a skilled craftsman and the barrel and breech even look as if they could still be fired.'

'So you think it might do well at auction?'

'I think it should do very well indeed. We have an auction coming up in our London salerooms in mid-September which will include a number of other items of antique weaponry, but this is head and shoulders above almost all the rest. If you're happy to let us include it in the sale – and these six-monthly events normally attract considerable interest among the arms collector community – I would suggest we put a reserve of twenty thousand euros on it.' She gave Sophie a smile. 'But I wouldn't be surprised if it were to go for twice that, maybe even more. It's a unique piece.'

'That's fantastic news.' And it really was. 'Would you like to take it away with you today?'

Paola shook her head. 'If you and I do all the paper-work today, I'll arrange for it to be picked up in a few weeks' time and taken straight to the UK.' She straightened up. 'Now, Chris also mentioned your having a mace.'

'A mace?'

Seeing the blank expression on Sophie's face, Paola dug in her bag and produced an iPad. She swiped through it until she found what she was looking for. This was a photo of a steel poker, a couple of feet long, with a nasty spiked end to it. Sophie nodded immediately.

'I know what you mean now. I think it's with some other bits and pieces he rescued from the pile I was going to dump in the bin.'

She led Paola back through to the kitchen and located the poker along with everything Chris had salvaged. When she handed the remarkably heavy metal rod to Paola, she saw her eyes light up. Once again Paola subjected this item to close scrutiny before announcing the unexpectedly good news.

'Don't be put off by its condition. What you have here is even rarer than the musket. It's a Gothic mace – a close combat weapon – almost certainly dating back to the fifteenth century. I'm sure it's originally German and we sold one like this last year for… just let me see…' She checked through her files before finding what she wanted. She handed the iPad across to Sophie and Rachel and pointed to what was demonstrably a remarkably similar weapon, albeit in perfect condition. 'You can see from the figure below that it sold in London for fifty-two thousand pounds.'

'Blimey.' Rachel caught Sophie's eye. 'Who would have thought it?'

Sophie was genuinely gobsmacked. 'And I was all set to throw it out.'

'If you'd like us to include it in the next auction along with the musket, it'll need to be cleaned and restored first. We can arrange that for you if you're agreeable and I'll get you an estimate for the work. It shouldn't be a particularly big job but it's essential for a good result in the sale.'

After concluding all the formalities, they sat down to lunch. Paola gradually loosened up in the course of the meal, removing her jacket and chatting amicably to Sophie and Rachel, with Jeeves stationed adoringly at her feet. Sophie suppressed a little feeling of jealousy by telling herself this was just because he had identified a potential new source of illicit titbits from the table. As the conversation proceeded, things suddenly got interesting as it became clear that Paola's affections didn't just extend to Jeeves. She had been with Chris on Thursday evening and it quickly emerged that she liked him, too. A lot.

'He's such a knowledgeable man as well as being such fun. What I like most about him is the way he's so unassuming, quite shy really, in spite of his good looks.'

While Sophie agreed with her, she struggled with conflicting emotions. Of course, this stunner might well be the woman Chris had mentioned as being somebody he liked but with whom nothing could happen – presumably because they were colleagues, as well as living a thousand kilometres apart? If so, should she give him a call and tell him what Paola had just said about him? At the same time, by doing this she would be pointing him in the direction of this other woman, just when she herself was beginning to think of him as something more than simply her best friend. This was a crisis of conscience she hadn't been expecting. She tried to sound nonchalant as she replied.

'I've known him for years and years. He used to go out with my flatmate at university. He's a lovely guy.'

Paola nodded in agreement. 'He is, isn't he? I think he likes me – although it's difficult to tell with him.' Now that she started to unwind, sophisticated professional woman Paola was sounding more like one of the lovelorn princesses in Sophie's book. 'But at least we've got our annual company retreat in the Pyrenees coming up next month and I know he'll be there. Hopefully I'll be able to find out what he really thinks of me.'

Sophie was feeling increasingly awkward by this time and was struggling for words. Thankfully her sister took up the conversation.

'What happens at a company retreat?'

Sophie wasn't sure she was going to like the answer but when it came it sounded innocent enough. At first.

'It's a week-long stay in a luxury hotel in the high mountains, in what becomes a popular ski resort in winter. In the mornings we have a series of lectures and presentations as part of our CPD strategy – you know, professional development; updates on everything from health and safety to sexual harassment in the workplace.' She looked up and there was a distinct twinkle in her eyes. 'It all gets far more informal in the evenings. It's amazing what a few glasses of wine can do to a bunch of men in suits – and a surprising number of the women.'

'Sounds like the ideal opportunity to get to know Chris better.' Rachel gave her sister a cheeky grin, seeing her squirm. 'But haven't you both been there in previous years?'

Paola nodded. 'Yes, but he was always with his girl-friend, but then they broke up and he came on his own last year. Only last year I was there with my boyfriend of the time. That all fell apart a few months later so this year I'll be there all by myself.' She beamed at the two sisters. 'I'm looking forward to seeing what develops.'

It came as a positive relief to Sophie when they drove Paola down to the station in time for her three o'clock train back to Milan. After waving her goodbye and thanking her again for her expert discoveries – if not her personal revelations – Sophie climbed into the passenger seat alongside Rachel who was driving. Jeeves leant over from the back seat and nuzzled her ear. Sophie turned to scratch his nose and did her best to put a brave face on things.

'Nice lady.'

Rachel was smiling broadly. 'With impeccable taste in men. Sounds like August in the Pyrenees is going to turn into Sodom and Gomorrah. Something tells me you should get a move on, sis, before Paola sinks her immacu-late red claws into Chris.'

The same thought had been swirling around inside Sophie's head since lunch, but she knew her limitations.

'I know when I'm outgunned, Rach. Look at her: she's gorgeous, she dresses like something out of *Vogue*, and she speaks the same nerdy antiques language he does. I don't stand a chance in comparison.'

'Don't be such a defeatist. You look great, you're every bit as bright as Paola and you've got a head start in that you and Chris go way back. You know each other so well already.'

'Maybe that's a problem rather than an advantage. Familiarity breeds contempt and all that.'

'I don't see it. Like I say, don't do yourself down.'

'That's easy for you to say. You've always had a way with people, with men, while I've struggled.'

'Don't give me that. You managed to land yourself the most desirable man in Rome.'

'Me and God knows how many other women.'

'Rubbish, if you want Chris, you just need to go for it. If it had been me, I'd have grabbed him and snogged him when he was here at the weekend. That way you'd have found out straightaway how he felt about you.'

'Yes, but you're you and I'm me.'

'Well, couldn't you at least have just told him straight out how you feel? I would have done.'

Sophie hung her head. 'You're right, I know you're right, but I lost my nerve... or something like that. I feel so silly, looking back. The problem now is how and when I can see him again before he heads for the Pyrenees.'

The more she thought about it, the more complicated it became. Was he going to come back over to Paradiso? Her problem – and it was a big one – was that, if he couldn't come over here, the only way she could go over to the UK to see him would have to be a day trip, flying there and back within twenty-four hours with only a very short time to see him and talk, because of Uncle George's pesky stipulation that she and Rachel needed to sign in together from the study every day. She took a deep breath, quite sure what she needed right now.

'I need the world's biggest ice cream. Feel like keeping me company?'

Her ice cream might not have made it into the *Guinness Book of Records* but it was mightily impressive all the same. The monstrosity that arrived, labelled by the ice cream cafe under the arches in the town centre as *Montagna Gelata*, contained at least ten, maybe a dozen, scoops of multiple flavours of delicious homemade ice cream, smothered in whipped cream and drizzled with raspberry syrup and caramel. The waiter reverently set it down on the table, along with a more modest-sized serving for Rachel, and even Jeeves looked taken aback. The waiter straightened up and gave Sophie a smile – she couldn't tell if it was as encouragement or commiseration.

'*Buona fortuna.*'

'Wow, Soph, if that doesn't sort you out, I don't know what will.'

Sophie began to work her way systematically through the mountain of ice cream and did her best to think rationally. Chris, her best friend, had a very suitable and very beautiful woman on his trail and maybe this was the woman he had indicated as somebody he fancied. From what Paola had said, she had little doubt that the company jaunt to the Pyrenees would inevitably result in his conquest – with or without persuasion – and she knew she had to act fast to pre-empt Paola's plans. Her sister was evidently thinking along similar lines.

'You've got to get him back over here before the company retreat and have it out with him, one way or another. When's the trip to the mountains taking place?'

'August.' Sophie's mouth was crammed full of ice cream and she had to take a mouthful of water and swallow hard before carrying on. 'Stupidly, I didn't ask the exact dates, and August starts in two days' time so I suppose it could be as soon as this coming weekend or, hopefully, not for a few weeks.'

'Well, that's easy to find out. Phone Chris and ask him.'

To give herself time to think, Sophie scooped up a spoonful of caramel and meringue ice cream with what looked like half a glacé cherry buried in the whipped cream on top of it. 'You're right. I can do that easily. After all, he'll be expecting me to call him to let him know what Paola said about the valuations.' Not without difficulty, she manoeuvred the heaped spoonful into her mouth where it gradually began to melt. As she did so, Rachel pulled a paper serviette out of the container on the table and reached across to wipe a splodge of cream off the end of Sophie's nose.

'Why not call him now? Strike while the iron's hot and all that.'

Sophie, unable to speak for the moment, just nodded. Rachel was right. That was the best thing to do. Or was it? She swallowed her mouthful and voiced her fears.

'I'll text him and get him to call me when he can, just in case he's in a meeting or something. The thing is, though, I don't want to get him to come rushing back over here just for him to tell me he fancies somebody else. And don't forget that I just *think* I fancy him at the moment. We haven't even kissed yet. What if he kisses me and it feels weird?'

189

'I understand that, but you've got to find out one way or another as soon as possible. You can't run the risk of letting him go to the company training week where, as sure as eggs is eggs, he'll end up in Paola's clutches.'

'And if he doesn't come here before the Pyrenees, what then?'

'Then, Soph, it'll all be in the lap of the gods.'

Chapter 17

The gods emerged victorious.

To Sophie's intense frustration, when Chris phoned her back later that afternoon in response to her text he informed her the company retreat was going to start in less than two weeks' time and he was up to his eyes with work – including four days in Scandinavia – and unable to come back to Paradiso even for a day. Even worse, almost immediately after the week in the Pyrenees he would be flying off to the USA and Canada for a series of big antiques conventions and wouldn't be back in Europe until early September. Regretfully, she agreed a provisional date towards the end of September for him to come and visit again but she knew, deep down in her heart, that it might well be too late by then.

She toyed with the idea of calling him back to suggest a brief meeting in London one day the following week – which would involve her jumping on one plane and then flying straight back almost immediately – but finally abandoned it. The time they would have together would be impossibly brief and with the additional danger of potentially ruining their friendship if she just blurted it out and it transpired that he didn't see her in a romantic way. She felt she just couldn't take the risk of screwing up their current relationship. In consequence, all she could do was to hope that things wouldn't go the way Paola intended at the mountain retreat, and did her best to dismiss him from her mind. This was far easier said than done, but at least she had other things to occupy her.

First, there were her regular short stories to write and then there was her book.

A direct result of this mess with Chris and the frustrating position in which she found herself was the discovery that it did at least stimulate her creative juices. Her next short story featured a love triangle with two suitors competing for the hand of one indecisive woman – who almost ended up losing both – while the one after that was a story of two lovers, separated by their jobs in different countries. As for her book, one evening the elusive first line for her book suddenly came to her and she hurried down to tell Rachel.

'I've got it. How about starting my novel with this? "Beatrice sighed as she leant on the battlements and stared out into the night sky. All her high hopes had come crashing down and she felt desperately alone." How does that grab you?'

'I like the idea of starting the book with what sounds almost like the conclusion, making the reader curious to read on to discover what's gone wrong. And Beatrice is a great name for a romantic heroine.' Rachel hesitated. 'There's just one thing. This isn't going to be autobiographical, is it? I'd hate to think you were feeling desperately alone with your hopes crushed. Try not to worry too much about this Chris thing. It'll sort itself out and, if it doesn't, you're a clever, attractive, soon-to-be very rich woman and you'll easily fix yourself up with a replacement.'

Sophie shook her head, although without much conviction. 'No, of course it's not going to be about me.

As for Chris and what might or might not happen, I know I'll be fine. I've got Jeeves and I've got you, remember.'

'That's the spirit. And besides, you and I are in the same boat, after all. I'm not seeing anybody at the moment, but I know that sooner or later I'll find someone new and it'll work itself out.'

Sophie paused. Might this be the opportunity she'd been waiting for to find out what exactly had happened between her sister and her ex? 'Rach, on that subject, do you feel like telling me what happened between you and your boyfriend a few months back? You said you'd done something stupid but that it wasn't what I thought. So I'm assuming you didn't leap into bed with some other man, but what could you have done to cause the break-up of the relationship after, what, two years?'

'Two and a half, almost three.' Rachel sighed. 'The stupidity on my part was to believe the lies of Donna, a woman I thought was my friend. She and I met up for a drink and a chat one evening after work and she told me she'd seen Gabriel with another woman, and stupidly I swallowed the story hook, line and sinker. I charged back home and started screaming and shouting at him – in my defence I had had a few drinks by this point – and he just clammed up and left without a backward glance. I only found out a couple of days before coming over here last month that the story was all made up. Another friend set me straight. It turns out Donna wanted Gabriel for herself and she was prepared to do anything to get him, including sabotaging my relationship with him and destroying her friendship with me, and I fell for it.' She raised her eyes towards Sophie. 'Like I say, pretty stupid, right?'

'So now you know it wasn't true, would you like him back?'

'It's not a question of me wanting him. I imagine he doesn't want anything to do with me after such a blatant lack of trust. You know me – I do have a tendency to fly off the handle a bit too easily. No, however much I might like him back, I'm sure he doesn't even want to hear my name.'

'And did he get together with this Donna woman?'

'From what I've heard, no.'

Rachel looked so down that Sophie couldn't resist reaching over and giving her hand a supportive squeeze.

'Tell me about Gabriel. Who is he? Why did you fall for him in the first place?'

Rachel paused for thought. 'He's an attorney. I met him at a party and we just hit it off. In many ways, he's not my type. No bulging muscles, no movie star looks, no sports car, no amazing moves on the dance floor; he's just a very caring sort of guy and I felt comfortable around him from the start. He has a firm sense of right and wrong – he specialises in human rights cases – and that's why I know my lack of trust must have cut him to the quick.'

'And he's from Florida?'

'Yes, he's a partner in a law firm in Orlando – Anderson, Cooper and Gomez. He's Cooper.'

'He sounds like a good guy. I think you should get in touch. Three years together is a hell of a lot to throw away. I know – I was with Claudio for about that length of time.'

'Yeah, but that's it, isn't it? You were with Claudio for years but you'd never take him back after what he did to you. I just know that Gabriel must feel the same way about me.'

'Rach, there's a big difference between you making a wrong assumption and Claudio sleeping with half of

Rome. Why don't you give it a try? Contact him. Go on, I would if it had happened to me.'

But Rachel refused to follow her advice. Clearly, she had made up her mind that there was no point in trying to crawl back just to be slapped down again. Sophie made another few attempts to get her to see reason, but they were all met with stone wall determination so, in the end, she let the subject drop. At least she now knew more about her sister, which was progress as far as relations between the two of them were concerned.

Armed with her first line, she now returned her attention to her novel and, at last, the words began to flow, but before she could throw herself fully into her new project, there was a more urgent one to be sorted out. She needed to find a builder. Beppe had suggested several and she had been contacting them over the past weeks but, as Signor Verdi had warned, they all turned out to be either fully booked or on holiday for the whole of August, if not longer. She was beginning to get desperate when Rita came up with a fine solution.

'My brother retired last year. He was a builder, and a good one as well. He might be prepared to do it if it isn't too hard for him. And if he can't, he might know somebody who can. Would you like me to have a word with him?'

Sophie was so grateful she almost kissed her, and when Rita's brother confirmed that he would come round that very afternoon to take a look she did catch hold of her and kiss her warmly on the cheeks.

When she wasn't writing, the other job to which both she and Rachel applied themselves was cleaning and pricing the items that would go on sale at the antiques fair at the end of August. Pricing involved scouring the internet for similar items for sale and taking those prices as a rough guide, minus a healthy discount in the hope of selling as many of them as possible. Gradually the pile of gleaming old bits and pieces, each with a neat price tag, started to grow.

And finally, there was the small matter of eight Spaniards due to descend upon them in two weeks' time. Fortunately it looked as though there would be just enough bedrooms for all. Rachel reckoned the group would consist of two couples and four individuals so, including their two rooms, that meant that all eight bedrooms would be occupied. They both gave Rita a hand to start getting everything ready and were mildly surprised to find that she was positively relishing the challenge.

'Your uncle often used to entertain people when he came here. We've had members of parliament, film stars and even a Nobel Prize winner. It'll be just like old times.'

Rita's brother, Giorgio, declared himself more than prepared to do the remedial building works and started almost immediately. Needless to say, this created considerable dust and disruption for Rita but she obviously had years of practice getting him to obey her orders and by the end of the following week, a matter of hours before the arrival of the Spaniards – or S-Day as Sophie referred to it – he had done it all: the lead work on the roof, the chimneys, the broken arches, and a few other bits and pieces he had spotted as he went along.

When S-Day Saturday dawned and Sophie returned from an early morning walk around the estate with Jeeves, she felt confident that they would be able cope with the influx. Rachel was still in bed – probably a wise precaution before what would be a long day – but Sophie didn't feel tired so, as the Spanish contingent were supposed to be arriving in the late afternoon, she decided to go for a longer walk that morning, before it got too hot. With eight guests to look after she wasn't sure when the next opportunity to take the dog out for a few hours would present itself. On impulse, she sent a text message to Dan, asking if he felt like keeping her company, and by the time she had emerged from the shower, he had replied, suggesting a route. This involved driving up into the hills for half an hour or so and then hiking up to a ruined tower which interested him for his book. Because she had Jeeves, she offered to pick him up in her old car which hadn't been getting much use recently.

Seeing him again immediately brightened her day and it occurred to her that as time passed, Chris might soon be in danger of having a rival for his best friend status with her. She hadn't seen Dan for a few days and she wondered if he had been away again. It turned out that he had been in Genoa and Pisa, studying documents at the university libraries, and had only got back last night. She told him all about the building works, her breakthrough with her book and the impending arrival of the Spaniards. She stopped short, however, of mentioning Chris and the Pyrenean retreat and Paola's interest in him.

Following his directions, she turned right at the bottom of the hill and headed inland. Before long the suburbs of Santa Rita gave way to open fields, rows of greenhouses and polytunnels. They passed through a decidedly more agricultural area before starting to climb into the first foothills of the Ligurian Apennines. The vegetation changed rapidly from cultivated fields to native woodland and they were soon driving up ever-steeper inclines into thick deciduous forest. According to

Beppe, these woods were rich in porcini mushrooms and, although the season had yet to get going properly, they kept coming upon empty cars parked here and there by the roadside, no doubt belonging to hopeful mushroom hunters in search of these valuable prizes. After twenty more minutes of climbing, they reached a spot where the ground levelled out into a little car park and Dan indicated they should stop.

When she got out of the car Sophie immediately felt the difference in temperature. It wasn't cold, but there was probably a difference of at least ten degrees between here and the coast and she almost wished she had brought a jumper. Reading her mind, Dan tapped her on her arm and pointed over her shoulder.

'Don't worry about it being a bit cooler up here. You'll soon warm up. That's where we're headed.'

She followed the direction of his finger and spotted a squat construction protruding from the top of a rocky promontory quite a way above them. She nodded to herself. It certainly looked like they had a hard climb ahead.

They set off and almost immediately came upon a granite boulder bearing a bronze plaque engraved with the names of half a dozen *partigiani* killed by the Nazis during the war. The youngest of the partisans had been only seventeen. Up here in the wilds of the countryside must have been ideal terrain for the resistance fighters and it was sobering to think of the blood that had been shed in what was now such a peaceful, idyllic spot. The path narrowed as it began to climb tortuously up the mountainside and they very soon stopped chatting. Dan led the way while Sophie and Jeeves followed. This was because he had read that there were poisonous vipers up here whose bite could be deadly to dogs or small children. Sophie didn't like the sound of that at all, so she made sure Jeeves didn't go charging off into the undergrowth. The idea of losing him was too sad to contemplate.

It took them three quarters of an hour to get up to the tower and fortunately the only reptiles they encountered were a few terrified lizards which disappeared into the crevices in the rocks as soon as Dan's shadow fell on them. As he had predicted, Sophie was far from cold by the time they got there. While he went off to clamber about in the ruins, she sat down with her dog beside her, fanning herself while she admired the view. From here she could see all the way down the heavily wooded valley to the sea in the distance – the reflection of the sun on it almost dazzling her. The trees did a magnificent job of blanking out any signs of human habitation and it felt remarkably remote. It was hard to believe that just half an hour from here the beaches were packed with noisy holidaymakers enjoying themselves. Here it was quiet – apart from birdsong – and very relaxing. She did her best to absorb the feel of the place so as to include it in her book – which was now well into its second chapter.

Gazing over the hills, she remembered what she had been trying hard to forget. Today would see the start of the auction house's annual mountain retreat and the opening skirmishes in Paola's battle for the heart and mind – or at least the body – of Chris. Sophie wondered yet again how he would react if Paola really did throw herself at him. Was she about to lose him before she had had a chance to tell him how she felt about him?

'Can you imagine what it must have been like back in the Middle Ages when the alarm came from the lookouts that a fleet of marauding boats from the other side of the Mediterranean had been sighted?'

Sophie looked up to see Dan standing right on the top of the ruined tower wall above her.

'Dan, for goodness' sake be careful up there.'

He carried on as if he hadn't heard a thing. 'The Saracens – as they called them here – would have killed or enslaved any local people they could find and looted their houses and fields. Everybody knew how dangerous they could be, so there would have been a mad rush to get away from the coast as fast as possible. It took us half an hour in the car to get up here. Think of the people back then, most of whom would have had to do the whole thing on foot, carrying what valuables they could on their backs and even driving their animals. Those were hard times, all right.'

'It does sound awfully hard and it would be just as hard to carry you down the hill if you broke your leg, so please try not to fall off that wall. It doesn't look too stable to me. I'd hate for anything to happen to you.' And she realised she meant it.

'Don't worry, I'll be careful.' He turned and she saw him disappear back into the ruins again. When he emerged a few minutes later he came over and sat down beside her. She looked across at him.

'Find anything interesting?'

'Nothing in particular. This place is little more than a pile of rubble now – but I came for the atmosphere as much as anything – you know, the view, the sounds, the scents, the vegetation. Although my book will be serious, factual history, I believe it's essential to get the feel of the places I write about. Hopefully it'll help the reader understand better what life was really like on the ground back then.'

'I'm sure you're right. In fact, I've been sitting here thinking about my book and this would be a lovely spot to include. It's so romantic.'

'Yes, you're dead right about that.' She saw him close his eyes and lean back against the sun-warmed stones of the wall, a little smile on his face. 'It sure is a romantic place.' His tone was dreamy and he looked very peaceful. 'You should bring Chris up here when he comes over in September. See if the magic of the place works on him.' He opened his eyes and glanced across at her, the little smile still on his lips. 'Mind you, I reckon you've already got him hooked.'

Sophie sat upright. 'I've what?'

'I could see from the way he was looking at you that he's under your spell. Not that it would be hard for any man. You're beautiful, you're bright and you're just a really nice person.'

Sophie could feel her cheeks glowing by this time and reached across and gave his hand a little squeeze.

'Thanks, Dan. And I think you're a sweetie, too.'

'So, are you planning on bringing him up here?'

'It's a lovely thought, but I honestly don't know.' She took a deep breath and decided to tell him the whole story. 'There's been a development on that front, quite a significant one.' In spite of her reservations, she went on to tell him about Paola, the upcoming corporate week in the mountains, and her fears for what might happen. 'She's an alluring woman and very suitable for him in many ways, and I'm afraid he's going to fall for her and that'll be that.'

'I'm sure you'd be more than a match for any woman.'

'I wish I had your confidence.'

201

'And this retreat starts today?'

'Yup, today.'

'And there was no way the two of you could have met up again before he set off?'

'No, I wanted to, but it wasn't possible. He was very tied up. I'm just going to have to let nature take its course and see what happens – although I'm not going to be holding my breath.'

'Have you at least hinted to him about how you might feel?'

Sophie had to stop and think for a moment. 'Not really... in fact, to be honest, not at all.'

'In that case I reckon you should throw him a bone at least.'

'What do you mean?'

'You need to give him some hope. From what you've just said, it's clear he has no idea you think of him as anything more than a good friend. You need to tell him, or at least give him an idea of how you feel.'

'But that's the problem, I don't know how I feel. I mean, I *do* like him a lot, but we haven't even held hands yet. What if the reality doesn't match up to my dreams?' Sophie could hear the frustration in her voice and he immediately picked up on it.

'It seems to me that the very fact that you're so obviously upset about the possibility of him ending up with this other woman proves that you do have feelings for him. Deep down, you do know, and I think you should at least give him a bit of a heads-up. He's a man, remember, and we're notoriously bad at reading the signs. Why not give him a call and tell him you miss him and can't wait to see him again?'

'I'm sure he knows that already...'

'What did I just say? He's a man for God's sake. You can't count on him being able to read between the lines. Can you honestly say you've told him you miss him?'

'Well, not in so many words…'

'Then do it.' He hesitated for a moment. 'Look, I'm sorry, this is no business of mine but if I were you, I'd call him and tell him. That way, at least, he'll know you're thinking of him and he'll know where he stands when this Paola woman comes on to him.'

'I suppose I could…'

'What do you have to lose?' He stood up. 'And maybe a lot to gain. Now, I want to take a couple of photos from up there.' He pointed to another rocky outcrop protruding through the trees a hundred metres or so above them. 'While I'm gone, why don't you make the call?'

'Tell me something before you go. Have you spoken to your friend Jennifer yet? Have you taken your own advice and told her how you feel about her?'

He looked back down at her and she could see he was embarrassed. 'You're right… I'm a fine one to talk. Here I am giving you advice and I still haven't had the nerve to tell her how I feel, even though I'm getting more and more convinced that she's more than just a friend.'

'You see? We're hopeless. Let's make a deal – I'll try to summon up the courage to speak to Chris if you promise me you'll do the same with Jen.' She held up her right hand towards him. 'Deal?'

After a momentary hesitation he reached back down and shook her hand. 'Deal. But it's five o'clock in the morning over there. I'll call her later on.'

'Well, just make sure you do.'

Once he disappeared around the side of the ruined tower, Sophie pulled out her phone and stared down at it blankly. Dan was right as far as Chris was concerned. She needed to say something to him, but what? After several minutes she took a deep breath and pressed his number. When he answered, his voice was metallic, with an echo.

'Hi, Sophie. How're you doing?'

'Hi, Chris, I'm fine. Your voice sounds funny.'

'I'm on speaker in the car. I'm on my way to Stansted to catch my flight to Pau. Today's the start of the company retreat in the Pyrenees.'

Sophie chatted to him about her book, the building work and the objects they had been preparing for the antiques fair, before finally taking the plunge.

'Anyway, I don't want to disturb you while you're driving.' She hesitated for a moment, still searching for the right words. 'It's just that, Chris… I wanted to tell you that I've been thinking about you a lot and I miss you. I can't wait to see you again next month.'

'I miss you, too, Soph.' She listened intently for any change in tone or sign of emotion. She heard nothing apart from the sound of a car horn in the background. 'Imbecile! Sorry, Soph, not you. Some prat just decided to turn off at the last moment and cut me up.'

'But you're okay?'

'I'm fine, thanks. Anyway, like I say, I miss you too.'

Sophie waited for more, but nothing was forthcoming and her mind went blank. She couldn't blurt out that she had started thinking of him as more than a friend but she wouldn't be sure until he kissed her and, indeed, she had no idea whether he might maybe feel the same way as she did, but if he didn't, or she didn't, she still wanted them to be friends. It sounded like gobbledegook in her head, let alone if she tried to express it out loud. So in the end all she could do was to wind things up. 'Enjoy yourself in the

Pyrenees.' *But not too much.* 'See you in September. Bye, Chris, and take care. I do miss you.'

'And I miss you too, Soph. A lot.'

After ringing off, she sat there for a few more minutes, doing her best to analyse what he had said – and what she hadn't said. Should she have been more direct, more open? When he had told her he missed her, had he meant it the same way she did? Being on the phone in the car hadn't helped. Maybe it would have been better if she had waited until the evening to call him but, of course, by that time he would have been at the hotel in the mountains, maybe even with Paola's elegant arms already draped around his neck, and unable to speak freely. In the end her only clue as to how he might feel about her came in the form of his last two words: *a lot.* He had said he missed her, but then he had added *a lot.*

That had to mean something, hadn't it?

Chapter 18

The first of the Spanish contingent arrived in one car just after five in the afternoon and the others an hour later. To muddy the waters, the two couples in the first car were both composed of a Fernando and an Alejandra. Tall Fernando was married to diminutive Alejandra, while bearded Fernando was engaged to normal-sized Alejandra with the red hair. In the second car came Lola and her brother, Juan, along with his two best friends, Sebastián and Pablo.

Lola – instantly renamed Lolita in Sophie's head – was stunning in a very ostentatious way and it rapidly became clear that both of her brother's friends fancied her. They were all very friendly towards Sophie and her dog and very appreciative of being invited to stay, and she was relieved to find that communication turned out not to be a problem. They all spoke some English – Lolita's brother Juan in particular was fluent – and Sophie soon discovered that if she spoke Italian to them and they answered in Spanish they could converse fairly easily and freely. As for Rachel, she just flicked an internal switch and poured out a stream of fast, fluent-sounding Spanish.

On Rita's advice and with her help, they had prepared a cold spread for dinner, but Sophie had forgotten that Spaniards tended to eat late. They all opted to go for a swim in the pool in the early evening and it was there that

Sophie discovered that Juan was built like the Incredible Hulk. His unbelievably muscular body was obviously the result of countless hours spent in the gym, and when she mentioned to him that there was a small gym here in the castle, his eyes lit up. For her part, as far as muscles were concerned, she could take them or leave them. She had never been a great fan of bodybuilders, finding many of them somehow grotesque, but Juan was friendly and remarkably gentle in spite of his bulk. She wondered what he would make of Uncle George's gym. Neither she nor her sister had ventured in there since arriving in Paradiso. It had just been too hot. Besides, she kept telling herself, walking Jeeves and swimming was all the exercise she needed.

When they emerged from the pool at close to eight o'clock, the Spaniards insisted on taking Rachel and Sophie to the bar across the road for an *aperitivo* which soon turned into several *aperitivi* and Sophie had to struggle to stop them plying her with drink. Luckily she remembered one of her favourites – a non-alcoholic aperitif that looked and tasted like Campari – and switched to this. The drinks came with complimentary crisps and Sophie saw a number of these disappear under the table as her mooching Labrador did his rounds wearing his 'I'm starving' expression.

They ended up sitting down to dinner at half past nine – which Rachel assured her was early by Spanish standards – and the meal was a great success. As the evening progressed, Sophie relaxed more and more, confident that the new arrivals weren't going to tear the place apart or prove to be a pain in the neck. They were a charming bunch and she could see why her sister had become close friends with them. She resolved to have a word with her later, to apologise for her original outburst when Rachel had told her she had invited them.

More by accident than design – at least on her part – Sophie ended up alongside muscleman Juan and chatted to him most of the time. She discovered that he was in fact an English teacher in a big high school in the suburbs of Madrid, which explained his fluency in the language. He told her he was teaching some tough teen-agers in a deprived area and she realised that this maybe also explained the muscles. He filled in the gaps as far as the others were concerned. Tall Fernando was a lawyer, as was his minute wife. The other Fernando was a doctor and his fiancée worked as a civil servant of some description. Lolita was between jobs – Sophie wondered if she might be into acting or modelling, judging by her appearance – and the two suitors for Lola's hand sold cars and pork products respectively.

In the course of the evening, Sophie began to realise that she could use these people as characters in her book and she soon had the car salesman and the ham and sausage purveyor down as knights competing for the hand of one or both of the princesses in her book. Fernando the lawyer soon morphed into the court chamberlain in her head, while bearded doctor Fernando became the apothecary. Juan would of course be the king's champion, feared all over the land for his feats of strength and skill in combat. She got into the swing of it and tried to decide whether she should model one of the princesses on Lolita and turn her into a man-eater. By the time she got up from the table and slipped out with Jeeves for his nightly walk, she had not only got to know them all but could genuinely say she was enjoying having them there.

The following day was *ferragosto*, the fifteenth of August, and Sophie remembered what Romeo, the hair-stylist, had told her: there was going to be a big party on the beach. She checked out the local Santa Rita website and saw that although there were events all day as varied as face painting for kids and sailing and windsurfing races, the evening looked like the best time to join in. After a lazy day, mostly spent by the pool, they set off at six o'clock. At the last minute, Sophie decided not to leave Jeeves on his own for the whole evening so she opted to take her own car. That way she could bring Jeeves and leave before the others if the event proved unsuitable for dogs.

Parking was a major problem and she ended up having to leave the car on the outskirts of town and walk for fifteen minutes or so to get to the seafront. The closer she got to the beach, the more the noise level increased and she muttered another little thank you to her uncle for choosing to buy a house way up above it all. It was clear that nobody living in the first three or four rows of properties by the beach was going to get much sleep tonight.

It turned out to be a lot of fun and, as there was a barbecue serving hotdogs and burgers and lots of little kids dropping things, Jeeves ended up eating far more than he should have done – much of it covered in sand. Sophie gave up worrying after a while, hoping that his digestive system would prove up to the challenge. They drank cold beer from cardboard cups and danced on the sand like Romeo the hairdresser had said, taking it in turns to keep an eye on Jeeves who wasn't really supposed to be on the beach. Dancing on the beach was an entirely different sensation and quite hard work, shuffling about in loose sand in her bare feet. She was feeling quite tired by the time she had danced with all the Spaniards, followed by Romeo himself, who appeared dressed in a gold lame suit and black shirt, unbuttoned to display the sort of chunky medallion she thought had gone out of fashion in the Eighties. He must have been boiling, but the demands of fashion clearly obliged him to wear this ensemble and Sophie was impressed at his dedication, even if his sartorial taste wasn't one she shared.

Finally pleading exhaustion, she took refuge on a bench up on the promenade and watched the proceedings with her equally tired-looking dog sprawled at her feet. The band was fairly good – and certainly loud enough – although the selection of numbers they played probably wouldn't have made it onto many UK playlists. Still, everybody from kids to pensioners appeared to be enjoying themselves.

She was sitting on the bench, sipping from a bottle of water, when she felt a tap on her shoulder. She turned to see Dan standing there and smiled up at him.

'I'm far too tired to get up. If you want a kiss you'll have to come down to my level.'

He leant down and kissed her on the cheeks before taking a seat alongside her, the Labrador now sitting with his head resting on Dan's bare knees. He stroked the dog and glanced over at Sophie.

'So, are you tired because you've been dancing?'

'I feel like I've been dancing with the whole beach. A continuous cycle of them. I'll have to introduce you to Rachel's Spanish friends who're staying with us. They appear to have boundless energy.'

'How's that going?'

'It's going fine and, in spite of my initial fears, they're a nice bunch. What about you? Have you been dancing with anybody special?'

'I haven't been dancing with anybody yet, but I'd love to dance with you if you feel up to it.'

'Give me another five minutes, would you? And then we'll need to find somebody to look after Jeeves. Otherwise he joins in and the results aren't pretty.' She caught his eye. 'So, did you call Jennifer and tell her how you feel?' He shook his head and she couldn't restrain a grin. 'I knew you'd chicken out.'

'I did call her, I promise, but it just felt so weird trying to say something as important as that over the phone. But I did ask her to come over to Italy and hopefully she's going to come in late September. Maybe it's best if I leave it until then...' His voice tailed off uncertainly and then he turned the question back on her. 'How about Chris? Have you heard from him since he arrived in France?'

'No, but I wouldn't expect to, really. We're close friends but we don't speak to each other every day. I suppose I could call him, though.'

'Why don't you?'

She mulled over the thought for a moment. While she did so, Lolita appeared, looking equally hot and tired. Her very short shorts showed off her legs – and bottom – to advantage and she had no doubt spent her time fighting off the attentions of her two Spanish suitors, quite probably plus a number of local men. She gave Sophie a little smile and pointed to the bench alongside Dan.

'I sit? Very hot.'

She sat down and Sophie introduced her to Dan, who impressed her by switching into fluent-sounding Spanish. While the two of them chatted, Sophie pulled out her phone and made a decision. She *would* call Chris. She would use the subterfuge of wanting his opinion on what price to put on an old copper bed warmer for the antiques fair. In fact, she reassured herself, this was a valid reason for the call. She and Rachel had been debating this earlier. She pressed call and waited. It took a while before he replied.

'Hi, Sophie, all well?'

She assured him all was well and hurriedly explained their query about the price to be on the label. As expected, he quickly provided a solution. After that, she did her best to keep the conversation going as naturally as possible.

'So how's life in the mountains? I'm at the beach festival at Santa Rita this evening and it's baking here.'

'I thought I could hear music. Well, if it makes you feel any better, we're submerged under a thick cloud here, you can't see your hand in front of your face, and it's pouring with very cold rain.'

'How are you filling your time if you can't go out?'

Sophie wasn't sure she really wanted to hear the answer to this. Out of the corner of her eye she saw Dan get up, with Lola at his elbow, and point towards the dancers. He mouthed the words 'going for a dance' before the two of them disappeared into the crowd.

'I'm actually sitting in the bar at the moment. Don't worry, I haven't been in here all afternoon. The hotel's got a gym and a pool so I've been for a workout and a swim. I met up with Paola and she said to say hi if I was talking to you.'

'Oh, right, thanks. Did you meet her in the pool?' Somehow Sophie had a feeling this meeting might have been orchestrated in advance by the elegant Italian.

'In the gym, actually. She really keeps herself in shape.' *I bet she does*, Sophie thought to herself. 'We ended up spotting each other, you know, helping each other with the weights. She can push a surprising amount.'

'Oh, good.' What else could she say? 'Anyway, as long as you aren't drinking yourself into an early grave.'

'No fear of that. And what about you? Is there dancing at the beach?'

'I've just sat down after what felt like hours of dancing. And in sand, it's exhausting.'

'Dance with anyone special? Your American friend for instance?'

'My American friend has just gone off to dance with Lolita. You'd like her. She's wearing spray-on shorts and a top that leaves absolutely nothing to the imagination. As for me, I've danced with three different Spanish men – one of them the size and shape of a barn door. I'm just glad he didn't tread on me.'

'Well, just as long as you're enjoying yourself.' There was a pause. 'And I wish I were there with you.'

This sounded promising. 'You do?'

'Yes, a bit of warm sunshine would be great.'

Once again he appeared to have fired and missed. Nevertheless, she decided to give him her message anyway – after all it was the reason for her call. 'Like I told you before, I miss you, Chris, and I wish I was there with you, rain or no rain.'

'And I miss you, too. A lot.'

And that was that. They said their goodbyes and hung up.

She sat and watched the dancers, easily identifying Dan's head rising up from the crowd. The band had chosen that moment to play a slow tune and she distinctly caught sight of Lolita's mop of lustrous dark hair against his chest. She hoped for his sake that he would be able to iron things out with the girl in America. As for herself and Chris, she had a horrible feeling matters were being taken out of her hands. She had had her chances to tell him how she felt – or rather, how she thought she felt – but she had blown it. If he ended up with Paola she couldn't really blame him. But, anyway, hadn't she arrived here convinced that she was happy with her canine companion and didn't feel the need to seek out another man? Was it the sultry Mediterranean air that was threatening to upset the applecart?

'Get a grip!'

She must have said it out loud.

'Sounds serious. How're you doing, sis? Here, I brought you a beer.'

Sophie looked up to see Rachel behind her. Unexpectedly she was alone. Somehow Sophie had expected to see at least one of the Spaniards at her side.

'Thanks for the thought, but I'll just take a sip. Apart from the fact that I'm driving, I feel knackered.'

Rachel took a seat beside her. 'So why are you sitting here snorting about getting a grip?'

'Men, Rach… or maybe me… probably me. I've just phoned Chris because I'm worried he's going to be seduced by the lovely Paola and yet I'm the girl who said she was happy on her own. What's wrong with me?'

'Nothing's wrong with you. He's just a really good guy. It's natural you should feel attracted to him. I do.'

'You do?' For a moment, Sophie had a sinking feeling. Surely her sister wasn't going to step in and take another boy from her…

'Yes. What's not to like?'

'So why didn't you make a move on him while he was here?' Sophie wasn't sure she wanted to hear the answer to this either. She saw her sister hesitate.

'Because you've called dibs on him of course and apart from anything else, to be completely honest, there's still Gabriel over in Orlando. I can't get him out of my head.'

Sophie caught hold of her hand. 'He was The One, wasn't he?' Her sister just nodded, her eyes on Jeeves at her feet. 'Well, Rach, like I told you before, you should do something about it. Honestly.'

Once again, Rachel just shook her head. 'It wouldn't do any good. I've just got to accept that it's all over and move on.' She looked up. 'Just like you're going to have to do if things don't work out between you and Chris.'

They sat in silence for some minutes before Rachel suddenly reached over and gave Sophie a warm hug and a kiss. 'It's not all bad, Soph. At least I've got you back now.'

Chapter 19

The evening ended with fireworks – but not just of an incendiary nature.

The official firework display started at ten o'clock and was impressive. It was fully dark by this time and the sky over the sea was lit up with magnificent multi-coloured swirls and shimmering stars interspersed with ear-shattering explosions. Sophie hadn't realised it was coming and as the first rockets whooshed up into the air from pontoons in the water, she dropped to her knees to comfort her dog and to grab his collar in case he should decide to run off in terror. She needn't have worried. Unlike his reaction to thunder and lightning, apart from a couple of louder bangs that had him pressing against her leg, Jeeves appeared to be as fascinated as everybody else by the display and even wagged his tail from time to time.

When it ended, Sophie left the beach festival and took Jeeves back up to the castle. Rachel also declared herself ready to go home and Sophie left her to round up the others, hoping they wouldn't drag it out too much. She was feeling quite weary by now and the idea of being woken up in the small hours by the revellers' return didn't appeal in the slightest. When she reached Paradiso, she drove round to the piazza in front of the castle and climbed out to open the main gates.

It was then that the trouble started. She had just unlocked the gates and pushed them open when she heard footsteps and then a voice behind her.

'*Ciao, bella.*'

She instantly recognised that voice and spun round in horror. In the light of the single street lamp he was unmistakable.

'Claudio, what the hell are you doing here? I told you not to come.'

'Yes, but I knew you didn't mean it. I just had to see you and I know you really want to see me, don't you?'

She stood there, rooted to the spot but, as he moved closer, her brain finally kicked into gear and she held up her hand to stop him. In the orange streetlight he was as handsome as ever, without a single hair out of place, but she could feel the anger bubbling up inside her like a volcano.

'What did I say I'd do if you came here?' She was almost hissing at him.

'Give me a kiss, hopefully.' He held out his arms towards her and she took a step backwards while reaching in her pocket for her phone.

'Never in a million years. As you appear to have forgotten, I said I'd phone the police.'

He assumed an innocent expression. 'Why? I haven't done anything wrong.'

Sophie made a quick decision. 'Then I'll call my boyfriend. He's on his way up here now.'

'Your boyfriend?' He didn't sound so sure of himself now.

Sophie glanced down at her phone and typed a hurried text to Rachel and to Dan.

Old habits die hard. It occurred to her as she pressed *Send* that she could have saved a few milliseconds by omitting the word *please*.

'Now there's no need to do that, Sophie. It's me, Claudio. I don't mean you any harm.'

'I should think not.' Even so, she took two more steps backwards.

'Listen, Sophie, I really miss you. Ever since you went off and left me I've been miserable.'

'Like hell you have!' She could feel the anger building again. 'Now, stand aside while I put my car away.'

She climbed back into the car, drove it slowly through the gates and parked. She toyed with the idea of locking herself inside it to wait for the cavalry to arrive but, going round to open the boot for Jeeves, she decided she owed it to herself to get out and face him. The dog jumped out and, to her surprise and delight, he didn't immediately trot over to Claudio to give him a friendly greeting. Instead, sensing something in the air, he stopped dead and stared suspiciously at the Roman. For once, his tail wasn't wagging and Sophie could hear what might even have been a low growl from him – something decidedly out of character. She took heart from his reaction.

'Please don't come any closer, Claudio. My dog's very protective of me.'

By this time she could clearly see that the hairs on the back of the Labrador's neck were bristling. *Good old Jeeves!* This did wonders for her confidence. Claudio was still standing by the gatepost, looking uncertainly at Jeeves but, as she tried to close the gates, he didn't move out of the way.

'So you're going to just slam the gates in my face after everything we've meant to each other?' There was an edge to his voice now that she didn't like one bit. She glanced at her watch. The text had only been sent five minutes ago. Even if Rachel and Dan had already left the beach, it would take a while longer before they arrived – assuming they had seen the message. Sophie choked back her anger – and a tiny tremor of fear – and did her best to keep the conversation on a level footing. For now, all that counted was keeping Claudio on the other side of the gates, so she tried to keep him talking for now.

'Tell me, why are you here, Claudio? Even you must realise that there's no chance I would ever trust you again or give you a second chance.'

'You give *me* a second chance? *You* left *me*, remember? I've come to tell you I'm prepared to take you back.'

Sophie couldn't believe her ears. Talk about thick-skinned. Deliberately taking a deep breath before replying, she tried to keep her voice as neutral as possible so as not to antagonise him. 'I left you because you were unfaithful to me, or are you trying to tell me that's not true?'

He shrugged his quintessentially Roman shrug, shoulders almost reaching up to his ears and with his palms splayed outwards in front of him. 'So I played around a little. We all do that. But you don't need to worry – the other girls mean nothing to me.'

'Clearly neither did I. And as for playing around, it's *not* what everybody does and it most definitely *isn't* what I do.' She pricked up her ears as she heard a car's engine approaching fast. He must have heard it too as he turned to take a look. Sophie took advantage of his momentary distraction to slam the left-hand gate into position. Now just the right-hand one remained.

To her delight, Dan's little Fiat squealed to a halt just outside, closely followed by one of the Spanish cars, from which Rachel and a bunch of others emerged. Dan came running across and Sophie was mightily relieved.

'What the hell's going on here?' Ignoring Claudio, he looked across at Sophie. 'Are you all right?'

She nodded as the two men turned to face each other and she knew she had to act fast to stop the situation spiralling out of control. On the spur of the moment she reached out her hands, beckoning Dan but addressing Claudio.

'I told you my boyfriend was coming, Claudio. Please go. It's all over between us and I really, truly never want to see you ever again.' She caught hold of Dan's hands and tugged him towards her, anxious to keep him out of the way of Claudio, who, she knew well, had a very short temper. 'Thank you for coming so fast, Dan.'

He took his cue and appeared quite unphased at having been described as her boyfriend as he encircled her shoulders with his arm and pulled her towards him.

'That's what I'm here for.'

A few seconds of silence followed while the two men sized each other up. To Sophie's surprise, the silence was broken by Jeeves who let out a real sinister growl. His lip curled and the streetlight reflected on his gleaming white teeth while his hackles were still up. It was clear that the hackles of both men were equally raised. The last thing Sophie wanted was for there to be a fight and she was about to dive between them when help arrived from a formidable source.

Into the space between the two men stepped the Incredible Hulk. Juan looked decidedly threatening, especially when, in true Hulk tradition, he pulled his T-shirt off – admittedly without tearing it into shreds or turning green, but still… He threw it disdainfully into the shadows, exposing ridge upon ridge of rippling muscles glistening in the orange light, and spoke to Claudio in a voice that, while calm, brooked no argument.

'Listen, *cabrón*, you have a choice. The lady wants you to leave, so leave. If you decide not to go, then I'm going to pick you up and throw you into the horse trough over there. Understood?'

The standoff lasted barely another handful of seconds before Claudio finally got the message. Without a word he spun on his heel and strode off towards his car which was parked outside the restaurant where he had, presumably, been waiting for her. He climbed in, slammed the door and gunned the engine, shooting off with a vicious squeal of tyres.

Everybody relaxed.

First things first, Sophie wriggled out of Dan's grip and ran across to catch hold of Juan and give him a massive hug – barely managing to get her arms around his broad back. 'Thank you so very much, Juan. You're my hero.'

She kissed him on the cheeks and hurried back to Dan who was now ruffling Jeeves's ears. She threw herself at him and hugged him tight.

'And *you* are my knight in shining armour. Thank you for being prepared to play the part of my boyfriend.'

She reached up and kissed his cheeks as well.

'My pleasure, Sophie. I'm here for you any time you need me. Just shout.' He glanced around at the others. 'But you didn't need me. Juan did all the hard work and you had your trusty hound to defend you. I had never thought of Jeeves as a guard dog before, but he was awesome. It's good to know he has your back.'

Sophie dropped to her knees and hugged the Labrador to her chest.

'Another hero. My big brave boy, Jeeves, you're a really, really good dog.'

He nuzzled her with his cold wet nose and wagged his tail gently. He already knew that.

Chapter 20

When she woke next morning it was almost half past eight, but Jeeves was still snoozing by the bed. It was very warm already and he had climbed out of his basket and was stretched out on the cool floor, eyes closed, so she sank back down onto her pillows and let her mind roam. One thing was for sure: if she had been looking for closure with Claudio, she had it now. Between them, Juan, Dan and Jeeves had made it clear to him exactly how she felt and now she ought to be able to relax as far as he was concerned. Then she thought about the other man in her life. It was pointless agonising about Chris for now. If he succumbed to the allure of Paola, so what? She had arrived here without a man and if she were to leave the same way, that would be fine – not least if she left with half the value of the castle in her bank account.

She and Rachel had been signing in religiously every evening, the building works had been completed, the top floor had been cleared and the new kitchen was due to be fitted the following week. All that remained after that was the grape harvest, the *vendemmia*, which Beppe had told her would take place around the middle of September, depending on the weather. Once that was completed and October the first dawned, the castle would be theirs.

Of course they would sell it. There was no way they could afford the upkeep of something as huge and valuable as this but Sophie knew it would be a sad day when it sold, although the idea of buying a smaller place as a holiday home definitely appealed if they had enough money. Apart from being the last palpable link to their wonderful Uncle George, Paradiso had lived up to its name. It really was a little piece of paradise and it would be hard to leave. The big unknown was what would happen next – at least as far as Sophie herself was concerned. Somehow a return to London, albeit with the possibility of getting herself a much bigger and nicer flat, or even a house with a garden, didn't have the same attraction. Once you've spent time in paradise, nowhere else really matches up.

On impulse, she reached for her iPad and Googled properties for sale here in Paradiso. There were only two. The first was a tiny studio apartment in the village, but the second came as a pleasant surprise.

It was Dan's house – or, at least, the house he was currently renting. She scrolled through the details, admiring the photos, and saw that it boasted four bedrooms and two bathrooms and was on sale for half a million euros. While that would have been wildly beyond her means a few months ago, if she and Rachel managed to sell the castle for the sort of money they were hoping to get, it would be more than affordable – and probably no more expensive than getting herself a bigger flat in London. Maybe, rather than a holiday home, this could actually become her real home. Suddenly the idea of staying in Paradiso began to crystallise inside her head. But for now, first things first: they needed a new kitchen, a successful *vendemmia* and the sale of the castle. After that would come the beginning of the rest of her life.

The week went quickly. The third day with their Spanish guests came and went without Sophie getting even a whiff of smelly fish and she was delighted they stayed on until the following weekend. Apart from the debt of gratitude she owed to Juan for his intervention with Claudio, she found she had thoroughly enjoyed their company – even Lola who turned out to be a sensible, grounded girl beneath the glitzy exterior – and was genuinely sorry to see them leave on Monday morning. They had brought a lot of life to the castle and as they drove off, she caught hold of her sister's arm and tugged her close.

'A lovely bunch of people, Rach. Sorry again for my initial reaction. I should have trusted your judgement. I'm afraid I was behaving like a know-it-all big sister all over again.'

Rachel grinned back at her. 'Thanks, but there's no need. I should have run it past you first, but I'm really happy you like them as much as I do. You know something? I'm seriously considering settling down in Spain once I've got my degree.'

'Nice idea and, for what it's worth, I'm seriously thinking about settling here in Paradiso once we've sold the castle.'

'You mean, set up home here with Chris?'

'Or on my own – with Jeeves. Somehow, I fear Chris is long gone.' The Pyrenean retreat had finished on Saturday and he still hadn't called.

'Still no word?'

'Nope.'

'And you aren't going to call him? You should do, you know. Or I'll call him if you like.'

'Please don't. Besides, you're a fine one to talk. What about you and Gabriel?'

They both lapsed into silence.

They didn't have much time for introspection as a large van drew up in the square and a man with a clipboard leant out of the window.

'Signora Elliot? We have a new kitchen for you.'

Rachel explained how to get round to the back lane while Sophie hurried off to open the rear gates. From there the van was able to back right up to the kitchen door. After that both girls dashed back into the kitchen and joined Rita who was already hard at it, emptying the kitchen cupboards and carrying everything through to the gym for now, as the dining room table was unavailable, being piled high with items ready for next weekend's antiques fair. The rest of the day was spent hanging dust-sheets across doorways, making coffee for the men, and doing their best to stop Jeeves getting in the way. The kitchen fitters took a distinct liking to the Labrador and when this extended to sharing their mid-morning snacks with him, he was forever at their heels. Sophie wouldn't have been surprised to find him inside one of the new units sooner of later.

In between all this, Sophie returned to her book which was going well. Taking her inspiration from recent events, one princess had to resort to the court champion to frighten off a former suitor who wouldn't take no for an answer. The other princess, on the other hand, was still pining for her beloved who had gone off to war before she had had a chance to tell him she loved him. She realised she was smiling as she typed. Her Creative Writing lecturer's mantra had been 'Draw on your own experience'. She was certainly doing that.

A few days later, after the kitchen fitters had finished for the day, she and Jeeves were splashing about in the pool when she heard whistling. She looked up to see Dan appear through the bushes and she beamed up at him.

'Hi, Dan. Come on in. The water's lovely.'

He gave her a smile and a wave. 'Hi, Sophie, it's just too damn hot today. I've been sitting at the computer for three solid days and I feel like I'm melting.'

He dropped his towel, shrugged off his shorts and T-shirt and dived in, surfacing alongside her where he was immediately assaulted – in a very friendly way – by Jeeves. After playing with the Labrador for a bit, he paddled across to Sophie.

'Have your guests gone?'

'Yes. They've been replaced by the kitchen fitters, so never a dull moment here at the castle.'

'And the antiques fair's at the weekend, isn't it? I was wondering if you'd like some help. I gather from Beppe it can get really busy.'

'We'd love that, thanks.'

'Have you heard from Chris? How was his week in the mountains?'

'He hasn't called.' Sophie shook her head sadly. 'I'm afraid I'm fearing the worst.'

'What? That he's fallen into the clutches of the antiques siren?' He snorted. 'No chance. You're the one for him, I'm sure.'

'You are? I'm not holding my breath.'

A bit later on, she persuaded the dog to leave the pool and she settled down on a sunbed while he rolled around from side to side on his back, trying to catch his own tail in his mouth while a puddle of water spread out around him. A few minutes later Dan came and lay down beside her. They chatted and it turned out that he had visited the church in Santa Rita to good effect.

'That baptismal font is mightily important for my research. The carvings look as if they really are representations of Saracens. You and Rachel have done me a great favour in finding it. It must have been left over from the original church that was destroyed in the earthquake.' He rolled onto his side so he could catch Sophie's eye. 'I'm not exaggerating if I tell you it might become the single most important indication I've found so far to support the main thrust of my thesis. Thank you both, so much.'

'I'm delighted we could help. Rachel and I had a lovely time that day and the church was a fascinating place for us to visit.'

'By the way, I've been meaning to say – you and Rachel look very settled now. There was an air of tension between you when I first met you but that seems to have cleared.'

'You're right. We've done a lot of talking and I can honestly say that things are back to normal between us now.'

'George would have been so pleased. He told me how upset he was that the two of you had lost contact.'

Not for the first time, Sophie realised that Dan must have been a really close friend of Uncle George's to know so much about the family. She wondered whether to tell him Rachel's version of why she had fled the country, but decided to leave that to her if she ever felt like telling anyone else.

'Yes, I've got my sister back and that's great.' At that moment her phone started ringing. Her heart skipped a beat as she saw it was Chris. Her immediate reaction was delight, tempered by apprehension.

'Chris, hi. It's good to hear from you. All well?'

'Hi, Sophie. It's all been a bit manic since coming back to work. Sorry it's taken me so long to get round to calling you.'

'So, how did your week in the Pyrenees go?' She didn't actually cross her fingers, but she did find herself holding her breath for a moment.

'It was great, thanks. I now know what to do if one of my colleagues decides to sexually assault me.'

'You what?' Sophie could hear her voice go up in pitch. 'What's happened?'

She heard him laugh. 'Nothing's happened. It was part of our CPD update. A guy from HR gave us a lecture about it. For the record, if something like that happens I must report it at once to my line manager.'

Sophie felt a combination of relief and mortification at jumping to the wrong conclusion. She tried once more to adopt a neutral tone. 'Good for you. I hope you never have to report anybody.'

'Speak for yourself.' He laughed again. 'Anyway, look, I've been meaning to phone you for the last three days.' This sounded promising, but as he continued it turned out to be less romantic than she had hoped. 'The music memorabilia auction's coming up next Monday and your LPs are in the catalogue with guide prices around the one-to-two-hundred-pound mark. I'll give you a call next week and let you know how it goes.'

'Oh, great, thanks.' Interesting as this was, what she really wanted to know was what had taken place in the Pyrenees. 'How about you? Did you have a good time in the mountains?'

'I had a great time. The good news is that the weather, after the first two days, was great – not too hot, not too cold – and we went hiking in the high mountains most afternoons.'

'We?' Sophie didn't feel ready to mention Paola's name.

'Me and some mates. It's absolutely gorgeous up there. I'll send you some photos. I was going to do it yesterday but I've been crazy busy here at work. I'll let you have them later in the week.'

'Great, thanks.' She took a deep breath and went for it. 'Did Paola have a good time?'

He laughed. 'Paola had a *very* good time. I'll tell you all about it when I see you.'

That sounded sinister but she did her best to rise above it. 'I can't wait to see you. Any clearer idea of dates when you might come back here?'

'Yes, that's the other reason for calling. I've booked the last week of September if that's still okay with you. I should arrive on Saturday the twenty-fourth and leave again on Sunday the second of October. I'll fly in and out of Nice and rent a car from there. That way I thought I could be there with you for your final day when you officially become the owners of a castle.'

'Terrific. I look forward to seeing you. It's Rachel's birthday on the first of October. We'll have to have a big party to celebrate both events.'

'Sounds like a great idea. It'll be really good to see you again. I've been missing you.'

'Me, too.' Had he meant he had been missing just her, or her and her sister? 'You' could be singular or plural, after all. The English language could be annoyingly ambiguous on occasions. But she had to concede that it did sound as though he had at least been thinking about her.

After ringing off, she looked across at Dan who had no doubt heard her half of the conversation. She relayed what Chris had said, in particular his comment about Paola having a *very* good time. Dan was quick to offer encouragement.

'But he didn't say who with, did he? Surely if he and she had hooked up he'd have said *we* had a good time. Don't worry, Sophie, I know it'll be all right.'

Sophie wasn't so sure.

Chapter 21

The antiques fair was every bit as busy as Beppe had predicted. From the moment the first visitors started arriving shortly before ten o'clock in the morning, it was non-stop all day. Sophie and Rachel had set up their table right in front of the main gates of the castle and it was piled high with everything from copper pans to hundred-year-old silk knickers. In the course of the day they sold most of the items and took a lot of money – so much so that they had to keep dashing back inside to lock the cash away as the little tin they were using as a cashbox filled with notes. The icing on the cake was the arrival at the end of the afternoon of the very canny owner of an antique shop in Monte Carlo, no less, who offered them a flat amount for everything still unsold. After a successful bit of haggling by Rachel, he got himself some bargains and they got rid of everything.

That afternoon Beppe had turned up in a borrowed van and ferried the junk pile by the back door to the dump, so the top floor was now clear. After the fair had ended, Sophie and Rachel took Beppe and his wife, Rita and her husband, and Dan out to dinner at the Vecchio Ristoro, to celebrate having ticked off another one of Uncle George's tasks, and they had a great night.

It would have been even better if Chris hadn't sent an email with half a dozen photos of spectacular mountain scenery. The trouble was that Sophie couldn't miss the fact that Paola, wearing short shorts and a broad smile, was in most of them, and in one of them her arm was affectionately draped around Chris's waist. Still, Sophie told herself, as long as her best friend was happy, that was all that counted.

Wasn't it?

Chris followed this up with another phone call on Monday, after the music memorabilia sale in London.

'The good news is that your handful of LPs has made over fifteen hundred pounds, even after the deduction of commission charges. Not bad, eh?' He was sounding very cheerful.

'That's brilliant news. Added to the almost three thousand euros we made at the antiques fair yesterday, that's amazing for a load of old junk.'

'What's junk to one person is a treasure to another.'

They chatted for a few minutes without Paola's name being mentioned until the subject of the antique arms auction came up.

'That'll be just before I come over to stay, so I hope I can bring you more good news. Paola was going on about your musket and mace at great length last week. She's confident both items will do well.'

'Will she be coming over to London for the sale?' Sophie tried to sound only casually interested.

'Oh yes. I'm looking forward to seeing her again. We get on really well together.'

Sophie grimaced. She had already got that message – loud and clear.

To reinforce her conviction that the hook-up between Chris and Paola was a done deal, she got a phone call the next day from Paola herself. This was to inform her that a courier would be coming on Thursday to pick up the musket and the mace and take them over to the UK for cleaning in readiness for the auction that would take place on the twenty-third of September. Along with this message came another that was unequivocal.

'Have you spoken to Chris? Did he tell you how much fun we had in the mountains?' Paola sounded decidedly bubbly.

'He certainly did. And he sent me some photos. It looks like you all had a wonderful time.'

'It's a great hotel and the food was as amazing as ever. Apart from all the hiking, there was lots to do and, like I told you, it all got a bit naughty in the evenings.' Sophie heard her giggle. 'Well, I certainly did.'

'So you enjoyed yourself?'

Paola giggled again. 'Yes, and I wasn't the only one.' Possibly remembering that she was talking to a client, her tone changed. 'Anyway, it was a great week. Get Chris to tell you all about it next time you see him.'

Somehow Sophie didn't think she would. She gritted her teeth and did her best to remain cordial. At the end of the call she turned to Rachel, who was sitting on the other side of the dining room table with books strewn around her. 'Well, that's it, Rach. The eagle has landed, cherry red talons first. She's got him.' She was unable to disguise the disappointment in her voice.

'I'm sorry, Soph. What a bummer.' Rachel got up and headed for the door of the gym which was their temporary kitchen. 'I'll make tea.' She stopped and checked her watch. 'What the hell, it's almost six. I'll get a bottle of wine.'

They took the bottle of cold white out into the garden behind the castle and sat in the shade while Jeeves wandered off to check that his territory was clear of cats, squirrels, lizards and other undesirables. He had developed the habit of barking at any he saw but he couldn't be bothered to do more than that. Clearly he was also feeling the heat. Rachel poured the wine and passed a full glass over to Sophie.

'Bottoms up. So Chris's gone over to the dark side, so what? The world's full of desirable men. Just you wait and see.' She took a sip. 'Are you going to be okay having him come to stay at the end of the month?'

'I'll be fine.' Sophie took a sip of wine and considered the question more fully. Yes, of course she would be okay, wouldn't she? 'He's still my best friend. It's not as though he's been unfaithful to me or anything. It's my own fault – I had my chance to say something and I bottled out. And like I've been saying all along, Paola's a very suitable partner for him after all.'

There was silence for a while before Rachel changed the subject.

'Today's September the fifth, isn't it? I was talking to Beppe and he reckons we should be able to start harvesting the grapes around the middle of the month – unless the weather changes drastically – but there's quite a lot of preparatory work to be done first. I'll be helping him with that but if you feel like pitching in when the *vendemmia* proper starts – he says Dan's offered to help as well – that would be really helpful.'

'Of course. And what happens to the grapes? Does he make the wine here or somewhere else? Is there a cooperative or something?'

'He does it all here. He's got a very smart set-up in that low stone building alongside the garage where the Merc lives. It all looks very hi-tech with stainless steel tanks and lots of pipes and gauges and stuff. I'll show you round one of these days if you like. He says he'll talk me through the process, and I can't wait.'

'And then you'll be able to start your own vineyard once we've sold the castle?'

'It's a lovely thought. By the way, shouldn't we maybe start talking to real estate agents about putting the place on the market?'

Sophie nodded. 'Definitely. I've been wondering that myself. There are loads of agencies down in Santa Rita. We'll have to ask Beppe or Rita which are the good ones.'

'Or maybe we might do better with one of the big international firms, seeing as it's a fairly important historical building with, hopefully, a hefty price tag. What do you think?'

'I'm sure you're right. Good idea.'

'I've just finished the assignment I've been working on for uni so I've got a bit more time now. I'll take a look on the internet and see who the big boys are. It's a pity I'm no longer talking to Gabriel. He and his firm do a lot of real estate transactions. He knows about all that stuff.'

'Well, why not use this as an excuse to get back in touch with him? You know you want to.'

Yet again, Rachel just shook her head. 'I know he won't be interested, Soph. It's like I told you. He's a very honest, very straight person and after I so clearly demonstrated I didn't trust him, why should he ever trust me again? Besides, it was all my fault and I'd die of shame if I ever had to talk to him about the way I behaved towards him. No, it's best just to let it go.' Sophie saw her pull herself together and plaster on a smile. 'It now looks as though you and I are both going to be unattached – but that's easily remedied. All we have to do is sell the castle, pocket the loot, and head for Monte Carlo where we can find ourselves a couple of toy boys.'

'How old do you think we are, Rach? I'm not thirty yet for crying out loud. A toy boy for you would probably still be in school.'

'I'm not that young, I'm going to be twenty-eight in just a few weeks' time.'

'While on that subject, I was thinking we should have a party to celebrate both your birthday and us completing our three months together, seeing as our last day of logging in is the thirtieth and your birthday's the next day. What do you think?'

'That's a lovely idea. Who do we invite?'

'I was wondering if some or all your Spanish friends might feel like coming back for the event? And, of course we need to invite Beppe and Rita, and I thought maybe Romeo from the hair salon with a few of his colourful friends. Then there's Mariarosa and her husband down in Rome if she can spare the time. She's a good friend. What about you? Anybody you want to invite apart from the Spanish brigade?'

Rachel shook her head. 'Not really. I've lost contact with most of my English friends and there's no point inviting anybody from the States. It's too far away and too short notice. Think of the cost of flights. Of course, there's Dan. He should still be about.' She glanced up. 'And what about Chris?'

'He'll be here then anyway.'

'And if he wants Paola to come?'

Sophie had already considered that. 'If he wants to bring her, that's fine by me. He's my best friend and I'm happy he's found somebody. I hope it works out between the two of them.'

She almost managed to fool herself.

Chapter 22

That evening after dinner, Sophie decided to do something radical. She settled down in her room, secure in the knowledge that Rachel was in the lounge with Jeeves watching *Raiders of the Lost Ark* for the millionth time. It was perfectly clear to her that Rachel was missing Gabriel, the man she had acknowledged as being The One for her, and would dearly like to hear from him but was too stubborn to make the first move. Sophie remembered that Rachel herself had offered to call Chris on her behalf the other day, so maybe this had indicated a subconscious desire for Sophie to do the same for her.

She racked her brain for his surname and managed to retrieve it from her memory: Anderson, Cooper and Gomez was Gabriel's law practice and Rachel had said he was Cooper. It was the work of a few moments to locate the firm's website and identify the direct email address of Gabriel Cooper, partner.

Slowly and carefully, Sophie set about composing an email to him. It took her over an hour and numerous rewrites until she was happy with it. In it, she explained to him who she was and the fact that she was writing without her sister's knowledge. As simply as possible she indicated to him that it was clear to her that Rachel was missing him and bitterly regretted how she has misjudged him, and yet was unwilling to contact him. After ten minutes' thought, she went back and replaced *unwilling* with *ashamed*, hoping it would convey the way Rachel was feeling. She told him they were currently in Italy on holiday and asked him if he felt like giving her sister another chance. Finally, after much deliberation, she pressed *Send*.

Twenty-four hours later there had still been no reply. It was looking more and more as though Rachel had been right in her belief that he wanted nothing more to do with her and she was starting to feel terrible for interfering. She should have just minded her own business. If Rachel ever found out, this would be yet another example of her meddling big sister thinking she knew best. It therefore came as a major relief when her phone beeped that evening just as the two of them were coming out of Uncle George's study after logging onto the computer. Sophie glanced at the screen, saw she had received an email from Gabriel and hurried off, ostensibly to the loo. She ran up to her bathroom, closed the door behind her and locked it before perching on the toilet seat to see what he had written.

> Dear Sophie
>
> Thank you most warmly for your email. You can't imagine how good it was to hear from you. I've been dying to get in touch with Rachel for weeks but her last words to me were that I should never try to contact her again and I have obeyed this instruction, although it has been hard.
>
> I miss her very much and desperately want to talk to her. Could I ask you to ask her to contact me by phone, email or text? Please do try to convince her that I miss her and

want to talk with her. What happened is no
big deal and we can work through it – at least
I know I can.

Thank you once again for your intervention. I am in your debt.

Kindest regards
Gabriel Cooper

Sophie almost whooped with joy. Her risky ploy had paid
off. She opened the door and ran out, calling to her sister
who appeared from the lounge looking worried. Jeeves,
alongside her, was looking equally perturbed.

'What's up Soph? Is something wrong?'

'Nothing's wrong. In fact, it's the opposite. Look.' She
thrust her phone into her sister's hand and waited for an
explosion of joy from her.

The explosion, when it came, was anything but joyful.
Stiffly, Rachel handed back the phone and spun on her
heel, heading for the stairs. When she was halfway up she
stopped and looked back down.

'You just had to stick your nose in, didn't you? You
always were a bloody know-it-all and you'll never change.
Why can't you keep out of my business and my life?' Her
voice disintegrated into what sounded like a sob as she
whirled around again and ran on up the stairs until she
was out of sight. A couple of seconds later Sophie heard a
door slam.

Silence fell on the castle and Sophie made her way
into the lounge, turned off the TV and put the lights
out. Followed by a subdued Labrador, she went along
the corridor to the kitchen, idly reflecting that the
fitters had promised they would have finally finished by
tomorrow night. She opened the back door and followed

the dog outside into the warm evening air. It was almost completely dark by now and an owl was calling from high up in a nearby tree, but she barely noticed. As she wandered around to the front and let herself and the dog out of the main gates, all she could think about was her sister's reaction. She followed Jeeves across the piazza and onto the path leading towards the headland, her brain churning.

What she had done had been with the best of intentions. It was patently clear that Rachel was missing Gabriel and wanted nothing more than to get back together with him. Surely Rachel herself could see that, and yet she had reacted so badly. Sophie kept asking herself how on earth what she had done could have been so wrong. Yes, she had been interfering with her sister's life, but hadn't she now got the outcome she so badly wanted? Why couldn't Rachel see that and accept that the result was the only thing that counted?

When Sophie and Jeeves emerged onto the open headland, she slowed and stopped by a rocky outcrop, leaning back against the still warm stone, her eyes ranging over the bay. With distant lights twinkling and the last vestiges of the sunset still tingeing the western horizon a deep violet, it should have been a beautiful view, but she barely noticed that either. She felt terrible. Her attempt to help her sister find happiness had blown up in her face. Now Rachel was unhappy, Sophie herself was disheartened and even her faithful Labrador, instead of running off into the bushes to hunt for sticks, had plonked himself down alongside her and was resting his big hairy head against her thigh, emitting plaintive little whines as he tried to work out what was wrong with his mistress.

'Bugger!' Sophie growled it out loud, but it didn't help.

Finally, after several long minutes she roused herself and her dog and turned back towards the castle. She knew she owed it to her sister to try talking to her. Back home, she found an unopened bottle of ten-year-old Torres brandy brought by the Spaniards and dug two glasses out of the heap on the ping pong table. She went back up the stairs, tailed by her dog, walked along to Rachel's room and knocked on the door.

'Rach, it's me. Can I come in?'

There was no reply. She tried the door handle, feeling sure it would be locked, but to her surprise it opened. The lights were off and the room was empty.

Rachel had disappeared.

Sophie stood there blankly for a few moments, wondering what had happened to her before some instinct made her look in the bathroom. She immediately saw that her sister's nightie was no longer hanging on the radiator and her toothbrush and toothpaste had disappeared from the shelf above the basin. A hasty check of the room revealed that Rachel's big beach bag had also gone, presumably stuffed with clothes.

Sophie hurried downstairs to the kitchen and immediately spotted that the Mercedes keys weren't hanging on the hook by the back door.

'She's done a bunk, Jeeves. Do you realise? She's gone.'

She slumped down on top of a dusty toolbox left by the kitchen fitters and felt a warm hairy body press against her leg and a big paw land on her thigh. She grabbed hold of it for a few moments before persuading him to lie down as she reached for her phone and typed a hurried text.

> Please come back, Rach. I'm really sorry. I
> didn't mean to meddle. I just want you to
> be happy. Please come back. x

After pressing *Send* she eyed the bottle of brandy for a few moments before deciding to be sensible. She got up, went over to the slick new fridge and poured herself a glass of cold red wine instead. She took it through to the lounge and as she sat there sipping it, there was just one thought going through her head: it was happening again. Just like six years ago, Rachel had left in a huff. The only solace Sophie could find was that her sister had left the majority of her clothes here so hopefully she wasn't about to do anything as radical as jump on a plane to the USA.

And then, of course, there was the little matter of the two of them having to sign in together before midnight tomorrow or lose the castle.

–

Sophie had a broken night. A couple of times she woke up, convinced she had heard a door, and even on one occasion went so far as to creep out into the corridor to check whether Rachel's room was once more occupied, but found it empty. Next morning, as the sunlight reached in through the open window and awakened her, the first thing she did was to hurry next door just in case, but there was still no sign of her sister. Feeling jaded, she returned to her room, pulled on shorts and trainers and took Jeeves out for his morning walk around the estate. She deliberately wandered down past the garage but there was no sign of the Mercedes. The bird had flown.

As the day progressed, she kept on calling and sending messages to her sister but to no avail. Rita came and went and the kitchen fitters finished and left, but Sophie hardly noticed. That afternoon she couldn't concentrate on her writing so she set off on a long walk with her dog. She toyed with the idea of calling Dan to see if he wanted to join her but decided she wasn't feeling very sociable, so she and Jeeves went on their own. The hours passed and she started having to come to terms with the possibility that Rachel might not reappear at all today and, of course, that would mean they couldn't log in and so, according to the terms of Uncle George's bequest, the castle would pass to some unknown beneficiary.

She sweated her way up the hill past the little chapel in the blazing heat and did a lot of thinking. Surely Rachel wouldn't be so pig-headed as to throw away potentially millions of euros out of sheer pique. The words 'cut off your nose to spite your face' came to mind and she wondered if her sister would really be so crazy. Inside her head, Sophie had already started making plans for the future based on inheriting half of what looked likely to be an astronomical sum. If Rachel really didn't put in an appearance today, things would irrevocably change. Yes, they would have the remains of the money Uncle George had left in the bank safety deposit box plus the proceeds from the antiques fair, the record sale, and the upcoming arms auction which should amount to a very handy sum indeed, but wouldn't be as potentially life-changing as if they sold the castle. Even a heaped bowl of ice cream at the little cafe in the next village didn't help and by the time she got back home again, she was feeling not only weary and sticky, but despondent.

She let herself in through the side gate and followed Jeeves up to the back door. However, as she reached the garage her heart leapt. The Mercedes was back. She dropped to her knees and hugged the surprised dog tightly to her chest.

'She's back, Jeeves, she's back.'

With a newfound burst of energy she ran to the back door and threw it open. There, sitting on one of the new ultramodern steel barstools in the empty, pristine kitchen was Rachel and she was smiling. Sophie's relief was palpable and she ran over to hug her sister.

'Rach, thank goodness you're back. Where've you been?'

Rachel was still smiling. 'I spent the night in a rather nice little hotel up in the hills above here and I've spent all day down at *Bagni Aurelia*. Lunch there was really rather good.'

Delighted as she was to see her sister looking and sounding so cheerful, Sophie couldn't help wondering how it could be that she had changed from bitter, angry victim to happy sister again so quickly. Yes, Rachel had always had the tendency to blow up dramatically and then return to normal equally quickly, but after a major shoot-out like last night, it was barely credible that she should now be so calm. Something wasn't right. She took a closer look at her, but could read nothing untoward on her face. She looked perfectly relaxed – and happy.

'Have you phoned Gabriel?'

Rachel shook her head but the smile didn't fade in the slightest. She still looked like the cat that had got the cream and Sophie's bemusement increased. 'No, but I will. It's only mid-morning over there now. I'm waiting for lunchtime. I need to be able to get him alone.'

That was perfectly reasonable and sounded quite genuine. Still, Sophie told herself, until she actually heard the two of them talking she wouldn't hold her breath. She went upstairs and changed into her bikini and, to the delight of her dog, headed for the pool with him. She spent an age floating about in the water, gradually recovering from the stress of the past hours and the effort of the long walk this afternoon. When she and Jeeves finally climbed back out again, she spread her towel on one of the sunbeds in the shade and stretched out with her dog alongside her. Within seconds she was asleep.

She was woken by her phone ringing. As she picked it up, she saw that she had slept for almost two hours and had been joined by Rachel who was sitting on an adjacent sunbed, still smiling. Sophie answered her phone and she saw her sister's smile change to a broad Cheshire Cat grin.

'Hi, Chris, how's things?'

'Erm, fine, thanks, Soph.' He sounded remarkably hesitant.

'You okay, Chris? You sound a bit strange.' As she spoke, she glanced across at her sister who was grinning from ear to ear and the penny began to drop. What Chris said next confirmed her fears.

'I thought I'd phone, Soph. You see, I got a call from Rachel earlier today.'

'Oh, God…' Sophie knew what was coming and all she wanted to do was to find a deep dark hole and disappear into it.

'She said some stuff about you… and me.'

'Oh, God…' Sophie realised she was sounding a bit repetitive, but she was struggling for words. 'What sort of stuff?'

There was a long pause before he managed to get the words out. 'About you liking me...' Another pause. 'A lot.'

Resisting the impulse to invoke the deity once more, Sophie made an attempt to play down what he had been told by her sister, who was looking as though she was about to explode with mirth. 'Of course I like you a lot, Chris. You're my best friend.'

'She said there was more to it than that. Was she wrong?' He was sounding a bit less hesitant now and she knew she owed him the truth. She took a deep breath.

'She wasn't wrong, Chris. Look, it's like this... I've started thinking of you as more than a friend. I have no idea how you feel about me and the last thing I want is to do anything to screw up our friendship. I know you and Paola are now an item and I...'

'Did you say Paola?'

'Yes, Paola, from Milan.'

'There's nothing going on between me and Paola, Soph. Whatever gave you that idea?'

'You did... and she did. You said you'd enjoyed yourselves so very much in the Pyrenees and she said she'd been very naughty. It wasn't hard to join the dots.'

'Well, the dots don't join up the way you think. Yes, we both had a good time in the hotel. Yes, if she says she did some naughty stuff, I'm sure she's right, but it wasn't with me. The word is that she ended up in bed with our boss.'

'Ah...' There wasn't much Sophie could think of to say to that, but fortunately he carried on talking.

'Soph, just so you know, I feel the same way about you and I always have.'

'But you were going out with Claire...'

'And you were going out with all sorts of other guys at Exeter and then, of course, your Latin lover in Rome until that finished last year. Why do you think Claire and I broke up?'

'She told me it was fundamental differences. She never really said much more. Are you saying I'm the reason you two split up? I'd hate to think I might have been responsible.'

'There was a lot more to it than that and I never so much as mentioned your name to her but, deep down, I've known it all along. Soph, you're the one I want and I'll always keep on wanting. And that's the truth.'

Sophie's mouth opened and closed ineffectually several times before she was able to form coherent words.

'But why didn't you say something?'

'For the same reason you didn't. We've both been too scared of screwing up our friendship.'

Sophie felt absolutely drained. She flopped back on the sunbed and stared up through the branches of the big old fig tree to the blue of the sky beyond. She had finally heard the words she had been waiting to hear: her best friend wanted to be more than that to her. There was just one big ugly fly flailing about in the ointment: how could she really know if she found him desirable until she had him in her arms? Still, it was a massive step in the right direction and she rejoiced.

'That's absolutely great to hear, Chris, and it makes me so happy. I've been trying to tell you so many times… I really miss you. I can't wait to see you again in, what, just about two weeks' time.'

They exchanged a few more slightly uncomfortable words before, by mutual agreement, they ended the call.

Sophie dropped the phone onto the sunbed beside her and heard her sister's voice.

'Stings, doesn't it?' Rachel still had that same broad smile on her face and Sophie struggled to suppress the overwhelming urge to push her into the pool fully clothed. 'It came to me this morning while I was sunbathing down at the beach. It seemed like the very least I could do was to help you the same way you helped me.' She winked. 'Glad to have been of service, sis.'

'Rachel, you little…!'

Sophie stuttered to a halt. When all was said and done, Rachel was right. She hadn't done anything more than her sister had done for her. And, all things considered, they had both got the result they wanted – for now. She took a couple of deep, calming breaths.

'Touché. All right, Rach, I suppose I deserved that.' She checked the time again. It was half past six. 'I make it lunchtime in Florida. Haven't you got a call to make?'

Chapter 23

The *vendemmia* started at dawn on the fifteenth of September. Beppe and Rachel had spent the previous days out in the vines pulling off leaves to expose the fruit and making a preliminary triage, removing as many rotten or unripe grapes as possible in readiness for the big day. Beppe was a firm believer in hand-picking the grapes, rather than using a machine, and in consequence, they were at it all day. Dan came along to lend a hand, as did Rita and her husband, and they all got down to work early. Jeeves, clearly confused by the behaviour of these humans out in the burning sun, trotted around, poking people with his cold wet nose and generally getting in the way.

It didn't take long before Sophie realised this was probably the hardest manual work she had ever done, constantly changing position, crouching, stooping and straightening up again, clippers in hand, as she carefully snipped the bunches of ripe grapes from the vines and laid them into a plastic crate at her feet. Drunken wasps didn't make the job any easier either and she had a few close calls. Once the crate was full, she picked it up, hoisted it onto her shoulders as Beppe had shown her, and carried it to the end of the row for collection by him with his little tractor and trailer. The only good thing about spending so much time in a crouch was that this did at least protect her from the sun which was still beating down fiercely, even though they were now in the middle of September. Rain was predicted towards the end of the month but, until then, the weather appeared to be set fair.

As she worked – and regularly stretched her aching back – her mind was free to roam. All in all, things were working out really well. She now spoke to Chris on the phone almost every night and although they weren't discussing anything particularly intimate, there was definitely a different feel to their conversations now. She still harboured the nagging fear that the reality of his touch might result in disillusion for both of them, but he would be here in just over a week's time and she would be able to find out once and for all if he was going to morph from friend to lover. It was a scary, but at the same time, exciting prospect.

As for Rachel, she and Gabriel had made peace and were spending long hours Facetiming each other. He had insisted on flying over at the end of the month to be with her on her birthday and to stay on for a few days' holiday. It looked like the beginning of October was going to be a joyous time. To add to their delight, there had been visits from representatives of two big international real estate agencies – one with an office in Milan and one in Nice. The result of these visits had been valuations of the castle in excess of ten million euros and the assurance that, in spite of the property market in Italy being generally in the doldrums, there were potential clients queuing up for such a unique property. Not wishing to tempt fate, Sophie and Rachel delayed asking them to start viewings until October dawned and Signor Verdi had rubberstamped the deal.

Around mid-morning, Beppe called a halt to proceedings and they all trailed willingly back to the shade of the trees by the cantina, the low building alongside the garage. Sophie took a look inside and saw the huge vats beginning to fill. She had been wondering if she might be required to take off her shoes and start trampling the grapes but he assured her this was all done mechanically. She was mildly disappointed until he told her that treading grapes could result in feet and legs being stained for days afterwards – surprisingly blue, rather than red, because of oxidisation or some such that Sophie's unscientific mind failed to grasp. She reflected that it was probably just as well that Chris's first sight of her since July wasn't going to be with a two-tone colour scheme.

She slumped down on a bench in the shade, clutching a bottle of cold water, and leant back, stretching her back and legs with a groan. A few moments later Dan appeared and settled down alongside her.

'Seriously hard work, isn't it?'

'You can say that again. I ache in places I'd forgotten I had places.' She gave him a weary smile. 'Thanks for helping out.'

'It's the least I can do. Besides, I need the exercise after all the hours I've been spending at the computer or I soon won't be able to fit into my clothes. I can't allow that to happen with Jen arriving next week.'

'So she's definitely coming? And have you at least hinted at your feelings for her?'

'Yes, after Rachel told me you'd opened up to Chris and she'd made up with her guy, I resolved to put my money where my mouth was and take a chance. We had a long talk and she told me she's been feeling the same way about me for years. Years! Why didn't she say anything?'

Sophie reached over and caught hold of his hand. 'We're all guilty of being afraid to reveal the way we feel. But at least it's out in the open now and I'm so glad for you. You must bring her to Rachel's birthday party on the first of October.'

'Thanks, I wouldn't miss it and I really want you to meet her. I'm delighted Rachel and her guy in Orlando have made up. And what about you? You aren't still afraid things won't work out between you and Chris, are you?'

Sophie shook her head, but it was without real conviction. 'It'll work out fine, I'm sure.'

He didn't miss much. 'Seriously, it *will* work out. Just try not to worry.'

By the end of the day they had picked all the black grapes and there just remained the considerably smaller patch of white grapes to do tomorrow. Rachel had had the bright idea of getting the restaurant to bring over an early dinner for everybody and they ate it outside by the pool, washed down with last year's wine straight from the fridge. At the end of the meal, as everybody drifted away, Sophie and Jeeves accompanied Dan back to his house and he asked her in for a coffee. They sat under his loggia, looking out over the lights of Santa Rita, and she mentioned that she had seen the house for sale on the internet. He nodded.

'That's right. They'll start doing viewings as soon as I move out in October.'

'Like us at the castle. You know that it'll become ours at the end of September if all goes well, don't you?'

He grinned. 'To be quite honest, that was my idea.' Seeing the surprise on Sophie's face, he explained. 'When George got his terminal diagnosis, I was one of the first people he told. He was remarkably phlegmatic about the whole thing, saying he'd had a rich, full life, but his one big regret was the fact that his nieces had quarrelled and he wanted to find a way of bringing them back together.'

Sophie was impressed. She already knew that Dan and Uncle George had been close friends, but she hadn't realised how very close. 'So it was your idea to lock us up here together for three months?'

At least he had the good grace to look a little sheepish. 'It worked, didn't it? I'm not as stupid as I look, you know.'

'You aren't stupid at all, but definitely devious. It was a marvellous bit of Machiavellian trickery and I compliment you on it, even though I was cursing you under my breath before I got here. And did you deliberately plan it so the last day would be the day before Rachel's birthday?'

'That was down to George. He saw a kind of synchronicity there.'

Sophie nodded. This was rather what she had been expecting. 'He never forgot our birthdays.'

'The thing is, he wanted to leave the castle to you girls, but he could hardly leave it to just one of you, so that meant putting the two of you together – and ensuring you stuck together. At the risk of appearing immodest, I'm delighted the results have been positive.'

'I don't suppose you know who owns this house you're renting, do you? Rach and I were talking about maybe buying a place here in Paradiso sort of in memory of Uncle George. We could use it for holidays or I might even set up home here if this book I'm writing were to prove popular and I decide to try to make it as a writer.'

'That sounds like a brilliant idea.' He paused for thought for a moment. 'The owner lives in Switzerland. I can contact him and see if he's interested in a private sale if you like.'

'That would be great. Paradiso has really lived up to its name and the idea of keeping a toehold here appeals greatly.'

'I know what you mean. You're right about it being a little piece of paradise. Compared to big cities like Boston or New York, it feels like being on a different planet – so calm, so quiet, so beautiful and so friendly.'

Sophie glanced at her watch and finished her coffee. 'Now, if I can stand up, I'm going home for a long hot bath and then I'm going to fall into bed.'

–

By one o'clock next day they had managed to pick all the white grapes and it was with a real sense of accomplishment – and considerable relief – that they all sat down to lunch. Beppe pronounced himself hugely satisfied with the quantity and quality of this year's grapes and he predicted an excellent wine when it emerged, ready to drink, next spring. Sophie wondered whether the castle would still be theirs this time next year or whether the new owners would find themselves with a liquid bonus in the cellar. On the one hand she hoped the place would have sold by then but, on the other, it would be good to taste the fruits of their labours.

At the end of lunch, after thanking everybody for their help, Sophie headed upstairs for a well-deserved shower and a siesta that lasted for almost two hours. When she awoke, she came down to find that Rachel had had a very good idea.

'How does a swim in the sea and a pizza sound?'

'They both sound great but what about Jeeves? I don't really want to leave him here on his own.'

'It's all arranged. Dan says he's too busy with his book to come with us but he'll be delighted to look after the dog. All we have to do is drop Jeeves there as we set off and bring a pizza on the way back.'

They drove down to Santa Rita in Sophie's car, leaving Jeeves with Dan on the way. Now that they were well into September the influx of holidaymakers had diminished to a trickle, and as a result the beach looked very different. Half the colourful parasols had already been taken down and they even found a parking space right alongside the promenade itself. There was an end of term atmosphere at *Bagni Aurelia* as the establishment was being taken apart, chairs stacked, umbrellas rolled up, the lifeguard's seat on top of the ladder removed and even the coffee machine disconnected as preparations for hibernation took place around them. The sea was still blissfully warm after the long hot summer and it seemed a pity that the season for places like this should be so short. Still, Sophie reflected as she floated around, it was a whole lot more peaceful and enjoyable now for locals like themselves.

They went to the pizzeria at just before seven and found it also only half-full. Rachel summed it up as they ate.

'Santa Rita's a funny place, isn't it? For two or three months of the year it's absolutely heaving, and then it just dies. I have a feeling it's likely to be a ghost town by the time January comes around.'

Sophie nodded. 'That's the lovely thing about Paradiso. It's been peaceful all summer up there so maybe it just carries on the same way all year round. At least I hope so.' She took a mouthful of her sumptuous *frutti di mare* pizza, laden with prawns, clams, octopus and squid, and washed it down with a sip of white wine. 'I suppose I'm going to find out. You're off back to Exeter to finish your degree and I'd better stay on here until the place sells. Besides, I have nowhere else to go at present anyway.'

'Of course, you could always move in with Chris.'

Sophie could see her sister was messing with her but she shook her head all the same. 'One step at a time, Rach. I still don't know if he and I are going to be physically compatible.'

'Come on, Soph. You know him so well; you love him to bits as a friend. Of course you're going to be compatible physically.'

'I wish I shared your optimism.'

Chapter 24

By the time Chris arrived on the twenty-fourth, Sophie had almost turned into a gibbering wreck. As the day progressed, her nerves had been getting worse and worse. What if he kissed her and it didn't feel right? What if her brain refused to accept him as anything more than a friend? Or, even worse, what if it all felt good to her, but not to him? What if she liked him but he didn't like her? His week's holiday with her could potentially turn out to be the most uncomfortable week of both their lives. Rita had prepared the same room for him he had occupied before, although Rachel had been making lurid suggestions about him occupying the other half of Sophie's huge double bed. Sophie had been quick to pour cold water on that. If kissing him was a big step, moving on from there promised to be an even bigger one, and she knew she was going to need time. When she heard the bell at just after five announcing he was at the front gates in his hire car she very nearly took to her heels and ran out of the back door and just kept on running.

But she restrained herself and went out to greet him. He was standing alongside his car, just outside the gate, and one look at his face told her he was as apprehensive as she was. This should have helped, but it didn't. Still, both of them managed to muster nervous smiles and she opened the gates and waved him in. He jumped back into the car, drove in and parked, and as he climbed out of the car, Jeeves very wisely decided to do his ice-breaker act. He charged over and jumped up so Chris had to stop and make a fuss of him first. Finally persuading the dog to return to all fours, Chris came across and held out his arms to Sophie.

'Hi, Soph. It's so good to see you.'

'It is, isn't it? I mean it's good for you… for me to see you, too.' She very nearly smacked her own wrist. 'You know what I mean… I'm glad you've come.' She was an almost thirty-year-old woman for crying out loud, not a tongue-tied teenager. Leaning forward, she kissed him on the cheeks and then enveloped him in a hug which felt marvellous. But that was as far as it went. For now.

She took him into the smart new kitchen, which he duly admired while she made tea and brought out the sponge cake she had made and iced earlier as a displace-ment activity. Rachel emerged from her essay writing and it looked as though she kissed him more warmly than Sophie had done.

'*Ciao, bello*. It's great to see you.'

'And, erm… ciao bell*a* to you, Rachel. That's what I should say, isn't it, seeing as you're a girl?'

'Dead right.' Rachel nodded and then dropped Sophie right in it. 'See, Soph, he *has* noticed that we're girls.'

'Rachel…!' Sophie turned her back on them, ostens-ibly to concentrate on the teapot but in actual fact to hide her blushes. Behind her, she was heartened to hear Chris reply confidently.

'It's never been in doubt in my head, Rachel. Specially your sister.'

Rachel gave a cheeky 'Ooh, I say…' before relenting and returning the conversation to a safer topic. 'So what are you two planning on doing this evening? I've got an assignment to write. Do you realise, in less than two weeks' time I'm going to be back at uni? Just think – me a student again...'

Rachel and Sophie had already planned this. Although Rachel did indeed have work to do, she was deliberately removing herself from the equation so that Sophie and Chris could talk... or more. Sophie set the mugs of tea on the table alongside the cake and explained what she was proposing.

'There's a village just a little way inland of here that's having its annual *festa del paese*, the local fair, this evening. If you aren't too tired after your journey, I thought we could maybe go up and take a look. Rita tells me it's usually a lot of fun. There are games, food and all sorts of other stuff to see. Jeeves can stay here and help Rachel with her homework.'

'Sounds perfect.' Chris gave her a smile that looked almost like his normal uncomplicated smile and Sophie felt her confidence grow, but only for a few seconds until he carried on. 'And now, if you'd like to sit down, Sophie, there's something you might like to hear.'

She was in the process of ferrying her tea from the worktop to the table at the time and it was a miracle she didn't spill it all down her front. She hastily took a seat opposite him and gritted her teeth. She needn't have bothered. What he had to say was not contentious and definitely welcome.

'Yesterday was the arms auction in London. I thought you might both be interested to hear how it went.' He pulled a folded sheet of paper out of the back pocket of his jeans and opened it on the table. 'You'll be pleased to hear that both items sold and they went for considerably more than the reserve. The total that's gone into your account after the deduction of auction fees is...' He glanced down to check the figure. 'One hundred and six thousand, three hundred and four pounds, fifty-three pence.' He looked up and beamed across the table at them. 'Fifty grand for each of you. Not too shabby, eh?'

'Blimey.' For once, Rachel sounded almost speechless.

'Wow, Chris, that's amazing.' Sophie was delighted to get words out. 'And we owe it all to you. Just think – I was going to throw the mace away, remember.'

'I'm delighted I could help and, listen, there's something else that just occurred to me in the car as I was driving here from Nice. Your plan is to sell the castle, isn't it?' He didn't wait for them to nod in agreement. 'Have you thought about what's going to happen to the furniture?'

Sophie and Rachel exchanged glances. They hadn't given it a thought.

'That's what I suspected. If you like, while I'm here this week I'd be happy – in fact I'd enjoy doing it – to take a look around and let you know what sort of value you might be sitting on. Would you like me to do that?'

'That would be brilliant.' The more Sophie thought of it, the better it sounded. She had no doubt that some of the furniture was quite possibly worth a lot. Then something occurred to her. 'We're hoping to buy a smaller place here in Paradiso for holidays and stuff so we'll need a few things for that but no doubt the bulk of the furniture can go.' She looked across at Rachel who was still looking shell-shocked. 'Isn't that so, Rach?'

'Absolutely. The place we're thinking of buying is the house Dan's renting at the moment. You'll see it tomorrow. He's invited us all to dinner.'

'Excellent news on both scores. I'm delighted you're going to keep a connection with Paradiso and I look forward to seeing Dan again. He and I've been corresponding recently. He's been very helpful with medieval queries.' There was a smile on his face as he reached for his tea. 'He tells me you've been dreading seeing me, Soph.'

Her cheeks flushed yet again, but she found the strength to reply resolutely. 'I'm always delighted to see you, Chris, and I always will be.' She looked hard into his eyes. 'I want you to remember that – whatever happens this week.' This time he was the one to blush.

'Then that makes two of us.' He glanced across at the cake. 'Is that just there for appearances' sake or do I get to try a bit?'

After tea and cake and half an hour chatting with Rachel, Sophie left the dog with her sister and set off with Chris for the little village of La Stella, barely ten minutes away by car, where the festival was taking place. To Sophie's surprise, considering how relatively empty the beach now was, the place was swarming with people and they struggled to find somewhere to park, ending up leaning precariously into a ditch. They left the car and followed the crowds heading for the sound of the music. A band was playing some unidentifiable tune with what sounded like a trumpet and an accordion featuring heavily in it. Marquees and tents had been erected in a farmer's field and numerous vendors' vans and caravans were drawn up in a semi-circle, sides open, offering everything from candy floss to grilled prawns on a stick – probably best not eaten together.

At the far end there were booths, stalls and sideshows and Chris insisted on stopping at the lucky dip. He paid the lady behind the counter and they each dug into the wicker basket and pulled out a numbered ticket. Sophie's didn't win anything, but his did. The lady disappeared behind a curtain and emerged with a sweet little teddy bear and handed it over to Chris. He in turn held it out towards Sophie.

'Here, a token of my undying affection.'

She took it from him and kissed it on the furry cheek. Then she leant towards him and kissed him softly on his cheek. 'I'll treasure it – even though I know you only gave it to me because you thought you'd look foolish wandering round with a teddy bear in your arms.'

'You know me so well.' He grinned back at her then, tentatively, held out his hand and caught hold of hers. 'Shall we go and see what else we can win?'

She gave his hand a little squeeze and nodded. They strolled hand-in-hand along the line of stalls and Sophie realised that it felt just fine to be walking along with a teddy bear in one hand and him in the other.

At the end of the line was a big tent, open all along one side, with a queue outside it. Inside was what looked like a production line of people, starting on the far left with three people, arms white with flour, busy making dough. The finished dough in turn was divided into round pieces, a bit smaller than tennis balls, and on the far right of this human chain were four steaming cauldrons. On closer inspection, these contained boiling oil and Sophie was reminded for a moment of her book, which had just reached an interesting scene in which the castle was being besieged by Saracen pirates. The boiling oil would no doubt have come in handy in repelling the marauders.

'Any idea what's going on?' Chris had to put his mouth close to her ear as the nearby band had suddenly struck up again.

Sophie shook her head. 'No idea. It looks like dough, but you don't normally see a queue like this at a normal bakery. Shall we join the queue and find out?'

They bought a couple of tickets and, as they did so, Sophie asked the man at the till just what it was they had bought tickets for.

'It's a local speciality, *pane fritto*. It's bread fried in olive oil, and its origins go way back. Some say it originated in North Africa and came over with the Saracen invaders back in the Middle Ages. Anyway, you try it. I guarantee it's unlike any bread you've ever tasted before.'

Sophie translated for Chris's benefit. 'It literally trans-lates as fried bread and he says it's unique.'

'Well, if it can generate a queue this long, it has to be something special.'

'I must tell Dan about the possible Saracen connection. That's his speciality at the moment.'

'Try eating it with a few slices of ham from that stand over there.' The ticket seller pointed over to where what looked like a whole carcass of an unfortunate – but no doubt delicious – pig was resting on a hefty wooden block. It had clearly been roasted and was covered in a glossy brown glaze and there was even a bright red apple in its mouth. 'Those folks come up every year from Lazio with their porchetta. You have to try it. And maybe wash it down with a glass of my cousin Alfonso's red wine.' Once again he pointed across to another stand. 'It'll be a meal to remember.'

It did indeed turn out to be a meal to remember, but not just because of the tasty ham, the excellent local wine, or the fried bread.

Once they had received their little brown paper bags, each contained three piping-hot rolls of fried bread, they bought hand-carved slices of roast ham and beakers of wine, and looked for somewhere to sit. All the tables around them were jam-packed so they walked across to the far side of the field where the ground began to slope steeply upwards into the woods and they found a fallen tree trunk where they were able to sit and eat, side-by-side. Over here, away from the band, the noise was less deafening and it felt wonderfully peaceful. It was almost dark by now but there was enough light shining across from the fair to allow them to see what they were eating. The still warm fried bread was exceptional; unmistakably bread, but with a brown crust that was delicious and not too crisp. The soft cream-coloured inside combined perfectly with the rosemary-flavoured ham. The wine, as the ticket seller had said, provided the perfect accompaniment.

As they finished their meal, Sophie felt his hand reach over and catch hold of hers again. She gave his a little squeeze and felt him pull her gently towards him. Before she even realised what was happening, he kissed her.

It wasn't the hardest, or the longest, or the most passionate kiss in the world, but Sophie was left in no doubt that if she hadn't had the support of the tree trunk beneath her, her knees would just have buckled. It felt so very right and her heart soared. When he drew back, she caught the multicoloured lights of the fair reflecting in his eyes. He was looking down at her and his expression was one of almost awe. She felt confident this was a good sign, but still, she needed to be sure.

'Chris…' She had to clear her throat before continuing. 'That was amazing. Please tell me it felt good to you too.'

'Unbelievable.' His voice was soft, his tone tender. 'I've always known it would feel so magical to kiss you but even in my dreams I never thought it could be like that. Sophie, that was the best kiss I've ever had or ever will have.'

Chapter 25

The next few days were idyllic. Sophie spent almost all her waking hours with Chris and was very rapidly coming to the conviction that she would also like to spend her sleeping hours him. They went for walks with Jeeves and down to the beach for long swims in the sea. She took him to the little restaurant in Albenga and back to the pizzeria, and they just talked and talked. She told him about her book, which was progressing really well at the moment, and he was as supportive as ever. He told her about his recent overseas trips and how much he enjoyed what he did. The more she was with him and the more they kissed and cuddled, the more convinced she became that this was the man for her and it seemed almost absurd that she had had such doubts.

As promised, Chris took a good look at the furniture in the house and made a number of interesting discoveries. Prime among these was the huge tapestry on the wall of the lounge. He studied it closely and took a load of photos before consulting a colleague in London who came back with the breathtaking news that, subject to detailed analysis, it looked very much like a medieval original which could well be worth more than the arms. Adding in various other old and valuable items, the figure Sophie and Rachel stood to make from disposal of these objects at auction was stunning and more than a little humbling. The sisters discussed it and decided that if all went well, they should consider setting up some sort of fund or charity in Uncle George's name to celebrate his life and to give something back to people who needed it more than they did.

Dinner at Dan's house the day after Chris's arrival was most enjoyable, not least as they met Jennifer for the first time. Sophie immediately took to her and couldn't have approved more of Dan's choice. It was clear to see that Jen had also taken the transition from good buddy to girlfriend in her stride and she and Dan looked and sounded inseparable. With Rachel's Gabriel arriving very soon, everything was working out and they couldn't have been happier.

Gabriel's flight was a few days later on September the twenty-ninth, and he planned to stay for the party on the first of October to celebrate Rachel's birthday and, of course, their successful completion of all the conditions of Uncle George's bequest. He was scheduled to land at Nice airport in the late afternoon and so Rachel drove across to pick him up. Sophie offered to go with her but, understandably, Rachel preferred to have him to herself so they could talk things over in the car on their way back to Paradiso.

The only disappointment that day was the weather which had finally broken and the rain had been bucketing down for hours. The garden and vineyards were awash and, however hard Sophie tried to keep him dry, Jeeves kept on slipping in and out and as a result soon emanated an unappealing wet dog smell. More importantly the weather was making driving conditions difficult, so Rachel set out good and early for what should have been, under normal circumstances, a journey of less than an hour and a half to Nice airport.

Sophie got a call from Rachel at five, saying she had arrived safely at the airport – although the spray thrown up by the big trucks on the motorway had been challenging – but Gabriel's flight was delayed by over an hour. Even so, she reckoned she should still be home by around eight o'clock. As Sophie read this, she felt a little flicker of concern. Neither of them had thought to bring forward their normal evening log-in onto Uncle George's computer and, of course, this had to be done before midnight without fail. The irony that they might have got all the way through the three months together only to fall at the final hurdle wasn't lost on her. It therefore came as a great relief when she received a text from Rachel at seven, telling her they were in the car and on their way home, hoping to be back in time for dinner at eight thirty.

Outside, the weather conditions showed no sign of improving and when Sophie and Chris took Jeeves out for a quick walk, the ground underfoot was inches deep in water in some places and all three of them were soon soaked to the skin long before they got back home. By this time it was half past seven so, after leaving Chris to dry the dog, Sophie ran upstairs to shower and change before hurrying down again to start laying the table and turn on the oven to warm the chicken and mushroom pie she had prepared as the main course.

Eight thirty came and went and Sophie's anxiety increased. She turned off the oven after an hour as the crust was blackening and the chicken drying out fast, and she and Chris sat side-by-side, waiting for sight of the Mercedes. Nice as it was to be alongside him, holding his hand and chatting, Sophie's apprehension continued to grow. Apart from the not so small matter of the computer log-in and the possibility of seeing their castle lost to them, she was growing ever more worried for her sister. In this weather, the *autostrada* would be treacherous and the thought of something happening to her was too terrible for words. With her parents gone, and now Uncle George too, Rachel was her last remaining close relative and she couldn't bear the thought of being parted from her. Chris was supportive and encouraging but she could see that even he was getting worried as nine o'clock arrived and there was still no word.

Sophie turned on the local news and the first thing they saw was a grainy picture of flashing blue and orange lights and the appalling news that one of the motorway bridges between here and the French border had collapsed an hour earlier, taking a number of vehicles with it and causing an unknown number of fatalities. Sophie's hand flew to her mouth and she instinctively reached for her phone. She called Rachel's number but a recorded message told her it had been impossible to connect her. She looked across at Chris, doing her best not to give in and burst into tears. He reached over and cradled her with his arm.

'Try not to worry, Soph. They'll be all right, you'll see.' He pointed to the screen where the pouring rain was still making the images hard to decipher. 'The emergency services are all there. If something had happened, we would have heard by now. They're probably just stuck in a queue. Just think: the collapse of the bridge must have closed the motorway so they're probably in a traffic jam somewhere.'

'But why hasn't she called and why doesn't her phone work?'

'You and I have both driven that piece of motorway. It's just one tunnel after another – and some of them are really long. She's probably stuck somewhere without a signal. Just give it time. It'll be all right, you'll see.'

Sophie managed a little smile of gratitude for his attempts to cheer her, but a cold feeling of dread settled in her stomach and refused to go away. She counted off the minutes, her mind turning over and over, and one thing emerged with clarity. Although there was now the very real possibility of their being unable to log in and, therefore, failing to complete Uncle George's prescriptive conditions, the loss of the castle and the massive financial bonus the sale of it would provide was nothing compared to the prospect of losing her sister. Just as their uncle had hoped, these three months had brought them back closer than ever, and if she had to choose her sister or the money, Sophie knew without a shadow of a doubt which choice she would make.

At ten o'clock, and every ten or fifteen minutes from then on, Sophie kept calling and calling, but still without success. Chris forced a mug of hot tea and a slice of her own apricot tart into her unresisting hands but she couldn't eat a thing. She sipped the tea, lost in her thoughts as the minutes ticked by, and it was almost eleven when finally her phone rang. She almost knocked it off the table in her rush to answer it, and the sensation of relief that flooded throughout her whole body as she heard her sister's voice threatened to reduce her to tears.

'Hi, Soph. There's been an accident on the motorway. We're…'

'Are you all right?' This was all that mattered.

'We're fine. We've been stuck in a tunnel since eight o'clock. We've been trying to call but there was no signal.'

'Thank God you're all right.' Sophie beamed across at Chris and, at the same time, felt tears running down her cheeks. 'I've been so worried.'

'Listen, Soph, there's a problem, a big one. We're still only at Arma di Taggia and we've had to come off the autostrada onto the coast road, but it's absolute chaos with all the traffic and it's stop-start all the way. I've got a horrible feeling we aren't going to get back in time to sign in. Soph…' Her voice broke. '…we could lose the castle.'

'It doesn't matter, Rach. Really, it doesn't. The only thing that matters is that you're safe.' She felt a cold wet nose nudge her knee and a large paw land on her thigh. She looked down and saw a pair of brown eyes staring up at her, clearly troubled. She caught hold of Jeeves's paw and squeezed it gently. 'You're safe, Rach, that's all that counts. Just drive safely and if you're late, you're late.'

When the call ended, she wiped her eyes and relayed to Chris what Rachel had said. He pulled out his phone and checked the map.

'Arma di Taggia is about thirty kilometres from here. Under normal circumstances that's barely twenty minutes. Maybe the traffic will clear or they'll get back onto the motorway. They can still make it.' He set down his phone and stood up. 'Anyway, like you say, the important thing is that they're safe. This calls for a drink.' A few seconds later he handed her a big glass of cold wine from the fridge. 'Now drink up and try to eat something. If she doesn't get back in time you can call the lawyer and explain. I'm sure he'll understand.'

Sophie took a big mouthful of wine and gave him a wry smile. 'I wouldn't be so sure. He struck me as a particularly pernickety sort of chap.'

'He'll understand; you wait and see.'

Rachel phoned forty minutes later to relay the inform-ation that they were once more back on the autostrada, heading for home. By this time it was a quarter to midnight and Sophie couldn't keep her eyes off the clock on the wall. Gradually, the hands crept upwards until, inexorably, they reached twelve. Sophie took a deep breath and looked across at Chris.

'Well, that's it. We've missed a day. Unless Signor Verdi turns out to be a whole lot more flexible than I think, we aren't going to become millionaires.'

He stretched his arm around her shoulders and squeezed her to him, kissing her lightly on the top of her head. 'I still think it'll be okay, but if it doesn't work out, so what? Whatever happens you're going to walk away with a lot of money, even if it isn't millions after all, but like you said the important thing is that you've still got your sister. You had lost her for a while, but now you've got her back and that's priceless.'

Rachel arrived at almost half past midnight, looking weary and despondent. Beside her was a tall man with a friendly face – albeit looking a bit strained under the present circumstances – and Sophie took to him immedi-ately. He, like Chris, was being very supportive and, by the sound of it, had been having the same conversation with Rachel in the car that Chris had been having with Sophie here. Sophie ran across to them and hugged her sister as if her life depended on it, close to tears. Her sister hugged her in return and they stayed like that for some moments before rushing upstairs to Uncle George's study. The Labrador followed on behind, clearly bemused at so much activity in the middle of the night. Sophie and Rachel reached for the computer, although Sophie's watch was telling her they were well into the new day. They looked on as the screen lit up and then, to their horror, the red outline of their hands began to flash and an error message appeared.

> Error: incomplete sequence. Failure to log in correctly previous day. Contact administrator.

Sophie removed her hand for the screen but kept hold of her sister's.

'It's too late to call him now but I'll text Signor Verdi and tell him what's happened. He'll understand, I'm sure.' She tried to make her voice as confident as possible although, deep down, she had a sinking feeling. It looked like the dream was over.

They trailed back downstairs and Sophie pulled out the lukewarm pie and the rest of the dinner she had prepared, but neither she nor Rachel managed to eat very much at all. Finally throwing in the towel at one o'clock, Sophie stood up and announced she was going to take the dog out for a quick pee and then go to bed. All of a sudden she was feeling immensely weary. Chris stood up and gently pressed her back into her seat.

'Leave Jeeves to me. I'll take him out for a quick run and then I'll dry him off and drop him up to your room in a little while. Why don't you go to bed? You look worn out.'

Sophie protested weakly but he insisted. As instructed, she went up to her room, brushed her teeth and fell into bed. In spite of her tiredness, however, she was still wide awake when she heard the door creak open and saw her dog come trotting in. Before it could close again, she called out.

'Chris, are you there?'

'I thought you'd be asleep by now.' His voice was little more than a whisper.

'Will you come here, please?'

He came in and followed Jeeves across to her bedside. She looked up, caught hold of his hand and smiled at him in the darkness. 'I really don't feel like being on my own tonight, Chris. Would you feel like keeping me company?'

He did.

Chapter 26

Next morning Sophie was woken as usual at seven by a cold wet nose from the floor nudging her bare arm. She glanced over at Chris's sleeping form beside her. There was a hint of a smile on his sleeping face and he looked satisfied with life. She would have felt the same way, had it not been for that damn computer and the collapsing motorway bridge. Without waking him she slipped out of bed and pulled on her shorts and sandals, doing her best to keep the happy dog from making too much noise as he bounced around, ready for his walk. Outside, she was delighted to find that the rain had finally stopped and the sky above was clear blue once more, although the ground underfoot was still running with water and scattered with puddles.

She and Jeeves went out of the front gates and across the square. At this time of the morning there was nobody to be seen and Sophie savoured the peaceful atmosphere of Paradiso, her enjoyment tinged with the realisation that her days here were almost certainly numbered. It dawned on her that Signor Verdi might insist upon their vacating the castle the very next day. That would be a most unwelcome birthday present for her sister and would pose the major problem of where to house the guests who were arriving from Toledo and Rome for the party. Thought of Rachel made her realise once more just how awful it would have been if she had lost her, now that she had found her again. No amount of money could possibly have compensated for that.

She and Jeeves splashed along the muddy track until they were out on the open headland. After the rain, the air was cooler and crystal clear. For the first time she was even able to make out the highest snow-covered peaks of the Maritime Alps away to the west. The sea was a brilliant blue and the trees and plants were looking brighter as a result of all the rain which had washed away the layers of dust accumulated over the hot, dry summer months. Paradiso looked like paradise all right, but somehow she felt sure it wasn't going to be their paradise for much longer.

Still, even that thought wasn't enough to dampen her spirits completely after the night she and Chris had just spent together. All her doubts and fears had been banished and she now knew with absolute certainty that he was The One. He was kind, he was bright, and she found him extremely desirable. He was also patently smitten with her and the icing on the cake was that he remained her best friend. It seemed ridiculous to her now that she could ever have doubted that they might end up together.

Back at home, she found Chris in the kitchen, making tea, and her heart leapt at the sight of him. Sidestepping the muddy dog's effusive greeting, he gathered Sophie in his arms and kissed her until she thought she was going to faint – not that she would have minded. Finally releasing her, he stared straight into her eyes.

'You're going to have to forgive me, Soph. I know you've got a lot on your mind and you're understandably worried, but I can't hide the fact that I've never been so crazily, madly happy in my whole life. Sophie Elliot, you're the very best thing that's ever happened to me.'

She leant forward and kissed him softly on the lips. 'Funny you should say that. I was thinking the exact same thing.'

'And now, to show my devotion to you, I'll do my best to clean and dry your dog. Tea's in the pot. Come on outside, Jeeves, you and I have a rendezvous with the hose and the towel.'

They disappeared out through the back door and Sophie helped herself to a mug of tea, sat down, and checked her phone. There was no response from Signor Verdi and she had a feeling this was a bad sign – although, she reminded herself, it was still early and her text to him had been sent in the middle of the night. She was still sitting there, staring at the screen when, to her surprise, Rachel and Gabriel appeared in the kitchen only a few minutes later.

'Hi you two, I thought you'd have a long lie-in after yesterday's ordeal.' Sophie couldn't help herself: she jumped to her feet and flung her arms around her sister. 'You can't believe how relieved I was to hear your voice last night, Rach. I was fearing the worst. I couldn't have faced losing you. Not again.'

Rachel, looking equally emotional, gave her a warm hug and a kiss. 'I feel the same way. Whether we really have lost the castle or not, you've got to hand it to Uncle George. His plan worked.'

Rachel made coffee and dug eggs and ham out of the fridge while Sophie got to know Gabriel. Just like Rachel had said, he was different from the hunks she had dated at university – still a good-looking guy, but much less flashy and much less full of himself than so many of them had been – and it immediately became clear that there was a good brain inside the head on his shoulders. She could see what had attracted her sister to him and she could also see quite clearly that he thought the earth of Rachel. Castle or no castle, log-in or no log-in, at least there was no doubting that both sisters had emerged from these three months with something a whole lot more important than money.

Sophie kept checking her phone but there was still no response from Signor Verdi. She was beginning to get a bad feeling about this when, around mid-morning, as they were all outside sitting by the pool, Dan and Jen arrived. He brought with him a bottle of champagne and some jaw-dropping news.

'I had a phone call half an hour ago from a mutual acquaintance.' There was a little smile on his face. 'Massimo Verdi – he was George's lawyer. You know him, don't you?'

Sophie looked up in surprise. 'Yes, but I didn't realise you knew him. I've been waiting for a call from him myself.'

Dan's smile broadened. 'That's why I'm here. He asked me what I thought he should do.'

He had lost her now. 'What he should do about what?'

'About your little problem.' He glanced across at Rachel and Gabriel. 'By the way, I'm relieved you two weren't involved in that awful bridge collapse – apart from getting stuck in the resulting jam for hours.'

'So he told you about that…?'

Rachel looked as puzzled as Sophie was feeling. Dan took pity on them and explained.

'You see, George and my father were the very best of friends. They knew each other from way back at school and they went into business together. I grew up calling him Uncle George just like you did. He used to come round to our place most Sundays for lunch and he always brought me a book to read. In fact, my love of history's probably down to him. When I told him my plan – my Machiavellian plan I think you called it – he asked me to come over and keep an eye on you two. He loved you both very dearly and he didn't want anything bad to happen to you.'

'He asked *you* to keep an eye on us?'

'I'm sorry for the secrecy but he made me promise not to say anything until you'd completed your full three months here. He wanted you to do it all by yourselves. I was waiting to tell you tomorrow at the big party, but in view of what happened last night, I don't think he would have minded me telling you one day early.'

Sophie and Rachel exchanged bemused glances and Sophie felt she had to come clean. 'That's amazing, Dan, but did the lawyer also tell you we missed the deadline for signing in yesterday? According to the strict terms of Uncle George's bequest, we missed out by one day, so it's not the happy ending after all.'

'Ah, but it is, you see. That's what I was here for. Although George trusted the guys who produced the little bit of software that logged you in every day, he had a healthy mistrust for the inflexibility of computers and he wanted me to be here in case anything like last night were to happen. It's patently obvious that his plan worked and you two are loving sisters once more. It would be criminal to deny you his bequest because of something over which you had no control. For him, family was all-important, and that's the way I feel as well. There was no way I was going to deprive you of what's rightfully yours.'

'Are you saying what I think you're saying?'

'Yup. In spite of your glitch yesterday, I was able to confirm to Signor Verdi that you have indeed completed everything George wanted of you and he's now able to go ahead and transfer the castle into your joint names, to do with as you please.'

Sophie knew she was probably looking totally blank but she was unable to do anything about it. Deus ex machina, in the shape of the handsome American, had just handed her and her sister a fortune. She sat back and did her best to digest what she had heard, as a sensation of exaltation came bubbling up inside her. Jen had looped her arm with Dan's and was hugging him tight and Sophie knew everything was going to be all right. Rachel jumped to her feet, quite sure about what was needed.

'I'm going to get six glasses. If ever a bottle of champagne was merited, it's now. Come to think of it, there's still Uncle George's bottle of Dom Perignon in the fridge. I'll bring that, too. I reckon my birthday party starts now, don't you, Soph?'

Sophie caught her eye and nodded. 'I feel like it's mine too, plus Christmas thrown in for good measure.' Catching hold of Chris's arm and hugging him close, she looked around at the others. 'I've got myself the most wonderful man in the world, a share of a medieval castle, a knight in shining armour all the way from America and the best sister a girl could ask for. I'm delighted I've finally got to meet Gabriel and Jen, and I've got my faithful dog at my feet. What more could I ask for? Apart from a glass of champagne.'

She felt a movement at her feet and felt a big black paw land on her thigh. A pair of big brown eyes stared up at her and, for a moment, it almost looked as though he winked. She looked down at him affectionately.

'And, Rach, bring a couple of dog biscuits, will you? We all need to celebrate.'

Chapter 27

366 days later

Jeeves hit the water with a splash. Sophie stood back and watched as he doggy-paddled up and down, clearly having a whale of a time. The same could be said about her over the last twelve months – not the doggy-paddling but the enjoying herself.

A lot had happened in a year. The castle had been bought by the owner of a world-famous fashion house in Milan for a whole heap of money, and with part of the proceeds Sophie had bought Dan's former residence here in Paradiso. Installing the pool had been one of the first changes she had made – partly for her own sake as she was now living here full time and partly for the benefit of her dog. Needless to say, she had not chosen Dario-the-cheater's pool company to install it.

Rachel was now the proud recipient of a First-Class Honours degree from Exeter University – and her sister's heartfelt admiration – and was about to embark on a three-year doctoral course at Florida State University. She and Gabriel had arrived a couple of weeks back and the first thing Rachel did was to show off the engagement ring on her finger. They were already making plans for a wedding next year.

Dan and Jen had wasted no time and were already married, and their big news was that Jen was expecting a baby next spring. Sophie and Chris had gone over to the wedding in New York a few months back and had followed it with a trip down to Florida along with Rachel and Gabriel. Now the six of them had congregated here in Paradiso once more to celebrate all these events, as well as to inaugurate the new charitable trust established by the two sisters to keep the memory of Uncle George alive. And, of course, it was Rachel's birthday. Sophie was also celebrating something else. Her book, *Behind the Castle Gates*, had just come out and she was basking in its unexpected – at least to her – success.

After persuading Jeeves to relinquish the pool and then taking evasive action to prevent him from soaking her as he shook himself, she rubbed him dry with the same towel she had found at the castle the previous year before calling everybody out to the loggia. Today there would be ten people for lunch as Beppe and his wife, along with Rita and her husband, had also been invited. Chris had fired up the barbecue and while he started grilling a mountain of meat, prawns and cheese, Rachel filled the glasses with Beppe's wine made with the grapes they had all helped to pick this time last year. Part of the deal when selling the castle had been that Beppe would continue to look after the estate for the new owners and Sophie and Rachel would get three *damigiane* of wine each year for the next ten years. Over a hundred and fifty litres of wine a year added up to almost half a litre a day, every day, if Sophie felt like drinking it, but so far she had been pacing herself. Although now firmly set on the road to becoming a professional writer, she had no intention of going down the Hemingway trail.

Knowing that most Italian men didn't consider a meal a real meal unless it included pasta, Sophie had made two massive steaming dishes of lasagne and she set them on the table for people to help themselves once they had finished their starters. The antipasti consisted of sliced ham, salami and a salad of fresh porcini mushrooms – found by Chris and her in the wooded hills to the north of them – mixed with rocket leaves, slivers of parmesan, lime juice and extra virgin olive oil. While everybody was digging in, she went over to the barbecue with a plate of salad and salami to share with Chris. She nibbled his ear and received a little kiss in reply.

'*Ciao, bella.*' His Italian classes were paying off. And they needed to. He had just heard that he was going to be heading up a brand-new branch of his company, specialising in medieval art and artefacts. Although this would be based in Rome, he would travel all over Europe and would be able to do a lot of work from home. And home would be here with Sophie.

'*Ciao, bello.* How's the food coming along?'

'Somehow I get the feeling our four-legged friend's going to do very well out of today's meal. You certainly haven't under-catered. These steaks alone would feed all of us and then some, without adding the sausages, prawns or all that cheese.' He gave her a quick peck on the lips. 'All well with the antipasti?'

'The table's gone very quiet and that's always a good sign. Here, I'll feed you some salami and porcini.' She fed him bit by bit and took a few mouthfuls herself while he continued with his cooking. She leant against him, savouring the moment. On her other side a slightly damp hairy body leant against her, nostrils flared upwards in the direction of the tantalising odours emanating from the grill. When Sophie and Chris reached the end of the salad she held up his glass to his lips so he could take a mouthful before taking a sip herself. Yes, no question, it really was good wine.

'Shall I go and fetch you some lasagne?'

He shook his head. 'I think I'll skip the pasta course. Having seen what's coming next, I don't think I'd have room.'

'Then I'd better go back to the others. We did invite them after all so I'd better put in an appearance at table.'

'Of course.' She was just turning away when she heard his voice. 'Soph, can you reach into the bag over there for me?' He nodded towards an anonymous little brown paper bag lying on the stone slab that served as a table alongside the barbecue.

Sophie reached in and pulled out a little square box, wrapped in silver paper and tied with a red bow. She gave him a puzzled look.

'I thought you'd already given Rachel a birthday present.'

'Yes, but this is for you.'

'A present? For me? It's not my birthday for another six months or so, so why…?'

He grinned at her. 'Stop asking questions and just open it, would you?'

She undid the bow and tore off the paper to reveal a slightly battered black velvet box. She glanced up at him. 'Is this what I think it is?'

'Just open the blooming thing, would you?'

She opened the box and inside she found an absolutely beautiful antique gold ring. Mounted on it was a little cluster of diamonds around a deep green emerald.

'Now listen, Soph. I want you to know that there's no pressure. Just because the others are all going legit, I'm riotously happy to just keep living with you any way you want, so you can wear it on any finger you like. In fact, if you don't like it, you don't have to wear it at all.'

Sophie suddenly felt sure she was going to cry. She struggled to speak. 'It's gorgeous, Chris. Where did you get it?'

'I bought it at our big jewellery sale last year.'

Sophie took it out of the box and turned it over and over in her fingers, seeing the sunlight sparkle and flash as she did so. 'I thought your big jewellery sale was usually at Easter.'

'That's right, April.'

'April last year, not this year?' She could hear the incredulity in her own voice. 'I was still in London then, moping about and looking like a tramp. Are you saying you bought this for me way back then? Are you sure it wasn't for some other woman?' She was sure she knew the answer, but she gave him a smile as she said it just in case.

'It was for you. I was all set to throw caution to the wind and ask you to marry me when you got the letter about inheriting the castle and announced you'd be leaving for Italy.'

'And you never said anything? Why wait until now?'

'I wanted the moment to be perfect. Here, now, in the sunshine, just you, me and good old Jeeves, with our friends just over there, strikes me as about as good as it gets. But I meant it about there being no pressure. Like I say, stick it on any finger or hang it round your neck if you like.'

She was still smiling, although she could feel the first of many happy tears already running down her cheeks. 'Let me get this straight: are you asking me to marry you, Chris?'

'Erm… yes, if you'll have me.'

She slid the ring onto her finger and wiped the tears from her face. 'Of course, I'll have you, you idiot.'

And she kissed him.

At her feet, a cold wet nose nudged her leg. Jeeves knew a happy ending when he saw one.

Acknowledgements

With warmest thanks to my editor Emily Bedford and all the lovely people at my publishers, Canelo. Special thanks also to my friends Laura Bambrey and Elaine Brent for being kind enough to read the book and comment. Much appreciated and very helpful.